Flight of the hilsa

AF663378

Amit Shankar

Vitasta

Vitasta Publishing Pvt. Ltd.
New Delhi

Published by
Renu Kaul Verma for
Vitasta Publishing Pvt. Ltd.
2/15, Ansari Road, Daryaganj,
New Delhi - 110 002

ISBN 978-93-80828-13-8
© Amit Shankar 2011
First reprint 2011

All Rights Reserved.

No part of this publication may be reproduced, stored in a retrieval system, or transmitted, in any form, or by any means—electronic, mechanical, photocopying, recording or otherwise—without the prior permission of the publisher.

All the names and the characters in this book are fictitious. Resemblance to anyone, living or dead, is purely coincidental.

Cover design by Sanya Shankar
Layout by Vitasta Publishing Pvt. Ltd.
Printed by Vits Press, New Delhi

I dedicate this book to Late Dr. Vishnu for giving birth to the present and to Vishu—the exuberant present in which a bright future blooms.

Closer to the meaning, you could just be dreaming

"What is happiness?" On the one hand, mortals spend their lives just trying to decipher this word, while on the other the blessed ones discover the treasure of this fulfillment in a jiffy. Not deluded by delusions, not failed by failures, these lucky ones soar above all challenges to discover and define their own truth, which leads them to acceptance—the source of all happiness.

Hilsa; a fish that swims upstream, against all odds, to lay eggs in fresh water and then travels back to its source—the sea, is a potent representation of people who take life on its face value, as it comes, and in the process achieve the ever elusive state of happiness.

But can one really strive to be happy when happiness should be a natural state? Can one really search for happiness when it should rest deep within? Can one link happiness to materialistic pursuits—a big house, a fancy car or a cushy, well paying job when in reality its breeding ground is contentment?

These ramblings pave the way for a potent yet diverse school of thought which approaches and explores happiness in acceptance of life's own truth. It believes that as mortals, we have a definite life purpose. To be a soldier or a sailor, an athlete or a singer, businessman or a lawyer; the roles could just be about anything. While essaying any of these roles, the truth of our life is to learn our respective lessons—of success, failure, poverty, riches, ignorance, knowledge and many more. It is the acceptance of our respective lessons which forms the foundation of this truth. And surrendering to this truth is the only way to experience the sublime happiness.

So let the Hilsa in you decide its own calling—fresh water or the sea, learn the intended lesson—calmness or turbulence, resistance or acceptance and embrace happiness like never before…forever.

Thank you and more...

I would like to thank my guardian angels for helping me marshal my thoughts in producing these ninety thousand plus words. Thank you God for being so kind and gracious in blessing me with everything!

My heartfelt thanks and gratitude to Shayantani Datta Sen for her endless hours spent on reading and editing the chapters, Bipasha Sen Gupta for all her tireless energy in finding me a publisher, Vagmi Kumar for providing me with his critical and honest feedback, Prashant Rana for his never failing words of hope and encouragement, Sanya Shankar for the brilliant cover design and for lending me her notebook, Amit Mukherjee for designing the entire communication and Subhasis Bhattacharjee for his web help. I would also like to take this opportunity to thank my publishers, Renu Kaul Verma, Sudesh and Santosh for having faith in me and bringing this story to you.

I Just Called To Say...

"Every night in my dreams,
I see you, I feel you
That is how I know you go on..."

The shocking pink-coloured D&G, limited edition Motorazr cellphone, kept on the ornate glass table top, came to life, with the honey silk voice of Celine Dion. Her powerful vocals, now turned into a squeaky mp3 ringtone, were getting stifled amidst a concoction of décor influences—the Raj, the Victorian and the French for starters. Not to miss the sporadic Moroccan, Arabian and Chinese travel memoirs thrown in liberally.

The king-sized Victorian bed had angels and fairies adorning the four posts, as if ready to embark on a flight to their heavenly abode. The impeccable, oversized, glossy mahogany writing table seemed to be the perfect companion in adventures beyond literary pursuits. The polished brass light fittings, the fresh scarlet orchids with a play of deep purple placed artistically in the huge Belgian crystal vase, the blue and green silk cushions thrown in the corner, the two over-stuffed, leather upholstered chairs sitting on a thick wine coloured carpet; all this and more was too carefully placed to impart the setting a casual look.

Though the faint drone of the air conditioner could do little to lessen Celine's misery, it surely did a good measure to chill the already cold Italian marble floor.

The door, which in all probability led to a Victorian styled washroom opened and a pretty, young and more than plump woman stepped out. As she did, a waft of lemon grass incense followed her; even after the door shut behind her, lingered and spread casually, just like the other artefacts in the room. Almost simultaneously, she looked at the phone display, smiled, said "Hello" and twirled the lock on her right temple. The morning sunlight wafting through the etched glass window caught her lock, turning it into various shades of burgundy.

"Hi Shwets, hope I didn't disturb you in the middle of something important?" There was a special emphasis on "something important," followed by a naughty giggle, indicating the deep carnal pointer of actions more intimate in nature.

Shweta let out a loud throaty laughter, which was completely out of sync with the demeanour of the period setting. But definitely it had a distinct tone of sincerity to it. "Shut up Avi," she chided the caller. "The day you get married to Sunny will you discover to your dismay that past the first few weeks, the so called 'something important' becomes as extinct as Rex the Dino."

Another round of laughter followed, this time in unison.

"*Arre*, did I say anything? It's you and your dirty mind working overtime." The caller clarified her innocent intentions.

"Aha, so I am the one with a dirty mind? Don't we all know that since the day you stepped into Delhi College of Arts, for all four years, you were the undisputed PQ—the pervert queen?" Shweta went years back to dig up some conclusive proof. "Remember the cigarette lighter in the curator's boxes?"

More laughter followed.

"Ok out with it, what made you call so early?" Shweta tried to steer the conversation to logical shores.

"Well, this call is to remind her highness that her humble friend Avantika Sengupta's painting exhibition is opening today, at the Epicentre, Gurgaon, and you, Her Royal Highness and your slave hubby, Prashant, have to be there to grace the occasion."

"Ohhhhhh. Good that you called up for that Avi, you are such a sweetheart."

"See I knew that you would conveniently forget this. That's why I had to give you a buzz." Avantika reprimanded her and the tone aptly conveyed the length of the road they had travelled together. She continued, "After marrying that pumpkin of a millionaire, why would you bother to remember boring engagements such as the opening of your friend's exhibition?"

"Shut up Avi," Shweta interjected in good humour. "And stop calling him a pumpkin. Poor thing, he is trying so hard to get back in shape. You know what, he is on a special diet and has also hired this personal trainer who has been a trainer to..."

"Not again Shwets, not now. Please, please, please! Don't you start rattling off names of the glitterati again," Avantika pleaded.

"Really, he is too good."

"So have you already tried him? Oh dear me, what's happening to my innocent baby?"

Shweta blushed and her cheeks turned amber red. The laughter came after a second. Maybe to conceal her embarrassment or it could have been just another innocent woman's giggle that has been a mystery for ages.

"Shut up Avi. You are impossible. I insist on re-christening you the 'Pervert Queen'."

"Sure let me be the PQ, my *Sati Savitri*. See you at 12 noon and get Prashant along." The click of the phone at both ends was drowned in hysteric laughter.

Shweta, still smiling while straightening an orchid stalk in the vase, was humming a tune under her breath. She proceeded to open her wardrobe, to pick a dress for the afternoon event. After much toying, she pulled out a heavy *chikan* cotton snow white *salwar-kameez*. Her smile broadened when she remembered Avi's reaction to her amber zardozi dress at the last exhibition.

Everybody Hurts

"How was your day Avi?"

"Another day, same old shit." The comment had equal portions of venom and whine. She threw the file and her satchel on the already cramped bed, kicked her *jootis* and walked towards the kitchen, scrambling for a song on her iPod and adjusting her earplugs. If Sunny was asked to list Avantika's one habit which infuriated him the most, definitely her iPod addiction would top the charts.

"Don't lose heart *Jaan*..."

Something snapped, she stopped mid way, turned around sharply and hissed—the snake thing now very pronounced. "Shut up Sunny and just stop using these *panjoo* prefixes of yours. Haven't I told you that I detest your unending vocabulary of *Jaan*, *Jaaneman*, etc? Why can't you just leave them at my door?"

The usually oblivious hum of the refrigerator suddenly assumed thundering proportion—that of a chopper blade; constant and loud. If the room were to be silent for another few seconds, the chopper blades would have crunched the gut out of every living soul.

Sunny was trifle embarrassed and hurt. He ran his thumb over his parched lips while the tongue made imaginary designs inside the cheek wall. His ear and the closely shaven face, the groomed and genetically blessed fair skin, were all various shades of crimson red. Avantika stared at him. Her eyes met his. He shifted his gaze. But within a few seconds the woman in her realized that she was being too harsh on him, and as a result, her stare became softer.

"I am sorry." The first peace restoration move came from her side.

"It's ok. I should have understood that you were having a bad day." Defeated, Sunny had no choice but to pull back graciously.

He continued, "But Jaa..., I mean, I genuinely believe that your work is good and it's just a matter of time the critics, the audience and the world accepts and appreciates it. You are a complete natural."

Good words or a pat on the back, like a peacemaker, always have a positive effect, on girlfriends too.

"Sorry Sunny. I really am." She moved forward and hugged him, her arms around his neck and her lips briefly grazing his neck. A sudden change of temperature and mood confused Sunny and he did not know how to cope with it. After all these years, he still had no clue as to what could trigger the ice princess in her or what could provoke the tigress. His hands hung limply, eyes trying to concentrate on a casual strand which had come undone from her ponytail, trying to fathom the best possible recourse. Should he nudge the passion switch within, or just let her guide him through her temperamental journey across the nape? He did neither and just managed to pat her back. His faint smile miserably failed to hide his bleeding male ego.

Wanting to look for a way out, Sunny blurted, "Can I smoke?"

Still ridden with guilt, Avantika opened her arms, which were encasing him and rolled her eyes, followed by an impish grin, "As an exception, yes."

Moving back towards the kitchenette, she peeped inside the refrigerator. After a few seconds of tinkering, she emerged with a half eaten tub of strawberry yogurt. She hitched her blue Fabindia gypsy skirt, stood on her toes and with a twirl settled on the small table which had a withered top. Her eyes had a million things in store then, besides the yogurt, which was obviously just a temporary solution to tame her wild and unruly senses. Between the drifting thick clouds of smoke, Sunny silently watched her.

"What did the journalist at the *Times* say?" He sounded concerned.

"Ah. A jack-ass that he is, he refuses to find any merit in my paintings. Bloody paparazzi. They all think that digging into free blueberry cheese cake at high tea hosted by clueless rich freak painters, who make neo-classical stuff of nude women, gives them enough expertise to judge art." She emptied her frustration, licking off the backside of the spoon of its pink gluey mess. "When I confronted him about the rude review, you know what he said?"

Sunny, like most men, did not know if he was supposed to answer that or stay dumb.

"The fucker told me that the review was at his kindest best. Bloody ass of the first order." She went on, not bothered by her audience's interest.

"They don't know shit about art, aesthetics or even life and some jerk assigns them to play the art critic." Her every word was filled with memories of bad encounters with the critics. "Critic my foot. My street mongrel could be a better one!"

She aimed the empty tub at the dustbin, but it landed a couple of feet away from its intended target, while the spoon could not gather velocity at all and landed at her feet. The cool yogurt did no magic as the mercury was still rising, rather, it was already over the top. In the balcony, Sunny stubbed the cigarette in a broken tea cup which had assumed the role of an ashtray and walked in. Settled on the bed, he reminicensed how this 6 x 4, low height bed has been a witness to so much—hours of scrabble, numerous coffee sessions, coffee spills, few pillow fights and many long nights, mornings and afternoons of love making. Was she still as demanding in bed as she used to be? Damn, it had been so long. He felt himself aching for her. He involuntarily stole a glance at her while she was undoing her ponytail, and running the fingers through her hair. He shrugged off the thought immediately. Somehow he knew that when your girl was having a bad day, carnal thoughts or actions were the surest way of driving her out of your life. And that was the last thing he wanted, at least as of now.

Confused, he picked the file which Avantika had kept on the bed. While leafing through it aimlessly, casually, he scanned the small *barsaati* apartment—home to his beloved Avantika. A small room with an attached kitchenette and a washroom, which was positioned as a studio apartment by the broker. His eyes flickered back to the file. He noticed that till a few months ago this file used to be bright and fresh. But its journey to numerous publication offices, clients, art enthusiasts, galleries, friends and colleagues had taken away its sheen.

He looked at Avantika who was examining her toenail. Was she losing her sheen, too? Nearing 30, she was not the girl he had met some eight years back; both physically and emotionally. Was it a natural process of change or it was something else?

He steered his wandering thoughts back to the file. As he flipped through the reviews, mostly the bad and the ugly ones, exhibition-announcing advertisements, some pictures of her paintings, he felt like a stranger—indeed a stranger in this relationship. Why was he forcing himself to appreciate this whole business of painting and art when he had no interest or inclination towards it? Was it his love for Avantika or was it the fear of losing her?

He looked up. She was engrossed in staring out of the small window, with her iPod earphones firmly securing her from any intrusion. He knew that now some old, white man named Roger Waters, Bob Dylan, Dio or Ian Gillan would be serenading her.

"Bye Avi. Catch you soon." No response. He gently closed the door and as he walked down the dilapidating staircase, the last thought to cross his mind before engaging his gleaming black-coloured Audi A4 in gear was the possibility of losing someone who never belonged to anyone.

Help Me And You Hurt Me

"But Mrs Lalani, I don't see anything wrong with them."

As she stood up, Avantika pushed back the antique silver stool. The lady being addressed placed the delicate blue China cup on the artistically carved silver and wood coffee table. The table was an experimental creation by one of her artists from Jodhpur. She adored the hand-crafted braids of wood and silver down the legs of the table and its two accompanying stools. Currently, she was intensely worried about the rough push which her darling stool had been subjected to by Avantika.

Avantika walked further down the hallway, towards her paintings, which were mounted on the wall facing Mrs Lalani. Under the strategically placed spotlight, they looked prettier and more inviting. A semi-clad urchin lay on his back, gazing at the full moon. His eyes were large and hugely expectant. The mellow bulb above the painting powered the light streaks from the moonlight and added a divinity to the kid's face.

"Oh dear, I'm so sorry. You need not take my honest opinion

to your heart."

Mrs Lalani drawled in her nasal American-Sindhi accent as she walked down the beige Italian marble floor. The big, silent hall reverberated with the steady rhythm of her stilettos, which were bearing the brunt of her fondness for Italian and Mughlai food. She was draped in a fitting ivory coloured dress, which was held together delicately by a few straps and a crystal brooch on her right shoulder.

"Now dear, if you look at this, 'Fondness', as you have titled it, I mean, it is so…" She squinted, searching for the precise expression but her vocabulary ditched her again. "Nevertheless, it is pretty in its own right, but if I were to articulate; though it's tough, it lacks… soul."

After glancing at the moon washed look in the kid's eyes, Mrs Lalani scanned Avantika's face for some instant reaction. But she just stood there, nonchalantly, adoring her babies, her creations, watching them in their full bloom.

"Dear, you need not be so shocked…"

"No I am not, Mrs Lalani. In fact, it is so nice of you to express your candid views. They are much appreciated." Mrs Lalani took the left handed compliment gracefully.

"Can I ask you a favour?" Sugar coat on each word was obvious. Before Mrs Lalani could oblige her with her consent, the favour was asked for.

"Could you please give me the names of the two buyers who bought my paintings at this exhibition?"

"Oh sure dear, if that makes your day, I mean, why not." Mrs Lalani pressed a few buttons on her mobile. "Here you go, Mrs Shweta Khemka and some gentleman named Mr Khurana. Sorry, I don't have his first name."

Avantika was transfixed in her *jootis*. Looking through the large French window, the Ashoka tree beyond and yet not actually seeing anything. Speechless, she just stood there. So during her last exhibition, her paintings could not find even two genuine buyers? Was she asking too much for her canvases? But she knew that at 30,000 for an oil canvas, it was a steal by any standard. Her facial expressions changed from hurt to that of betrayal and gradually metamorphosed into anger, the bitterness of which steadily crept into her throat.

Being the woman that Mrs Lalani was, letting go of any opportunity to prove the divide between the 'haves' and 'have nots' was not one of her virtues. With her attention still transfixed to the big, illuminated screen of her phone, like a proud mother, whose heart was overflowing with love, she could not help but express the same. "Now keeping all data is so easy with my Vertu. Didn't I tell you that I had gone to Dubai to attend a seminar on contemporary art and painting? Picked this darling during that trip. At just $6,000, isn't it worth every dime?"

Avantika's pre-occupied mind was too busy to appreciate her ostentatious display of technology.

"Sure Mrs Lalani. Could you be kind enough to please look up your Vertu for the telephone number of this gentleman, Mr Khurana?" The candy floss tone was slowly waning.

"Sure Darling. Here you go… 9810144466."

The number clarified whatever little doubt that existed in her mind. After all, this was a number she had dialled a million times before finally saving it on her mobile phone.

"Thank you Mrs Lalani. Much appreciated." She paused her candy floss flow, just to garnish it with a dash of her trademark venom. "And by the way, even a basic Nokia phone worth ₹ 1,500, like the one your driver carries, can save names and numbers as easily as your three lakh Vertu. Have a good day Mrs Lalani."

Before Avantika hailed an auto, she dialled that familiar number sequence with both her thumbs as she wanted to sort things out today itself.

Knockin On The Heaven's Door

The white Honda Accord came to a halt on the gleaming asphalt tarmac. A step away from the parking, the soft green grass was rolling, pausing only for the flower beds and the marble stepping stones. Even before stepping down the car, one could hear soft '*gayatri mantra*' wafting from the hi-tech, aesthetically concealed speakers. It was obvious that in modern times, there was a shortcut to *Nirvana*, provided if one was ready to part with the *Maya*.

"I still don't see any reason to be here with you."

"Simi, can you please stop bickering and arguing over this?" Requested the man, getting off from the other side of the car. He was in his late 50s, robust, short-cropped salt and pepper hair, smartly dressed in a white polo T-shirt, black trousers and loafers. He indicated the driver to unload the basket of fruits from the boot.

The woman, Simi, appeared to be in her early 40s and heavily influenced and inspired by the glossy, glam, fashion magazines. Attired in a leopard print top, black tights and leopard print boots, amidst the serenity of the *mantras* and silently moving attendants in saffron and white, she stuck out like a sore thumb.

The driver handed over the basket to one petite, barefoot girl, who seemed barely a day over 20, dressed in a white *salwar-kameez.* The girl glanced at them and smiled. The smile plastered on her face was duty bound and with her eyes she indicated that she had to be followed. Her expressions seemed to manifest more out of routine than anything else.

"Will you ever know how to dress Simi? You look so gawky," the man mumbled.

She followed him and the girl in silence, with a constant scowl for company and entered the foyer and then a hall which was dotted with more attendants and followers. The volume of the *gayatri mantra* was more pronounced there. A heady concoction of roses and marigold, along with a variety of incense overwhelmed the olfactory senses. The petite girl had disappeared towards the front of the hall, which looked like the main area for the congregation.

An attendant in saffron indicated the corner where they needed to take off the shoes. Simi bent down, trying hard to unzip her boots. She looked around for a place to sit so that she could squeeze her ankles with her fingers, out of the tight boots. But the corner was stark and she continued to fight a losing battle, hopping on one foot. The irritation on her face highlighted the crow feet wrinkles, deftly hidden beneath layers of makeup.

"I am going to screw the happiness of that son of a bitch." Her face distorted more, making her look tackier.

"Simi, please," pleaded the man accompanying her in a hoarse whisper. "We are at the ashram to seek blessings from *Maa*, not to curse your shoe designer."

"You and your blessings." Her voice seethed with contempt. "Did I want to come here? Why do you have to drag me here every time? Don't you know I hate all this drama, especially that bogus *Maa* of yours?" Maybe her last remark was uncalled for as it was hastily retracted by the fear in her eyes. But suddenly, God was kind to her.

"*Jai jai sai raam, sai raam sai raam.*" The shrill ringtone jarred the moment. The man who was washing his hands in gurgling water, in a basin, shaped like a fountain, quickly wiped his hands using the paper tissue kept there and answered the call. 'Hi Beta. I am at the *ashram*. Can we talk later?" He whispered.

"Sure thing. Just called you to remind that today is Mamma's death anniversary." A female voice on the other side updated him.

"I know I know, that is why I am here to seek *Maa's* blessing for your Mamma's soul and for us, too."

With every passing second, Simi was turning more and more restless. She had finally de-shoed her feet, rinsed her hands and was patiently walking very slowly, with him, to keep pace with the flow of the tele-conversation. They were now halfway down the hall, amidst silent people and chanting of *shlokas*. And then her patience just snapped.

"Can we please wrap her first?" She said, pointing towards the end of the hall, her hands in a folded *namaskar* posture, as if mimicking someone. Her high pitched tone turned a few heads with looks of disapproval. Suddenly, the response from the telephone crackled. "Dad, don't tell me that on Mamma's death anniversary you are at the *ashram* with that bitch?" The scorn and hatred in the tone made the man hold the phone away from his ears.

The expressions of disapproval around Simi were gradually turning to disgust. She stared at her black net stocking for a split second, then her purse for another. Her distorted face resembled that of a fancy witch in a nursery fairy tale book. With a deep exhalation, grasping the clutch and still looking like a haute couture scare crow, she paced ahead, trying to lose herself amidst the crowd which had now begun rocking to *bhajans*.

"Avi, this is no way to speak of Simi. You owe her an apology."

"Apology?" The voice on the other end was genuinely shocked.

"Do you really think it's me who owes an apology? On my mother's death anniversary, who also happens to be your late wife, you are going to pray for her soul with that whore of yours. And to top it all you are telling me that I owe her an apology?" Avantika's voice got hysterical.

"Avi please stop it, please," he pleaded. "What is wrong with you? Tell me? What makes you hate me the way you do? For God's sake, I am your father damn it."

"Thank you for telling me this. You know Dad, you are no different than those *panjoo* bastards who think they can buy anything... love included."

"Avi!" he shouted to a dead phone.

The decibel level, the blood pressure and temper all were soaring. Simi was lost in the crowd ahead, the pitch of the *bhajans* were now reaching a crescendo, the room was dotted with shades of saffron and whites, and multitude of nodding heads and clapping palms.

The Living Hell

"Shiela, are you ready?"

The commanding voice boomed across the big colonial bungalow—tennis court-sized rooms, high ceilings supported by wooden beams, ventilators with coloured ropes hanging down to move them, fans attached to elongated iron rods, stuffed trophies of deer, bears and leopards looking down with frozen fear in their eyes.

The inanimate echo vibrated in the vacuum; so did the little girl aged eleven, named Avantika Sengupta. She crouched by the stair rails on the first floor landing. From her vantage point, she could see the living room and the anteroom beyond. The left panel of the living room was flanked with gleaming shields and trophies while the right one with the sinister looking leopard skin. In the centre of the room stood Major Sengupta, 32nd Armoured Corps, her fear evoking, tyrant father. Hands on his hips, dressed formally in a dark suit, indigo silk shirt and matching handkerchief, half submerged in the left breast pocket of the jacket.

She mentally cringed, half knowing how the scene would unfold in the next few minutes. This made her crumple to half her size, with fear, helplessness and humiliation.

"Sheila," the voice re-thundered. "I want you here, all dressed up, in the next sixty seconds." This time the tone was more menacing.

A petite woman, dressed in a printed *kurta* and jeans walked in. Even the deep-rooted hatred in her big brown eyes failed to dampen their spirit or lessen their beauty. "SG, I have an exhibition coming up this Saturday; therefore, I cannot make it this evening. Moreover, I don't enjoy your parties anyway." Her voice and stare were soft yet firm.

"Too bad you don't, but I am sure that you understand that we live in a society. And being social animals, we have to follow certain social protocols, discharge certain social obligations, especially in the armed forces. And attending parties as a couple is very much a part of it." The tyrant thundered. The lady smiled.

"I fully appreciate your theory on the social animal bit, with just a minor modification." SG looked at her curiously.

"Just don't use social as a prefix." She laughed.

"Major Sengupta, you are an animal or maybe even worse." Her laughter got hysterical. "You are a blend of a hyena and a rattlesnake." The shrill laughter continued unabated, through the cold and unsmiling eyes.

The little girl wished if she could close her ears also. But unfortunately, she only had two hands.

"You wretched woman, how dare you speak to me like this?" His voice seethed with rage. "You are very well coming along with me. Go and put on whatever makes you look presentable."

"See Major Sengupta, I have already hurt the animal in you." Sheila taunted, knowing the consequences well. "See, it's coming out. There it is. Bring it on. Let me see what you have got today. Are you afraid of me, you sissy? I wonder how your seniors and friends claim that you are one of the most fearless officers that the armoured corps have ever seen. Are you?" She launched her sharp, poisoned darts.

"Come on braveheart. Come on, try me." She instigated him further. "I am not like any of your other girls who would walk out on you. I am your wife. Come to your darling wifey whom you have caged in this zoo of yours. Come baby. What are you waiting for, bring on your leash, my ring master."

Taunts leaped at the tyrant like gun shots, hard and fatal.

"What can you do to me that you have not done to me before? Come baby, come." As a heady and terrifying mix of laughter and excruciating cries filled the room, the little girl, Avantika, did not know what hurt her mother more: the leather belt with brass buckle or her husband's insensitivity towards her needs. She helplessly watched her mother laugh, writhe, claw and sneer like a mad woman. "You have taken the colours from my life, but you cannot take them from my soul."

In the midst of foggy eyes, once again the little girl reiterated her resolution; to become what her mom had wanted for herself—a painter, with loads of name and fame, successful by the standards of any man, any society.

Part Time Lovers

Art Café.

Quite a fancy name for a place where it was hard to judge what was more nerve wrecking: its tacky interiors or the mindless menu. Every single piece of furniture was unique or offending in its own way. Instead of a normal table base, one could find anything from an iron sewing machine stand to a potter's wheel. All chairs were of different size, shape and needless to say, colour. The walls looked as if someone had thrown garish red, purple and green paint on them. Some random posters, ranging from jazz to old Hollywood blockbusters, lent the place a confused creative touch. To complete its disdain for any thing even closely aesthetic, the place served ridiculous combos too. Finest coffee to something as crass as Maggi, an assortment of flavoured *hookahs* to something as mundane as butter toast and it just got crazier as each of these assortments had a French name.

Sunny looked around as if trying to figure out a thematic cohesiveness, if any, or maybe a cosy corner. The café buzzed with a motley crowd, largely youngsters; typically the college kinds—weird hairdos, jeans, sneakers and tattoos.

He glanced at the menu which was hanging from terracotta figurines on each table. His table had a delightfully happy looking, over-baked mermaid and the menu parchment hung listless like her necklace.

As he scanned the area, the builder-cum-architect in him could not resist the simple calculation. 3,500 to 4,000 sq feet of space! Considering the way that area had picked up, it would be pegged anywhere between ₹ 40,000 to 50,000 per sq feet. Gosh! He was exasperated. Why do people spend a fortune for vending out coffee and sandwiches? Why can't they do something more rational, like a commercial venture, maybe setting up a mall?

Putting a stop to the inane mental calculation he tried focussing on the objective of his visit. Was he early? Not really, he told himself. Anyway, to be doubly sure he looked at his watch; a Breitling Navi-timer, a gift from his Dad on his 30th birthday. Well, Dad never had time, so maybe he wanted to gift me his time, in the form of a watch. His mind sprinted from one topic to another; this time to the closely-contested debate with Avantika, over the Breitling watch. Avantika's point was simple. Why should someone spend four lacs just to keep time when HMT, Titan, Timex and Casio did the same, and at just a fraction of the cost? He wondered why she could never see his side of the story; maybe a difference in point of view.

"Would you like to place your order, Sir?" The last word was a decibel too pronounced to jog him out of his reverie. He looked up. A sweet guy, dressed in brown T-shirt, holding a small note pad and a pen was smiling.

"Well, I guess a cappuccino would do for now, buddy."

"Sir, should I add anything to eat?"

"No, nothing as of now." He replied with a smile. Avantika thought he looked really cute when he smiled. Shuttling back and forth between now and the years back, he wondered if he had reduced smiling as well. Oh Avantika! Why was she changing everyday?

Sunny was still flirting with the past; nestled amidst the ever-growing chaos, only to be multiplied manifold by the ongoing metro construction, there used to be a small coffee house—Madras Café. Playing with the mermaid on the table, he could not remember having seen it lately. It used to be the melting pot of Delhi's artistic community. Painters, poets, artists, renowned or struggling, used to inhabit it for hours, debating over issues which made little impact or were of little consequence to the outside world, over cups of *chai*.

This was the place where he had first bumped into Avantika. Fond memories brought a smile on his face. He had walked in to meet a painter to collect some samples for one of Dad's commercial projects. Crowded as it always used to be, there were no vacant chairs. God! How he hated the dim, smoky chamber, buzzing with murmurs and guffaws till his eye caught a table with a pretty girl on it. Though now on second thought, he remembered that it was not the girl but the vacant chair that had caught his eye.

"Mind if I take this." He still remembered his exact opening line.

"No, and get a life and brush up your pick-up lines," was the curt reply.

He was embarrassed and blurted out something to the effect that he was genuinely looking for a chair and nothing else.

"Have you ordered something?"

He had not realized it when she had walked in, located him, and was already pulling the chair and placing her petite frame on it. He snapped back eight years forward in a fraction of a second. Oblivious to his past and present mental rambling, she yanked her earphones and placed her iPod in her satchel. Travel in the auto had made her skin look flushed in the Delhi heat. Wisps of hair had come loose of their binding and were now tucked temporarily in the clutches of the glares which she had plonked on her head. He looked at her face, wondering if she was really as beautiful as he thought or did it all exist only in his mind. Though after seeing her pictures, his mother was of the firm opinion that beauty lies in the eyes of the beholder and that people indeed fell in love.

"Sorry, the traffic near Andheria More was real bad." Her eyes scanned the wall, taking pot shots at the paintings on them, which she always found obnoxious. She involuntarily turned up her nose at the vast display of the black and white series. Varied styles or lack of it just framed and put on the walls. When would her work adorn some fancy restaurant, some gallery, some swanky office or a plush living room?

"That's ok, and I have ordered my coffee." His mono-syllabic acceptance of the growing traffic snarls got her back into the conversation.

"Why can't they fix the traffic signals and these damn roads for good?" She cribbed. Sunny smiled. He was used to her habit of blaming everything—the road, the system, the urchins, the government, just about everything, but her own self.

Hey, but he loved her. Didn't he? So why was he thinking on these lines? Why should she blame herself? Wasn't she the epitome of beauty and brain? At 5'4 or maybe 5'5, with big black eyes, straight hair, a serene face, dusky complexion, she looked quite interesting to him, or so he thought till a few months back. Dump it!

"Avi, this is a nice place. I wonder how you always manage to find these?

"Shut up Sunny. I know why you like it." Avantika replied playfully. He started to wonder the reason which made him like the place because his statement was just aimed to please her. Or did she like his opening line?

An opening line after all these years?

"You like it as it is one of the few places where you can still sit and smoke while having your coffee or sandwich." Avantika presented her the explanation. How come he never thought of it? Never too late. He started searching for his cigarette pack. Murphy's law struck. He had left the pack in his car.

"So how was your meeting with the client?" Sunny placed a direct question.

"Don't know if it was good or bad. He told me that he would get back to me. Going by my experience, no one ever gets back."

"Avi, Ah… the cynic in you. Why do you have to be so cynical all the time?"

"Am I? I am just stating a fact." She nonchalantly looked at the menu without a spark in her eyes.

The boy walked with a cappuccino and placed the cup on the

table. Sunny looked at the cup and the fancy design the coffee froth had. Some kind of fern graphic. How does fern get into coffee, he wondered.

"Can you get another cappuccino for me?" She instructed the boy.

"Sure ma'am. Anything to eat?"

"No thanks."

Sunny jogged his mind, trying to find the right opening line for the conversation he intended to have.

"You wanted to talk about something?" Avantika did the needful.

"Well yes." He shifted his gaze as he watched the young couple sitting on the sofa, cuddling up. He tried to guess if it was love or just physical attraction. Damn them, he felt as if he were sitting on a dormant volcano which was already hissing through the fissures. He shifted his focus back to Avantika. Her Raybans were now tossed on the table, her shoulder length hair still loosely encased in the ponytail. Her rust coloured Fabindia *khadi kurta* complimented her bronze skin well. And though he could not see her lower torso, but he knew that it would be covered in faded jeans and a *jooti*.

"I was having a conversation with Dad yesterday. He was asking about my plans."

"But you are already handling his business, aren't you? What else?" She quizzed.

Sunny smiled, a feeble smile, which had shadows of the next line which he was all set to deliver and mentally trying to map the smoke which would erupt from the fissure.

"Yes, the career seems to have settled down good. Now, with this new independent project, I am pretty fine. But he thinks that now I should get married and settle down." His throat gulped an imaginary lump and he licked his lip, as if he was anticipating a major showdown. His eyes were glued to her face.

"Your coffee ma'am." The young boy placed the large coffee mug with multicoloured sachets of sugar. Avantika did not even care to acknowledge it. She looked at Sunny, in the eye.

"Get married then. What's the problem?"

"But Avi, it concerns you... I mean us." His voice wavered.

"Let me make something very clear. To me, life is not about getting married and making babies." She delivered her point straight, without any pretext. "If it is about having sex, we are having it even now, aren't we? So why do we need to get married? And if you ask me, this whole institution of marriage sucks."

She picked her cigarette deliberately from the pack, fumbled around for the lighter and finally lit it. "It bloody sucks big time."

He knew that the lava was burning within the forced calm in her voice; the cigarette lighting was probably just a way to buy time, choosing the correct words and to fend of the urge not to blast off.

"It's just not natural. Take a look around and you will find that ninety-nine per cent of the couples have the strangest reasons for living together, and my dear friend, love does not figure in that list. They get stifled, mess with their individuality, but keep sticking to their partners without love, without purpose even when their marriage loses its entire soul. I want to achieve what I have set my eyes on. To me, my life has a purpose and I shall not rest till I achieve it." She took another deep puff and stared into one of the black and white paintings, behind his head, intently.

He was hurt, sorry and angry—all rolled into one. After giving eight honest years to the relationship, he felt as if the whole thing was slipping from his fist like quicksand. Was unconditional love nothing but a mirage? Though he acknowledged that being a part of her parent's unhappy marriage had scarred her mental makeup. So, like a shrewd business negotiator, he steered clear of that point and brought up the next one.

"But for how long do you want to keep on trying this painting stuff of yours?"

"What do you mean by how long?" She snapped and almost choked on the smoke. He knew that he had set off the panic button.

"I mean it has been more than ten years Avi, but it's going nowhere."

"Don't you think that it is my life and therefore I have every right to put in ten or hundred?"

Tempers were rising. She was losing control of her self-imposed calm. Even he was a changed man; in no mood to quit without presenting his point of view.

"Avi, sure it's your life. But even then, like a sane being, you should realize that your so-called 'life purpose' is serving you no good. Maybe, life has something better in store for you, something different. Unless you pause a chapter, you would never know."

She watched him. He took it as a sign of acceptance.

"Maybe life wants you to settle down, enjoy life, have a family and be happy. Look at your friends. Look at Shweta, your batch mate, happily married and a mother of two."

This time the cynic in her smiled.

"So you think that someone who is married and has two kids has every reason to feel happy about life in general?"

"Of course, that is the way life is. That is what we are supposed to do. Go to school, then college, settle in a career and get married, have kids and raise them. Our grandparents did that, our parents did that and now it's our turn. Isn't it what we call the circle of life?"

And finally it erupted, the only difference being that instead of spewing hot lava, hot Brazilian coffee flew around. The tall white mug hit the stone floor. It refused to take the insult lightly and promptly disintegrated into hundred of pieces, some small and some big ones, flying all over the place. People sitting around took cover from the coffee assault, looking at her and wondering what could have provoked such a petite, demure and coy girl.

"Circle of life? Bull shit! And don't you dare count me in when you say it's our turn. Like your grandmother, mother and millions of *panjoo* women, do you want me to get up and put on red coloured, gawdy lipstick even before I brush my teeth? Do you think I will do *pairi pauna* and start and end every conversation with *Jai Mata Di*? Mr Khurana, you *panjoo* men want a woman to flash your ill-gotten money by making them wear diamonds, sending them off to moronic kitty parties, while you menfolk go screwing around town."

He experienced a surge of mixed emotions. Embarrassment, anger, helplessness, hatred and pity. His face was red and he could feel the ebb of heat waves pulsate in his ears.

"Mr Khurana, your grandmother would have done it, so would your mom. But for sure, I won't do it."

She dipped into her satchel, pulled out a 500 note, still staring at him, slapped the note with a bang of her palm on the table. The mermaid quivered at the unexpected violence. She weaved her way between the tables, towards the bright sunlit door of Art Café.

Embarrassed, he fumbled in his pocket for an imaginary cigarette packet, or just about anything; anything which could temporarily take away the scorching heat of the scores of eyes trained on him. Without success, he finally donned his Bvlgari shades, as casually as he could, and started his trek towards the exit door.

Patch-Up

"*Arre*, you are overreacting," Shweta tried to console Sunny who had no other place to go when Avantika left him bruised and bleeding.

"Don't you know how Avi is? Believe me, she loves you immensely and truly. It's just that she is a little wired up. Her last exhibition is not helping her cause either. Between you and me, don't we know that we were the only ones who bought her paintings?"

They were seated in the verandah with a checkerboard floor, overlooking a well-manicured garden, dotted with white painted wrought iron chairs. Shweta was curled up in the oversized, overstuffed cane swing which hung from the ceiling. She was filing her nails and curled them inwards to inspect them and then carried on with the next finger.

"But Shweta, she is almost thirty and not getting any younger. Why can't she understand that maybe, I am saying maybe, she is not cut out to be a painter." Sunny kept the empty coffee mug back on the table after he presented his rationale.

"Ramdin, marinate the chicken and please keep the salad back in the refrigerator." With a slight detour, Shweta got back to the conversation. "Sorry, sorry. To celebrate Prashant's company crossing the 500-crore mark, we are organizing a small party, only for close friends."

"And surely we are not a part of the privileged few?" Sunny cribbed.

"Don't blame me, ask your darling Hitler. I called her and as expected, she flatly refused. Ask her." Shweta got offensive.

"You don't owe me an explanation. I was kidding." Sunny surrendered.

Suddenly out of nowhere, Shweta's eyes lit up with some bright idea.

"Hey, you know what, let me put Avi on the speakerphone," she beamed, throwing the filer on the table and picking her mobile phone, "let me help you guys sort this mess out, for once and all."

"No no…" Sunny dashed to stop her as he knew the consequences of this seemingly innocent gesture. But it was too late as the quick dial had already started the buzz on a distant telephone.

"Hello Ms Sengupta, how are you?" and without waiting for a reply, "you are now on the speakerphone, in the esteemed company of her highness Shweta Khemka and Mr Sunny Khurana." Shweta chuckled, failing to mimic the emotionless, steely voice of an office telephone operator.

"Hi Avi." Sunny greeted her meekly.

"Shweta, what is this business all about? Didn't I tell you that I will be with a client for the rest of the afternoon? You know, I had to excuse myself to take your call." Her voice was curt and business like.

Sunny could feel as if a lump of cold sticky gelatin was stuck in his throat, trying to push its way down the food pipe, trying to flee from the problems of the outer world.

"Avi, stop overreacting. And yes, this thing is as important as your client meeting." Shweta tried to take control of the call. "It's time you understand that there is more to life than paintings, paint and your easel." With an overdrive of energy, she groped for vocabulary and similies which applied to this context. "How can you leave the canvas of your life devoid of colours in an attempt to fill colours on an inanimate canvas?" Continuing with her literary masterpiece, she continued, "Can you understand what Sunny is going through? Do you have any idea what is he trying to tell you?" After a theatrical pause and letting the moment sink in, she very softly chided her friend, "My poor baby, I know you are much tensed. See baby, I really don't blame you for blasting Sunny, but all I am trying to say is…"

"Shweta, all what you are trying to say or do is interfere with my life right now. Can't you see that both Sunny and I are adults? As two adult individuals, this is something between the two of us. I would appreciate if he had discussed it directly with me, instead of running to every Tom, Dick and Harry with his white-flag-sympathy campaign."

"Avi, you are getting it all wrong," he pleaded.

"Sunny, one moment." It was Shweta. "Thanks Avi for letting me know that I am just an outsider between you and Sunny. Let me ask you my real name and the status as well. What am I? Tom, Dick or am I Harry? Answer me Ms Avantika Sengupta?"

"Shwets, stop overreacting." Avantika knew that her hyper-sensitive friend had taken things a little too far.

"I never meant anything like that and you know it. You are my sweetie pie. All I was saying is that I expected a little more maturity on Sunny's part. Ain't relationships all about understanding and trust?"

"It has been eight long years, Avi. I have lived with your every whim, given in to your every demand…"

"Sunny, please," Avantika snapped. "Stop playing this martyr-tyrant story with me. And by the way, which whims of mine are you referring to?"

He realized that he had goofed up again.

"You got me wrong babe." His voice took a u-turn, laced with love, which stemmed out of fear of losing her.

"And for God's sake, I am not a babe. Please stop using these moronic, Americanized adjectives when you know that the context is far from being true. Do you think I am a babe? Do you even know what babe means?" She thundered.

"Avi, he did not mean…"

"And now that you have said it, I think you have always been looking for a babe, never for a woman with real dreams and desires. A hottie, whom you could flaunt, fuck and make babies with."

"Avi, please don't give me this again. Have I ever stopped you from pursuing your dreams? Tell me. And why do you think that there is something wrong in getting married and bearing kids? Don't all women do the same? Didn't Shwets get married, made babies? Is that a sin? Avi, why do you always make me feel guilty for loving you?"

"You know what Sunny, maybe you should have married someone like Shweta, or better, her only."

Love And Hate Collide

The room was small, like any other middle class bedroom. One wall was lined with cupboard while the other had a small sliding window which looked out from the 12th floor apartment. A queen-sized bed was placed in the centre, flanked by two side tables. Both tables had identical red and white lamps. Weak housekeeping was obvious as both bulbs were of different colours and wattage. The constant use of the tube light mounted on the wall, to soften the dark maroon coloured walls, had resulted in a dark grey spot on the ceiling. The stark white marble floor added some mellow tone to the otherwise overbearing character of the room.

Simi was sitting on the bed, examining her finger nails with no particular interest. Wearing a pink crumpled cotton shirt, which was unbuttoned and a grey laced skirt which was carelessly hitched high on her thighs, she looked frightfully ordinary without the company of Christian Dior and Maybelline.

"Darling, soda or water?" A voice rang from the other side of the door.

"For how many years have we been together?" She shouted back with deep contempt, without budging her sight from the mini research she was conducting on her nails.

"And in all these years, you could not even understand that I hate it when you sit on that bed of yours, and plan to get drunk." Came the reply. "Now, move that pretty butt of yours and bring it to the living room. The living room is the place where you are supposed to have your drink, unless you are celebrating some special occasion in bed with champagne. But I am not blaming you darling." The pause in the sentence was punctuated by the click of a cigarette lighter and then a quick inhalation. "I know the real culprit is your civilian genes." The man shouted back playfully, bordering on a guffaw.

"I am not coming anywhere. And just in case you are still not aware, I always have my afternoon drink with tonic water." She replied.

"Got you Darling. Now be a good girl and hop out of the bed."

"But I am not dressed up. Can't you get it here?" She argued.

"Don't you know that I like you more when you are undressed? You can leave the buttons of your shirt still undone." There was a tease in his voice.

"Aren't you a horny rascal?" Her voice said that she took the compliment well and as a result, swung her legs to the cold marble floor.

"Tell me?" She strutted out of the bedroom, into the living room, still buttoning her shirt with one hand, while the other was trying to settle her unruly tresses. The walls were white, and the intermittent columns were highlighted roya blue. Bamboo chik, also in blue colour, covered the big glass panels on the door and the windows. The bamboo furniture was painted enamel white and had mustard bead cushions propped on them to offset the monotony of white. The side table had various arrangements of bamboo shoots. Small potted ferns along the length of the room complimented the colour scheme. For someone like Simi, the house seemed to be well done.

Colonel pulled her in his lap.

"Ouch. What are you doing?" She protested meekly. Colonel smiled and kissed her cheek.

She smiled. "Whenever I see your lust being replaced by love, I get scared."

"You women are impossible." Colonel smiled and kissed her cheek again. "I don't think any man in this world has a clue as to what it takes to stop you from complaining."

She kissed him back, got up and picked her drink which was standing amidst the bamboo shoots, placed herself on the chair, adjacent to the sofa, and placed her leg on Colonel's lap. "Cheers" She said and took a large sip of gin with tonic.

Colonel smiled back slyly, sipping on his Black Label. "You wicked woman, you know what I like, don't you?"

"You know what Colonel, at times I feel that I am the luckiest woman on this earth. But then there are times when I am forced to think just the opposite."

"And what evokes these contrary thoughts in you?" Colonel was looking at the stretch of the bare expanse of her legs, topped with the crumpled skirt which lay in folds and creases, the shirt was stretched at the buttons. A slight smile touched his lips to remember the wild time she gave him less than an hour ago. He was still holding his glass with one hand, while the other massaged her feet.

Simi smiled, with clouds of nostalgia getting over her. "I mean, it almost sounds like a story out of Hollywood. A couple having a turbulent marriage till the wife decides to seek some professional help..."

"...without knowing that this so-called professional help would steer her life to a different course by falling for her dashing husband." Colonel completed her sentence and ended it with a hearty laughter and an extra squeeze to her red painted toe.

"Shut up, you scoundrel. You trapped this innocent girl," Simi clarified her status while taking a long gulp from the glass.

"Should I remind this innocent girl that it was she who was eyeing this dude right from day one?"

The last line did not register with Simi. She was lost in her own stream of thoughts. Emotions changed rapidly on her face. Her eyes softened and voice trailed. "You know what, at times this whole thing makes me feel so guilty." She shifted on the chair, pulling her feet from Colonel's lap and curling them under herself. "I mean your wife had come to me seeking help and I cheated her. Poor thing, post that she could never recover." She gulped down another large sip of the gin-tonic concoction. The burning sensation of sweetened alcohol made her mind go off the chain of thoughts, albeit temporarily. "I have always led my life my way. Did things I wanted to. Whatever I did, I never had any second thoughts or guilt. But for this one." She had a faraway look in her eyes. "Yes, I liked you instantly. Yes, I fell for you; yes, I wanted you very badly. But all this cannot justify the heinous crime of holding your wife's hand and knowingly leading her towards a dead end." Her eyes got moist. She emptied the gin-tonic, in a contemplative mood and placed the glass on the table.

"Simi, stop blaming yourself," Colonel tried to assuage her. He picked her glass and walked to the bar. "Whatever happened was a part of the destiny. We just played our parts." Handing her the glass, he said, "go slow hon."

"Even if it were for destiny, I can't live with the fact that I was instrumental in your wife's suicide. I was supposed to help her, guide her and..." She pulled up her knee and buried her face and started sobbing.

Colonel's mood was bordering on exasperation. He gulped the scotch in one go and thumped the glass on the table, out of sheer frustration. He had been a part of this scene a zillion times—as a participant, an audience, a party, a mute spectator, and, therefore, he knew that only some divine intervention from '*Maa*' could resolve this. His thought gave the situation those few extra seconds for a self heal, while he stood there, as if waiting for the moment to get over.

"You know, every action has to be judged not only on its merit but also on its pay off. What did I get after all this?" Simi looked up with hurt eyes.

"Simi, don't start it again. Please." His voice was calm but firm and he kept facing the window. He could never get himself to face these situations head on. This part of women was still like a puzzle to him, which he could never solve.

"What do you mean by 'don't start it again'?" Her face changed from that of a victim to that of a tormentor. "It does not give me any pleasure in repeating the same saga over and over again. Why can't you marry me and put a full stop to this story? And why can't you face me and look at me in the eyes?"

"Simi, please stop being dramatic." He turned and leaned on the window, facing her tear-streaked, horror-struck eyes.

She banged the loaded glass on the table. The crystal glass snapped and the heavy glass base disintegrated and flew from the table and landed at the far end of the room, like a meteor. The body of the glass was still in her hand. The table drooled of gin-tonic, which had also splashed on the mustard bead cushions. Colonel watched her, maybe with pity in his eyes. Her extreme action did not evoke any emotion in him. He merely removed the glass from her hands and walked off towards the kitchen.

She screamed towards the kitchen door, "I'm tired of playing your slut. I gave up everything for you; my career, my family, everything that I had. To be what? Your mistress? You come and go whenever you feel like. What am I supposed to do here? Wait for you to get horny? I know you don't love me any more. You never did."

Her voice got hysterical as her eyes followed him walking out of the kitchen. "I should have known that how can a man, who induced his legally wedded wife to commit suicide, love and marry someone else." Her hoarse voice was whimpering, crying and mumbling nothing in particular. Her dark kohl-smeared eyes were following Colonel as he picked up the car keys and the jacket. His eyes were loaded with pity, just as he kicked the thick glass base out of his way and walked away.

We Don't Need No Education

"Why do all college canteens have the same gastronomical assault menu cards? Samosa, Patty, Bonda." A much younger Avantika cribbed.

"Is the *bong* babe craving for *macher jhol*?" Younger Shweta giggled.

"Fish cutlet could have saved my day. But I know hoping to find any thing like that in this city infested with crotch scratching men is like finding a virgin in Thailand." A round of laughter filled the small make-shift canteen of Delhi College of Arts. With red coloured plastic chairs and weather beaten wooden tables, it was the only place where irrespective of the courses—fine arts, applied arts, sculptor or painting—students got together to discuss and enjoy something even bigger, life.

"Avi, tell me something. Do you really hate Delhi and Punjabis due to your so-called progressive and evolved genetic code, as you choose to call it, or does it have anything to do with some past memories?" Chintan, the Punjabi dude of the group, posed a simple question. She looked at him while her mind processed the right answer. To facilitate the same, she pulled out a pack of Navy Cut, lit one and allowed the nicotine to soak every cell of hers, turned the chair, back to front, and sat astride facing him, with the sun on her face.

"You know Chintan, maybe you are the cutest *panjoo* I have ever known." Elated, Chintan took a bow while the group cheered and clapped.

Avantika continued, "and to answer your question, I guess it has to do with the truth. Now, look at yourself. Born to well-to-do doctor parents; Mom, a gynaecologist, and Dad an ophthalmologist." Chintan had the quizzical look planted all over his face as he tried to figure out the context she was trying to establish. "Both operate out of the same clinic, which is your garage converted into an office-cum-OT. Your domestic helps double up as compounders for both, your Dad and Mom. The same set of house helps-cum-compounders help in carrying out an abortion, delivering a baby, helping during a cataract operation and also cooking *chapattis* in your kitchen."

Chintan could not make out head or tail of her statement. "So is there any thing wrong? What is that you're trying to say?"

"See that is the point. A *panjoo* would not even notice anything wrong with that." Avantika sounded caustic. "For God's sake, how can a domestic help be the compounder or vice versa? How can you call a servant chopping vegetables to dispose of an aborted foetus and then send him back into the kitchen? Can't you see my point?"

Chintan's face turned red. Shweta, the perpetual peace maker since the time she knew Avantika, anticipated rising tempers and to diffuse the tension, she deployed humour and diversion tactics. "Ms

Sengupta, this is also known as full utilization of manpower resource. By the way, what should I order for you?" Her effort proved abortive as it infuriated Avantika further. "No, it's called unethical practice and exploitation. And every single Punjabi is doing the same. Karol Bagh to Ludhiana, these wretched creatures thrive on unscrupulous methods, practices and corruption." She fumed.

"Why single us out?" The Punjabi genes in Chintan got up to defend and survive. "If we are the only ones to be blamed, then why is Bengal not free of corruption? Why is it decaying under the able and progressive leadership of the Red flag?"

"Chintan, don't take it personally dude. Avantika did not mean to hurt you. She was just trying to give an example." Shweta played Mother Teresa to the hilt.

"No Shweta. She wanted to prove how mean my parents are. She suffers from a superiority complex which stems out of ignorance. One Rabindranath Tagore and a Netaji is all that they have."

Shweta was surprised to see Chintan's reaction.

"Look around yourself Avi, open your eyes. The biggest painter is not a Bengali, nor is the hottest music director. None of the top musicians or the poets are even remotely Bengali. On the contrary, the administrative services, the foreign service, the management cadres, even the armed forces, all are full of gallant and sharp Punjabis."

Avantika took a deep drag of the Navy Cut, filled her lungs with the thick smoke. Maybe nicotine did her some good as she smiled back.

"Sure thing Chintan."

This casual remark frustrated him even more and he decided to get back at her with more vengeance.

"And if you were as progressive, evolved and a self-respecting woman that you portray yourself to be, before running down the entire Punjabi clan, you should have realized that even for you, it takes a *panjoo* boyfriend to foot your bills."

A face turned pale and another red. Avantika got up and walked away, silently, as if carrying the world on her frail shoulders. Since that day, '*panjoo*', though a six-letter word, turned into a four-letter word for her.

Give And Take

"Dear, now art is big time money. It's serious business." His tone had the precise balance of conviction and sagacity. "And therefore, you have people like me to ensure that this business goes well for both, the artists as well as the art collector; investors as I prefer to call them."

Avantika silently studied the man sitting behind the large marble top desk, on a big leather upholstered chair. His face was fair, round and puffy. Courtesy the umpteen rounds of 'scotch-soda' combo followed with artery clogging butter chicken, the once high cheek bones were now buried under layers of fat. However, his well-defined beak like nose, thin lips and white long side burns definitely imparted him an aristocratic look. The piercing eyes beneath the gold rimmed glasses were alert. His crisp white linen shirt with real mother of pearl buttons and sterling silver cuff links announced his love for understated style.

Why was she there?

Surely not to attend a lecture on 'the art of investing in arts.' She cleared her throat and regained her composure. Her eyes caught her hand on the arm rest of the chair and she noticed that her red Fabindia *kurta* was going well with the raw silk upholstery. Good contrast, she thought.

"Well sir..." The gentleman sitting across her smiled and made a polite interruption. "Oh dear, the Queen never knighted me. Too bad! So till the time she does, you can call me Chow. My friends call me the same."

Avantika smiled, though a forced one. While flashing the same, her mind tried to figure out how could someone with a name as ancient as Surender Singh Chawla hide behind a façade of a degenerated nick like 'Chow.' Damn these *panjoos,* she mumbled to herself.

"Well Chow I fully appreciate that if someone as seasoned as you has a point of view on art, it has to be with merits. Though I am of a little different opinion, but it really does not matter." She tried putting her best foot forward. "No dear, every point of view matters. Believe me, it does. And especially if it is that of an artist. " He replied in his cultured voice.

"Well, Chow, actually when I came to you, I had a very specific agenda. I know that you are a busy man and your calendar is cramped with appointments. Therefore, I would hate to get into a debate with you and waste your precious time." At times, she wondered how tough times softened even someone like her.

"Oh dear, you don't worry about my calendar or appointments. All of this can wait as I am sure that your agenda ought to be as exciting as you are."

He smiled. Only this time both his smile and voice betrayed his demeanour to reveal the lust-laced edge. Also, his eyes caressed her cheeks, lips and lingered for a few luxurious extra seconds on the upper part of her *kurta* before settling on her eyes again. She knew for sure that he was not trying to figure out the knit pattern of her *kurta*.

She got uncomfortable and her left hand moved involuntarily to rub off an imaginary speck off her chin with her thumb, thus casually covering her modesty. For a second, she was surprised at how the caustic body language of a complete stranger could rob her of whatever little self-confidence she had. Shifting back in the chair, she tried to adjust her emotions, which were swinging between embarrassment, anger and need.

"Well sir, I have come to seek your opinion on my paintings. For some reason, even after all these years, they have failed to catch the imagination of the critics, gallery owners and even the art enthusiasts. During my own short career, I have seen mediocre artists and their works fetching astronomical prices, where as..."

"...your exhibitions fail even to generate any enthusiasm or footfalls, leave alone fetching a single dime? Am I right Ms Sengupta?" Chow completed her. Truth is never sugar flossed and so was the statement made by Chow. Like any other occasion, this time too, truth produced a long and eerie spell of silence.

"My statement might sound curt, but then it is a mere reflection of the crumbling state of thousands of artists. This large bunch leads a dark life with no future just because they presume their paintings to be the last word in the domain of art and fail to go with the ways of the art world." Chow's statement reeked of deep-rooted hatred towards artists who did not cringe and bow before the powerful brokers of the art world.

"But sir, as artists, shouldn't the freedom to express be our right? Whether it goes well or bites the dust could be another story."

"Ahhhhh. Do I see the famous communist Red flag coming up?" His laughter was cynical.

"Ms Sengupta, as children of the Supreme Creator, the God, we have a right to so many things. Even our Constitution promises the same. Right to education, right to speech, a right here and a right there." His temper, though well restrained, was rising. "But do we get them? No. They are mere words." He continued. "Art is marketing. Hard core marketing. It's a discipline. And like any other discipline, it has its own complexities, numbers, formulae and ROI."

She was hit by a speeding truck. All what was said sounded gibberish and so alien. Wasn't painting an expression, a divine expression where the world was the canvas and nature and imagination the paint brush?

The perfect accented voice of Chow disrupted the construction of Avantika's rosy world. "For your benefit, let me apprise that like a brand, artists have to be positioned, packaged, priced and then sold. Big time brands or artists don't happen by chance. It is all planned. Every single detail. What they will paint, what will they wear, where will they put up their first to nth exhibition, who all will be the attendees, who will buy their paintings, which media will cover it, when will they go to Paris and when to Milan. Everything to the last T."

A chill was descending from the base of her head and progressively plunging down the spine. The shock of losing a cherished dream was getting on her and she had this overwhelming urge of running out of the room and crying aloud. After all, if this was what it took to succeed, she could see all her years going down the drain. For the first time a sudden surge of loneliness gripped her. She felt so cold and lonely. No one to hold her hands, no one to guide her and not even a shoulder to cry on. What a waste of life and time. No career, no friend, no future. What the hell had she been doing all these years?

"Have you heard of rock star managers, or closer to home, film star secretaries?" Chow's voice dropped to a whisper. Without even bothering to look at her, he continued, "similarly, there are agents who take care of a painter also. And let me warn you, it is not the painter, but the agent who can make or break a painter's career. No wonder these agents charge a fortune."

He smiled. Maybe the thought of dollars comforted him.

"And how do I get one, if I decide to go for one?"

"Come on dear. Don't be mean. I am right here, in front of you, at your service."

Avantika smiled, a fake one. The rising repulsion was written on her face and it was only growing. "If I may, what would you charge?"

"Oh dear, we can take it as it comes along. That can be negotiated. Everything on this earth is not measured by the moolah, and with a painter as pretty as you, we can work out a cash and kind deal also."

It took a second for her meekness to turn into courage. "Chow, I want to tell you something which I feel from the bottom of my heart."

"I'm listening." He smiled.

Avantika moved forward, leaning on the table, and whispered, while Chow's eyes were glued to the soft depression, the red Fabindia *kurta* made on the edge of the table across him.

"Mr Surender Singh Chawla, you are a first rate bastard and a second class pimp."

The words hammered on the ear drums of Surender Singh Chawla even long after Avantika left.

A Bad Day

"I am glad that you decided to come over. Trust me, we will have a blast. You have been working too hard and this change of place will surely do you good. I swear, Delhi gets on my nerves." Sunny deftly manoeuvred his Audi A4 on the chaotic South Extension road. "This place, my friend's farm house, is an absolute bliss. The best part is that Raj, this friend of mine, and his family are away to Europe on a vacation. But with all the servants available round the clock, I promise we will have a great time."

Sunny had a charming smile hanging on his lips as he looked at her suggestively and looked away when he wasn't sure if her eyes were reciprocating the same. He picked up a light whistle along with an old Kishore Kumar number on the FM. Life was looking good today, after a long time.

As the car stopped at a red signal, Avantika looked out at the sea of humanity, which had converged on the sidewalk to cross the street. There were so many of them, from so many parts of the country. Each burdened with their own dreams, desires, abilities and shortcomings.

Her eyes flirted over the teeming and bobbing heads which trotted on the zebra crossing. The sari-clad woman with a baby on her hips and a worn fabric bag slung over her shoulder rushing to probably attend an ailing relative or work, the tall girl in her early 20s in denims and a tee, with a spring in her walk and knapsack on her back, head nodding to music from the earphones, a woman in the gaudy lipstick and *churidar kurta* with a plunging neckline showing off the negligible wares they held, while her eyes constantly flickered to catch the attention of a well-to-do customer, preferably in a large car. Every one was so different from the other, yet in the crowd they mingled so seamlessly. If people have different faces, then why doesn't the crowd?

Her focus shifted inside the car as her fingers caressed the leather seat. It was smooth, almost like silk. She wondered if money could also smoothen life. She did not have any answer, at least for now. The signal turned green and Sunny pressed on the accelerator and they sped along. She watched the big stores whizzing past, looked to her right and her eyes stopped at the man at the wheel—Sunny Khurana.

He was quite good looking. Fair, tall and with sharp features. He could easily pass off as a film star. To know what she looked like, she did not even need a second opinion. Dusky, 5'4, big eyes, which were always brushed with thick *kajal*, sharp features and the typical Bengali length hair—long and black. She could be described as presentable, at the most, average on a good day. She knew that her friends wondered why Sunny adored her, especially Shweta, who constantly reminded her that he was perfect husband material and she should not let him go.

But then at times she wondered if there was really a term as

'Husband Material'. To her, if life was a journey, which needed a companion, the companion should be fun to be with—intelligent, compassionate, understanding, and if it happened—Bingo! And if so did sex—Double Bingo! Why did the companion need to be good looking or rich? Why were other trivialities accorded so much importance in a relationship?

An irritating knock on the car's window disrupted Avantika's chain of thoughts. She jerked involuntarily to find two eunuchs, smiling at her. Clapping hands in their traditional style, for some reason, they always looked menacing to her. She cringed with fear. Sunny laughed. "Don't worry. Poor things are harmless. Give them a tenner and they will go away." His cool demeanour worried Avantika at times. How could he be so indifferent to things which disturbed her? Was he extra cool or did she overreact? Or was it just a difference of sensibilities and sensitivity? The eunuch persisted with their window tapping.

Avantika opened her satchel, searched for a tenner and when she found none, pulled out a fifty. The eunuchs smiled when they realized that their persistence was about to get rewarded. She pressed the button to roll down the window, maybe by a few millimetres, and slipped the note through it. Black fingers with garish red colour nail paint snatched it away. An aura of the outside world seeped inside the sanctum of the car—the sharp but smooth essence of jasmine, the intoxicating and heady mix of petrol and diesel, unidentifiable stench of fruit peels and vegetable waste from the roadside vending cart. Thank God, the ordeal finally ended. She took a deep breath after rolling up the window.

The car slowed down as it turned into a lane.

"Avi, just give me a minute. Let me grab my laptop and I shall be back." Sunny parked the car in front of his gate—a thousand-yard *kothi*, as he called it, and not waiting for a reply, half jogged, half walked inside the premises. Avantika looked past his receding figure. The tall iron gate had a massive brass circular plate which proclaimed '*Jai Mata Di Sadan*.' The brass plate was certainly polished every other day to keep up the sheen and to keep the persistent pollution at bay. Beyond the gate, the cobbled driveway was flanked by two rows of large trees on either side. Beyond the greens, a white double-storey house built on the lines of Roman architecture loomed. Big white columns, sweeping arches and loads of space everywhere. Avi soaked in the silence of the lane while admiring the grandeur of the *Gulmohar* which stood majestic in its fiery bloom.

Her eyes saw a servant running out of the gate. Please God, she did not want to go in and meet anyone; not his mother, at least. Either her silent prayers were not answered or the divine had other plans in store. In anticipation of the servant coming to her side of the car, she rolled down the window again.

"*Namaste Madame. Memsahib ander bula rahi hain.*"

Slavery in its worst form still existed, she thought. As she stepped out of the car, her mind was trying to figure out the plight of the poor servant. Did he know the meaning of the word '*Memsahib*' or its origin? Only a conceited *panjoo* would have initiated him into this '*saheb*' and '*memsahib*' circus.

She walked through the cobbled driveway, then through the path in the garden which led to a flight of wide white marble stairs that led to the luxurious patio. The verandah was lined with identical potted plants and the furthest wall had over hundred masks hung, in all shapes and colours. There was this six-foot wooden tribal mask, which she remembered Sunny had mentioned picking from Namibia. She tried to identify some others like Venetian papier-mâché, Durga, Kathakali, Nathau, rest all were a conglomeration of colours, shapes and emotions and strangely she had an uncomfortable feeling about the whole place. For some odd reason, she stopped at the door, and adjusted her *kurta*, her bead necklace and the bag. She knew that there was not much she could do with her green *khadi kurta*, broad bangles, seven-year old pair of Levis and the pair of *mojri jootis*. But then there was no harm in trying. Maybe the opulence of the house was making her nervous.

The door opened and she saw another brain dead '*saheb-memsahib*' type standing there, smiling. Purely based on courtesy, she smiled back. Was she nervous? Shut up, she told herself. This was not the first time that she was visiting his place. But then on second thought, she was visiting his place the first time with his parents around. All other unaccounted visits happened during unearthly hours, amidst darkness, when she never had the time or opportunity to look around in this part of the house.

"Hi Avantika, come on in please."

The voice alone reinforced her feeling that something was not right. The perfectly pitched voice belonged to a middle-aged woman in her late 50s, short hair dyed a brilliant shade of blue-black, in a sweat shirt and track pants. A fleeting image reminded Avantika of Betty of Archie's comics. Even from some 40 feet away, Avantika could see the big diamond rocks adorning her earlobes and another one sitting at the base of her neck. Out of the blue, she started figuring out which film star had said that whenever she received diamonds from her husband, she knew that he had cheated on her. Damn her meandering thoughts. She ought to put a check on them.

"Hi Mrs Khurana. Good afternoon."

"Afternoon dear and it is good to see you. It has been really long. Where have you been?" Mrs Khurana hugged her. It was a formal, cold hug which betrayed the literal meaning of the word 'hug'. Avantika's artistic sense was assaulted by her loud perfume. Her eyes met Mrs Khurana's. She smiled. 'Avantika, don't be conscious, don't be nervous,' she told herself. 'Come on, gather up your nerves, and strike a conversation. You are the intelligent one. Go for the kill. Turn this socialite *panjoo* woman to dust.'

"Nice perfume Mrs Khurana." She started with her earnest endeavour.

"Thanks Avantika." She smiled and lightly squeezed her fingers as an acknowledgement. Kind words always work.

"You know, during this Europe trip of mine, I was at a small store in Austria and I chanced upon this hand-made, made to order, personal fragrance. I just could not resist. Though it cost me a fortune, but who cares."

"Sure. It's really nice." Her soul cursed her for lying so blatantly. Being nice was acceptable but this was an outright lie as she knew that the first whiff of the European fragrance reminded her of women of lesser virtue, stalking Park Street after sunset. 'Not fair Avantika. Don't be mean. Try another line. Come on strike a conversation.' She tried controlling her meandering thoughts.

"Hey Avantika, isn't this the kind of *kurtas* which used to be available at Fabindia? Wow, do you still get these things for 300 bucks?"

Avantika had no clue of her reaction. Though the initial one was that of murder, the second one was milder where she wanted to tell that high school dropout, whose only claim to fame was that she married the guy who didn't stop at anything to make money, to fuck off.

The servant rushed in.

"Sunny Baba, Sunny Baba, *gaadi bahar nahin hai. Lagta hai chori ho gayi.*"

"What? The Audi?" Mrs Khurana shrieked and stared at the servant. The servant's nod was affirmative. Sunny came rushing down the stairs and darted towards the gate, where he had parked the car. Mrs Khurana followed him. Not sure as what to do, Avantika too followed to become a part of the confusion. As they stood at the gate, the gleaming piece of metal and cutting-edge technology was gone.

"Oh dear, call up Gupta uncle. Tell him to get all the borders sealed before they take it to Rajasthan or UP."

Sunny was frantically dialling numbers.

Avantika stood there, in complete silence, trying to figure out if there was any way in which she could be of any help to them. But she knew of her limited networking.

"Avi, when you got off the car, did you lock it?" Sunny enquired while still punching numbers on his phone. She tried remembering if she did. But she knew that her frequent auto travel had made her oblivious to locking and unlocking of car doors. Shit! Was it her mistake? Damn! A mistake worth 30 lakh. At least that was the price

Sunny had told her when he had bought that car. Should she accept her fault worth three million or should she play the pretender? Truth will make her face the music and lie, her conscience.

'Take your pick Ms Sengupta. Move fast.' Her mind coaxed.

"I am sorry. Maybe I did not." She stuttered.

Her frail frame could not handle the expensive guilt and its ramification. She held the iron grill of the tall imposing gate.

"You can't be serious Avantika." The deep cultured voice of Mrs Khurana gave away to her real self. She walked towards Avantika, almost menacing, grabbed her hand so hard that it hurt. Her face was red with raging rage.

"Do you think your sorry could get back our car?" She screamed like a true refugee, Punjabi woman, surviving in one of the non-descript rehabilitation colonies in North Campus, Lajpat Nagar or Shahdara for that matter.

"Mom, it's ok. It was insured." Sunny tried to pacify his stomping mother who had assumed the form of Goddess *Kali*.

"What do you mean by that? You think you can set this house on fire just because it is insured? Or do you think you can push me down the Eiffel Tower because I am insured? What sort of logic is that Sunny?" She lambasted him. Anyone who came to protect Avantika would have been treated in the same manner.

"Mom, I was just trying to tell you…"

"Mr Sunny Khurana, I hope you know that insured piece was worth three million. Three million, which most people can't make even during their entire lifetime."

Intentionally or unintentionally, during the last bit of her sentence, her eyes stopped at Avantika for a second longer than needed. And letting the disdain and scorn for someone not reflect in her eye was an art which was not mastered by Mrs Khurana.

Avantika was hit by a sledge hammer, blasting her self-respect to shreds. Her rarely used tear ducts celebrated the occasion of their use. With tears till the brim, her eyes looked more beautiful and her face more vulnerable. She looked at Sunny, expecting him to take her side, defend her and be her man. Sunny noticed her need but also realized the futility of any effort to pacify his mom. He sighed, looked the other way, pretending to dial another number.

She controlled herself and the vulnerability on her face was replaced by conviction and strength, which were more like her. Now, instead of being just a painter, her resolve was to be a successful one, as living with a burden of three million on her soul could be suffocating. As she walked away from the imposing gate of Greater Kailash, her inability at number crunching was highlighted as despite all her efforts she was not able to figure out how many paintings she needed to sell at ₹ 30,000 each to make three million.

It All Comes Back To You

Never in her lifetime did Avantika believe in anything possessing the slightest hint of religion. Idol worship, fasts, *havans*, the hocus-pocus of birth charts, astrology and palmistry included. Maybe her stand of being an atheist stopped her from delving into anything which was remotely religious in nature, as to her religion was illogical. Therefore, it was highly unlikely that she would digress from her path to explore and experience something as alien and unheard of as hypno-therapy and past life regression.

But either blame it on her repeated failures or the persistent hard sell by Shweta that she agreed to try it out. She had her initial session with a nearby therapist, who did her *chakra* cleansing and healing. But owing to Avantika's dominant left brain, her therapist could not access her subconscious mind which held the root cause of her repeated failures and misfortunes. That was the time when Shweta insisted that she should visit Chauhan sir, her family friend, mentor and guide. According to her, her hubby's soaring fortune in chemical trading was due to Chauhan sir's blessing and guidance. Also, to strengthen her sales pitch, she blurted out the names of some twenty odd celebs who were a regular at his *ashram*.

Avantika could see his exalted stature clearly in the form of the numerous certificates, neatly framed and put on the wall of his huge and modern bungalow in Gurgaon—address to the *nouveau-riche*. As she sat in the healing room with Shweta, she could feel the air of serenity around. The walls were painted virginal white and the big windows had thick beige coloured silk drapes on them. The wooden flooring imparted a certain warmth to the big room which had a high back chair, a small work station, a lazyboy in dark tan colour and exactly seven stain glass paintings with strange mystical motif on them. The sterile aroma of camphor coupled with the rhythmic drone of *Om* chanting heightened the soothing vibe.

Skeptic, apprehensive and confused, the atheist was surprised when she saw Chauhan sir walk in. Her entire imagery around Godmen and astrologers and the likes was shattered in a fraction of second. Built like a bull, Chauhan sir's fair complexion was graced with a broad forehead and a strong nose. His bulging biceps and chest muscles moved restlessly under his tight white T-shirt. The wavy, shiny and long curly hair was tied neatly in a pony. He looked like a WWF hulk. The big red *tilak* on his forehead further accentuated his hypnotic aura.

"*Namaskar* Shwetaji. How are you? How is Prashantji? Please make yourself comfortable." His deep voice accentuated his charm as he settled into the high back chair. Shweta walked towards him, bent down and touched his feet. Avantika did not know what to do. She stood there in awe and confusion. Her eyes transfixed to his face.

"So Avantikaji, how are you?" He looked at her directly.

Avantika's heart missed a beat as he turned on his Mac notebook which was perched atop the work station. While it booted, he moved closer to the screen and put on his silver rimmed spectacles. The delicate frame, perched precariously on his nose bridge, added the required intelligence quotient to his robust charm and aura.

"Have you heard of hypno therapy and past life?" he enquired. His kind yet deep baritone eased off her defence mechanism a little.

"Well, yes. In bits and pieces." She blurted.

"Sir, I told her whatever little I knew." Shweta came to her rescue.

He smiled.

"So what brings you here?"

"Well, I mean…" She fumbled.

"Sir, actually we are here…" Shweta tried to play the wonderful friend that she was but there are some journeys which ought to be taken alone, without any co-passenger. Probably past life was such a journey, as Chauhan sir raised his hand, signalling Shweta to slow down. She got the clue, touched his feet, and walked out of the room.

He looked at Avantika and smiled. His eyes still had the same question which he had asked a few seconds ago.

"Actually I am here to know about my future. I am a painter and for some reason, for long, success has been eluding me. Also, on the personal front, things are not quite right. Be it my relationship with my father, boyfriend or anyone else." She rattled off.

"Avantikaji, Sai Baba is very kind." He folded his hands and closed his eyes, expressing his gratitude to the divine power. Avantika noticed for the first time that she really liked the sound of her name when he said it.

"I am sorry but I don't get you."

"He has got a miracle for everyone. When your therapist forwarded your case to me, I had no appointment for the next two months. And then, one night Baba appeared in my dreams and ordered me to see you. Let me tell you something, whether you take this session or not, you always have Baba's blessings with you. He will always guide you and be your guardian angel." She could not corelate all this as the current mess she was in had pushed her into being a complete non-believer.

Maybe he read her mind.

"Avantikaji, as we all know, this life of ours is an aggregation of our past lives and *karmas*. And the next life will be an aggregation again. That is why it's called the *Karmic* Cycle. It goes on and on till we can break it by surrendering to the supreme being and striving towards our respective *moksha*. But it takes a lot to do the same. Giving up negative emotions like lust, hate, greed, desire and uniting oneself with the Supreme Power, using the umbilical cord of love."

She nodded in acceptance.

"Contrary to the popular belief, no therapy or past life regression is not for propagating shortcuts to happiness, making predictions and advocating sure fixes. It has a bigger purpose and a role to play." He continued, "therefore, let me clarify that I am not into predictions. I am just a medium who will help you meet your angels and guides. The entire journey and the conversation will take place between you and your angels and guides. They will show you things they want to, and it's they who will not let you see certain parts. It will be your own personal journey and I will just help you by facilitating it."

What the hell, she thought. If he was not going to predict the future, then why did she take all the trouble of coming to Gurgaon? Again, somehow, he deciphered her thoughts.

"Avantikaji, you have come to Gurgaon with a purpose."

"Sure sir, I mean *Panditji*…" She got confused with the choice of prefixes which aptly demonstrated the quandary in her mind. "But more than the talk of higher self and the higher path, I just want to know about my future. Please forgive my impudence, but I can't help it as I am in a very bad state." Her eyes got clouded with tears.

He got up and offered her a glass of water.

"Can you read a book without learning how to read alphabets and words? Of course not. So before we move to the specifics, you need to understand life in bits and parts. This will give you the right perspective. And having the right perspective alone will reduce your worries, tensions and stress by more than fifty per cent. Life is so simple, so beautiful. Every step is planned by our divine father on the basis of our past *karma*. Like a smart Father, He wants us to learn lessons from this life so that we don't repeat the same mistakes in our next life too. But being mere mortals that we are, we accuse him of being harsh on us. You do the same. Don't you Avantikaji?"

She nodded.

"Please come and make yourself comfortable." He pointed towards the Lazyboy and took out a small chain with a locket kind of a thing attached to it. "This is a pendulum, and with this, we will check your *chakras* first."

With his deep, soothing commands taking over her mind, she gradually slipped into a state of absolute peace and bliss, feeling like a feather, floating effortlessly, where she could see a better future waiting for her.

As she walked out of the bungalow, she was completely dazed. She could not believe that she actually saw things which she never dreamt of in her entire life. Was she dreaming or did she actually see them? However, the good part was that on the basis of her ramblings during the sessions, Chauhan sir assured that her future was bright and the best part of her life and career was just around the corner.

Like a child, she only remembered about the candy part but failed to pay any attention to the fact that it was bad for her teeth.

The Turning Point

"No it's ok. Showcasing your earlier work won't be necessary. Mr Khurana has personally vouched for you and your work. As this hotel is his project, he better be sure of his recommendation." Mr Lancolne smiled. A nice, warm and genuine smile which was a part of the overall warmth he exuded.

For a man of his stature—worldwide CEO of one of the largest and leading interior design firms—he was indeed a trusting and compassionate soul. In his early 60s, his lean frame was dressed in a grey silk short shirt, which definitely seemed to be an India purchase, and light blue denims. The tan loafers complimented his casual style. His silver hair was sharply combed back to a slick tail held together by a black band, highlighting his sharp features.

Avantika mentally reprimanded herself for taking Sunny's advice seriously and dressing up in a business suit for this meeting. Her brand new black business suit and a string of pearls at her neck was so unlike her and made her look and act so uncomfortable. The more she thought, the more she cringed and wanted to sink inside her suit.

"Sunny, I hate you," she thought.

But maybe she was being too harsh on him. He had been pestering his father for last two weeks to fix this meeting. To ensure that she pronounced the French name right, poor thing also tutored her for two days. During the two days, she was told that it was not pronounced as 'Frankois Lankolne', but 'Francuaa Leson'. No wonder, she could never muster the courage to order food at the expensive French restaurants Sunny often took her to.

The very thought made her smile. After long, very long, she felt that she still loved him. But was it this meeting which made her feel good about him or was it something else?

She snapped back to present as she watched Mr Lancolne twirling the coffee cup on the table. The well-manicured fingers truly belonged to a creative genius. She smiled and nodded and adjusted the lapel of her jacket. Was it a size small?

"Mr Lancolne, if I may ask, as the designer of this project, what kind of paintings would you like for the hotel? I mean, do you have any particular brief in mind?"

"Well, as I have told you, this is going to be a luxury boutique hotel with 30 rooms. Very European in look and feel. If I were to articulate, very Brit in nature, less the ostentation. To give you an example, something like an English cottage. Cosy, warm, lots of wood, candles, fireplace, wooden floor, rugs and trophies."

"Something on the lines of a log cabin? Or maybe a hunter's cabin?" She tried to help him with his visualization.

"Yes and no. Well, to a large extent, yes, but more plush and with modern conveniences." The conversation warmed up with his smile.

"So do you think, the paintings need to be around hunting, wild life or..."

"Though it would be your call, but if I were the painter, I would have taken the more universal appeal of the outdoors; the fauna, the flowers, the butterflies, the birds and the bees, the waterfall, the river." His eyes got nostalgic. "I am sorry." He smiled and apologized. "The mere thought of outdoors carries me away to the French countryside." All his words were trailed by softness and complimented his conversation style.

Was it his simplicity that made him such a successful and a respected name in the interiors business? Avantika wondered. Running a vast business empire would require him to be astute, shrewd, manipulative, deep into finance and what all. Then why was he not like the businessmen of Delhi—loud, uncouth, lecherous, stingy and mean?

"Mr Lancolne, I know you are a very busy man and I really appreciate your gesture of meeting me at such a short notice." She hesitated. "But if you can spare me a few more minutes, I would love to take you through a similar series which I have with me."

Such a soft statement coming from Avantika was like a shower in the Thar. Needless to say, good manners, genuine smile and simplicity were his soft spots.

"Certainly lady," he adjusted himself in the chair so as to have a better look at the paintings which were to be presented on the centre table. She opened her big portfolio bag and fumbled as she could feel his eyes watching her clumsiness. 'Oh God, I can't sit here all day fumbling like an idiot', she thought.

"Take your time. I am in no hurry." His soft and gentle voice helped her to focus more as she finally found what she was looking for. She pulled out a few 8 × 8 cards and handed them over to him. He flipped through them casually. Then again, he went through them, this time with more interest. Did she see a twinkle in his eyes? Avantika thought to herself—had a worldwide CEO lost all senses to get enthused to see paintings by an amateur? After all, that's what she was when she did these 10-year old paintings. She chided her enthusiasm. As she adjusted her focus back on him again, she saw the 8 × 8 cards spread in front of him. He was juggling them around in a sequence and then another, with both hands. Did she read his face right, as she was not used to appreciative glances of people around her paintings.

"Where did you paint these?" His voice had a distinct tone of admiration.

"Shantiniketan. I was there on a college trip then. Shantiniketan is in West Bengal, it is…"

He cut her short with a dismissal wave, "I know. It is where Rabindranath Tagore got his inspiration from." He adjusted his posture.

"Don't take my words on this, trust your instincts, but these candid, innocent, vibrant and soulful expressions would be just perfect for this project."

Did he use the word soulful? During her short meeting with Mr Lancolne, Avantika knew that he was articulate enough to realize the difference between the right and almost right word. And if he did use the word, which he did, he meant it. So who was right? The critics who branded and labelled her work as 'soulless and terribly staid' or this design guru, who would have seen the world and life more than all the critics put together?

Her dizzy steps took her out of the room, clutching her leather bag and the portfolio. There was a lightness in her head and steps. She could have danced all the way to the lobby. She desperately needed some nicotine in her system.

"Auto." She waved her hand to stop one.

"Defence Colony." Before the auto driver could say yes or no or haggle on the fare part, she got in, put on her earphones, and for a change, instead of Floyd or Led Zepp, opted for the more soulful 'Wonderful Tonight'. As he crooned, she wondered, how the same guitar sounded so romantic, as if it had a bleeding heart when Dave Gilmour, Jimmy Page or Eric Clapton caressed it and how it created a complete pandemonium when one of the shredders wielded it.

The auto took a wrong turn, and knowing Delhi auto drivers, it was an intentional one, to fleece the commuter. She felt like checking the auto driver as she was in no mood to pay him any extra for the forced Delhi *darshan*. But then she thought, maybe it was a good time to introspect and plan. Introspection amidst all the noise, chaos and mayhem of Delhi traffic? She was sure that some philosopher would have supported her viewpoint by telling her that if a man experienced the most severe bout of loneliness amidst a crowd, then why couldn't she plan amidst all the chaos? Point taken, she smiled.

Her mind went back to her meeting with Francois Lancolne. Was it a good one? Did he really like her work or was he just being kind? Did it mean that finally she would be doing something worthwhile? Would her talent finally adorn the walls of a boutique chain of hotels? All this, she found very hard to believe. Her fingers ached to dial someone's number.

Sunny or Shweta?

Sunny was the obvious choice as he was not only her boyfriend but also the one who had fixed this meeting. She scrolled down the phone book till she reached the entry, Sunny Khurana.

And as if out of nowhere, a Honda City pulled beside her auto. The tinted window rolled down and a guy in his teens looked at her. The blaring *bhangra* music which leapt out of the rolled-down window ached to establish its supremacy by beating the unbearable decibel being produced by the chaotic traffic. All these years in Delhi had taught Avantika to ignore such indecent and unruly *Delhi-wallahs.* She followed her strategy. But the car driver was persistent.

"Hey baby, wanna lift?"

She ignored.

"Come on baby. Don't be shy."

Though the music was almost deafening, but even in that loud music, his words were slicing her ear drums. In the side mirror, her eyes caught the face of the auto driver who was smiling. A lecherous, taunting and a typical MCP smile.

She looked at the Honda City driver and then at the smiling face of the auto driver. She could feel the volcano of rage simmer and then blast.

Phaaaaaaaaaaaaaaaaaaaaaaaaaaaaaaat

The slap caught the auto driver off guard. The inertia of the pain, the fear of getting toppled over and the reflex action of trying to avoid it; it all happened simultaneously. This made him lose control of the auto, which was plying at high speed, skid sideways and hit the Honda. Metal against metal produced a loud metallic screech. The

Honda hit the pavement with a loud bang. Courtesy all the concrete, it was thrown back on the road. The driver tried to control the car. Avantika held on to the frame of the auto rickshaw. After wobbling dangerously for few times, it finally landed.

"M******************" screamed the car driver. He was not to be blamed or branded as *Delhi-wallah*, as hurling profanity under this kind of extreme situation would have been the most preferred and natural reaction worldwide. The auto driver did not know if he should look back to confront the passenger who had just slapped him or should deal with this rowdy driver first. He chose the latter and hurled back a profanity; Newton's third law in action.

Avantika's face was blanched. She held tightly on to the auto frame as her last strand for survival.

"Stop the auto." She screamed as she saw a PCR van parked ten metres ahead at the junction of India Gate. "Stop it I say." She screamed louder. Probably the youngster in the car also saw the PCR van, as he sped away hurling profanities at her. As the car zipped past, she tried to make a mental note of the number. But instead of staying focussed on the number plate, her eyes got transfixed to the tinted rear glass of the car, where bold, red letters proved her theory bang on.

It read *PUNJABI PUTTAR*.

That Is What Friends Are For

"Avi, I am going to ask you something and I need your honest answer." Her voice was dull, strained and very unlike Shweta.

"Shwets, all well? What happened?"

"I want to... well, do you mind if I..."

"What is the matter darling? No, I don't mind anything. Just tell me what is it?"

"Can I move in with you for the time being?"

"I didn't get you. Come again." The question was obvious as Avantika could not get the context of her request.

"Avi, I am asking you till the time I get a house of my own, can I stay with you?"

"Are you crazy or what?" Avi held the unlit cigarette in her hand and left the lighter on the table and started pacing the room.

"Avi please. I am in no mood for any *gyaan* or lecture. Just a yes or no would do."

"Come on Shwets, you need not ask me, but at least tell me what happened?" her pacing velocity gathering momentum.

"Nothing. Where should I tell the cabbie to take me?"

"You are in a cab?" This revelation made Avantika realize that something had to be terribly wrong. Her dainty friend, who was born to rich parents and married to a richer guy, loathed the very idea of using any form of public transport. "Tell him to take a left from the Defence Colony flyover and keep on following the road till it hits a dead end."

"Ok ok. I know my way from there. See you."

It was obvious that she was struggling to make herself heard over the din on the streets. Always used to travelling in the quiet hum of the plush airconditioned cars, this was a nasty exercise for her throat.

"No no, you don't hang up. Talk to me. Tell me what's going on. Tell me now Shwets." Avantika knew of her hyper and extra-sensitive nature. Owing to her long association, she very well knew that under stress or mental turbulence, Shweta was capable of taking steps which even she would repent, only if she were still alive to do the same.

"Avi, I am in no mood, please." For a change, her perpetually soft voice had an erratic edge.

"Ok you don't talk to me, just answer my questions. Ok?"

The verbal silence on the other end was an indication that the deal was made. "Had a fight with that millionaire pumpkin of a husband, did you?" There was a long silence on the other side of the line.

"Look Shwets, you are breaking your promise. If you don't want to talk that's fine, but you did promise to answer my questions, didn't you?"

"I am not going back to that shithole. I've had enough." The action was stated, but not the reason.

"That's fine. I am not asking you to go back. You can stay with me for as long as you want." Avantika tried to cheer her up, more so because she wanted to keep the conversation going till she reached her place. "We will have a blast of a time. We can go to the UPSC Bhawan and have *paani-puri*, do shopping at Karol Bagh and then have *Roshan Di Kulfi* and, of course, get drunk at The Rodeo. You remember these places?"

The sob on the other end of the line was ascending, both in intensity and volume.

"Shwets, what happened?"

Silence.

Avantika cursed herself for initiating the dialogue. If this conversation would have happened face to face, at least she could have sensed her mood and steered it, or at least offered a hug to make her feel better.

The dam holding up Shweta's pent-up feelings, frustrations and desires cracked and a deluge followed. Instinctively, she turned around to pick the tissue box only to see a glaring hole in the rear panel from where the speakers had been yanked out. Her *kurta* sleeves, *dupatta* and the back of her hands kept dabbing the stream of tears.

"Don't stop yourself. Let the tears roll. They will do you good and you will feel better."

"Every day, right from early morning till late in the night, I did whatever it took to keep my family happy. Playing the perfect *bahu*, the all-rounder wife, the smart mother. Not once did I listen to the woman in me. I always told myself that now I am more of a daughter-in-law, a wife, a mother and more."

Avantika felt sorry for her friend. That was the least she could do for her.

"Every single breath, every strand of thought, every bit of me was centred around my home. This sari would suit *maa*, this shirt would look good on papa, this suit Shruti will love, this tie would go well with Prashant's suit." The sarcasm in her voice made it clear that she was referring to her in-laws side. "Working day in and day out, managing the household, their whims..."

"Shwets, please don't get worked up."

"Damn it, I have every reason to get worked up Avi. After seven years of marriage, when I caught my husband cheating on me, there was not even a single soul to support me. Not even my own parents."

Avantika was taken aback. Not because she found the fact startling but because she was trying to figure out who would be the girl who would have an extra marital relationship with a creature whose lower half was shaped like a pumpkin and the face had a close resemblance to a wild mongoose.

"Can you believe Avi, on his business trips he was sleeping with hookers?"

"Ah…" Avantika sighed. She was not widely off the mark. No one was having any affair with that repulsive creature. It was all paid!

"Shwets, you have kids, you have responsibilities. You just can't walk away like this. Did you try to initiate a conversation with him? I am sure he would be sorry for whatever he has done."

"Avi, you too? If this bastard had slept with one and regretted it, maybe I would have blamed it on the testosterone and accepted his mistake. But he has got permanent hookers in every city that he visits."

The deafening noise of honking cars told Avantika that her friend in distress had reached the Mooolchand flyover and would be arriving within the next 10 minutes. She looked around. Her so-called studio apartment was in a mess. Unmade bed, coffee mugs strewn on the floor, canvases, paints, ash and ashtrays, cigarette packets and matchboxes and… God, she had a lot of cleaning to do. Her Virgo friend was already too stressed and such a messed up sight would surely lead to a cardiac attack.

There was silence as Avantika did not have any words of comfort. "And do you know how slyly this slime ball bastard saved their names on his mobile?"

Avantika racked her brains. Office? Friend? Auntie? Leave it. She knew that she was bad at this guessing game and then figuring out some pervert's mind was not up her street.

"Car Rental!" Shweta exclaimed.

"For the Mumbai whore, it is Car Rental Mumbai 1, Car Rental Mumbai 2. For the Bangalore one, it was Car Rental Bangalore 1 and so on. It so happened that Meenu wanted some local help in Mumbai during her trip this week that I pulled the numbers from Prashant's phone. Who knew, I was on a mission to help myself. Mumbai Car Rental... my foot!"

Good Lord. How original. She yawned. Suddenly, she started feeling a little stupid and uncomfortable. Sharing her space with anyone didn't make her too happy.

But then isn't this what friends are supposed to do?

The Final Countdown

The black *sherwani* wearing *Durban*, sporting an obnoxiously large and bushy moustache stopped the autorickshaw ferrying Avantika and Shweta and told them politely that auto rickshaws were not allowed inside the Delhi Golf Club.

They both got down and after paying the auto driver walked towards the brightly lit building. The sight of the colonial styled façade took Avantika years back. Back to her army days when many of her evenings terminated at the army club seeking refuge in the library in an effort to steer clear of the interested looks of young officers and eliminating all chances of encountering Dad's wrath. Snapping back to the obnoxiously mustached *Durban*, she wondered, if it were the uncanny resemblance of the building of her past that made her uncomfortable or was it something else? Maybe time would answer the same.

On the other hand, Shweta wondered what was wrong with her normally exuberant and chirpy friend, Avantika. Since morning, she was not her usual self and was fidgeting and bothering over trivial issues which never featured in her list of importance. Like what should she wear, should she wear *kajal*, should she carry some flowers and the list was endless. She did not even haggle with the auto driver over the fare. Was she nervous? But knowing her, this one emotion did not gel with her.

As they walked silently towards the big, arched porch, they could see expensive cars driving up. The turbaned guards were rushing to open the doors of the cars carrying distinguished citizens, attired in expensive clothes. Avantika was still busy in trying to decode the mystery when she knew well enough that in the coming ten minutes or so it would be solved in any case. But why this sudden invitation by Mrs Khurana? Why at the Delhi Golf Club and not at some other, less formal place? Why today? Though Shweta had tried her best to answer them as logically as she could, but something told Avantika that this time there was definitely something more to it which no logic could fathom.

The Ivy Room was their destination. They took the stairs to the main lobby, the huge glass door swung open, courtesy the efforts of another burly mustached guard. As they were ushered in, they noticed the brightly-lit interior. The bar, which was right ahead of them, was decked up with numerous bottles of various shapes, sizes and colours. Bartenders with slick smiles hanging at the edges of their lips were serving the thirsty patrons perched atop tall bar stools. White attired waiters were silently balancing China plates, loaded with starters and deftly placing them, picking glasses, placing soda jars and refilling glasses. The only noise which their activity seemed to generate was perhaps the clink of the ice when it hit the glass. Hearing the ice almost brought Avantika back to the Ivy Room and almost involuntarily, her eye searched for two things—Old Monk and a place to smoke. Hard luck on both the fronts as Old Monk was not on the shelf and the 'no smoking' sign was painted on fashionable fish motifs and was placed at various locations. The longing for a whiff of nicotine intensified. Fighting the urge, as she looked around to locate Sunny, a waiter stepped up to her.

"May I have your name Ma'am?"

The tone was cultured, but the smile plastic. Without even acknowledging his existence, Avantika continued her search across the room, hoping to spot the expected faces. There they were! She waved and walked towards the round table where Sunny was seated with his family. Shweta, who knew that her friend and formal niceties were poles apart, mumbled a 'thank you' to the waiter and followed.

Sunny got up to greet and escort them. Mr Khurana senior adjusted his blue silk tie knot and his better half plastered the perfect welcome smile.

"Dad, meet Avantika and her best friend, Shweta."

They smiled. Avantika noticed that Mr Khurana had a handsome, rugged, yet, pleasant face.

"Hello Avantika, hello Shweta. Please be seated. I was really looking forward to seeing you all this evening."

Avantika did not know what to say. She just smiled. Her eyes met Mrs Khurana's.

"Evening Mrs Khurana."

"Good evening Avantika. Good to see you again. Though I hope this time it is not as eventful as the last one." Mrs Khurana let out a throaty giggle, dripping with sarcasm. The figure of three million hit Avantika again. Damn her! She needs to start working on the hotel project fast. At least that will give her some amount to contribute towards her kitty of three million. She struggled to act and look normal by not letting go of the smile from her face.

"Oh dear, what a day it was." Mrs Khurana made a general announcement to nobody in particular. She looked at Avantika and asked, "you remember dear?" Before she could reply, Sunny tried to steer the conversation.

"Mama, please. Don't start your sob story again. Have you met Shweta?"

"Shweta, meet my Mom. And Mom, this is Shweta, Avantika's best friend."

"Hi Shweta."

A cursory glance at Shweta was enough for Mrs Khurana to notice that they had a lot in common. Rich and upper class families to start with, obnoxious-sized solitaires on their fingers, followed by another pair on their ears, not to miss the expensive watches which were prerogatives of a select few.

"Hi Auntie. Thanks for inviting us over. It is really very kind of you." Shweta spoke addressing the entire Khurana family.

"Oh not at all dear. I am glad you could make it."

Sunny looked at Avantika and he knew that she was feeling out of place. He wanted her to enter the conversation before her mom and Shweta hijacked it.

"Avantika, did you tell Dad that you met Mr Lancolne?"

Before anyone could respond, Mrs Khurana did.

"Though we were expecting her call, but never mind. Knowing a gentleman that Mr Lancolne is, he did the needful."

Avantika looked at Sunny, confused. Sunny gave his mother a glance and then followed it with an apologetic look.

"Now come on, stop intimidating them and offer the girls some wine." Mr Khurana played the good host.

Deep in his heart, Sunny thanked his father and immediately handed the drink menu to the ladies. Avantika knew that her favourite, Old Monk, would not feature on the expensive hand-made paper menu card. So she did not even bother to have a look. Shweta strained her eyes to read the cursive fonts.

"Sunny, stop playing passing the parcel and order a *Dom Perignon*. I am sure your friends will like the heritage and relish its eternally young spirit."

Mrs Khurana declared that she indeed was the de facto captain while she inspected Shweta's beige and sea-weed green Ritu Kumar *kurta* held by the small Swarovski clutch at the neckline.

"So Shweta, what do you do?" Mrs Khurana enquired. "To me, you don't look like a painter. Are you?"

Her questioning smile to Shweta was definitive, but everyone present knew the smile was not directed at her. What were painters supposed to look like? Avi wondered. Famished, dirty, with a beard and *jhola*, smoking *bidis*? The communist in her was rising as she could see the divide coming up. The age-old divide between the capitalists and the communists. She felt a little stifled and nauseated.

"No, I am a homemaker. I leave the working part to my husband. He is into exporting bulk drugs," Shweta elaborated.

"That is a fast growing sector. Smart guy your hubby is." Mr Khurana proved that he was an avid follower of numerous news channels and business publications.

Even after whatever happened between Shweta and her husband, praise for him made her feel good. Was residual love the reason?

"What is your spouse's name?" Mr Khurana enquired.

"Prashant, Prashant Khemka."

"By any chance, are you guys related to Sunil Khemka of the Khemka Group?" Mr Khurana was getting curious, as a common interest, common name, common workplace always generates excitement.

"He is my father-in-law." Shweta blushed.

"Small world indeed." Mr Khurana smiled after proving that his trail was right. "I know him quite well. As a matter of fact, I was there at your wedding also. Remember me?" He quipped.

"Ah VK, you are not a Shah Rukh or Amitabh Bachchan that the poor girl would have spotted you while getting married." Mrs Khurana reprimanded him.

They all laughed. But Avantika, who scraped a smile, realized she was making patterns with her thumbnails on her forefinger. She desperately wanted to go out and let nicotine soothe her nerves. A drag or two would also do, but then she knew that this was not the best place for it.

The silent waiter served the bottle of legacy, along with an array of accompaniments with dexterity.

"Cheers." Mr Khurana raised his glass. "To health, happiness and life."

Surely, Old Monk was a better bet, was the first thought that hit Avantika's cerebral cortex, as the sweet dry champagne coated her taste bud. She was sure that this bottle would have cost a fortune; of course by her standard not Mr Khurana's. Just to get over the funny taste, she took a slice of the crab cake. She stared at her finger. Her nails were short trimmed, without a hint of colour. They looked so unkempt and crude when compared to the other ladies on the table. She glanced at Mrs Khurana's fingers. She had delicately balanced the champagne tulip on two fingers, her nails a radiant pink, one large stone glistened on one finger while the other had a large band with a sprinkling of diamonds which looked like hundreds to Avantika. She quickly washed down the delicate starter along with the thought of glittering paints and stones!

"So Avantika, tell us about yourself. We have been hearing a lot about you," Mrs Khurana enquired.

"And all good things." Mr Khurana smiled, tried putting her at ease. "Tell us about your family, your future plans."

Avantika looked at Shweta and then at Sunny. She felt trifle confused, suffocated and nervous. Without Shweta, her saving grace, she would have never made it past the first thirty seconds. A long spell of silence followed as she had no clue as to what to say. She moved around the last morsel of the crab cake around with her tongue, tried to hold the glass as delicately as she could, realizing three pairs of eyes were on her. She needed the nicotine more than ever. Just a puff would clear her mind. God, just one puff, she prayed.

"For how long have you been painting Avantika?"

Mr Khurana offered her a sitter. She would have been seven or maybe eight. Or was it when she was in the fifth standard? Like a moron, Avantika actually started calculating the number of years. Her silence was embarrassing Sunny. This was not the girl he knew her to be. 'Come on Avi, say something, please,' he prayed.

"Ever since I have known her. And we have known each other since the sixth standard. Right Avi?" Shweta proved again that good friends go a long way in making life comfortable. The palpable tension on the table dissolved.

"Why don't we place our order first? Right Avi? I am starved." Sunny came to her rescue. But Mrs Khurana was relentless.

"Sunny, we have come here all the way to meet her, to know her better, and to do that we need a dialogue. I am sure the food can wait. Right Avantika?"

No one had any doubts.

"Can you excuse me for a moment?" Without even waiting for an answer, Avantika got up from her chair. The need to light up a Navy Cut was too strong now, almost uncontrollable. Shweta looked at Mrs Khurana and let out a sheepish smile. Sunny looked at Avantika, with concern, and tried demonstrating the same.

"You want me to come with you?" He volunteered and pushed his chair and was half standing.

"Sunny, why you would like to accompany her to the ladies' room is beyond my comprehension." Mrs Khurana's statement was cold and curt.

Sunny, still not upright, gradually pretended to slick his hair to a side and eased down on the chair gradually. His eyes were remorseful as he glanced at Avantika, and then, in turn, looked at his mother with a wounded puppy look and stared inside his glass. The lights got too bright for his comfort.

The waiter politely enquired if they would like to place their order. Mr Khurana obliged and rattled off the family's favourite dishes on the menu. He took his time to explain the dishes to Shweta loudly to cover up for the dour silence which was otherwise obvious. Mrs Khurana continued to examine her nails, as if she could stare them into a different colour. Sunny seemed to search for answers to all his questions in the half-filled glass. Shweta tried to look as interested in the dinner menu, while observing the mother and son duo, trying to figure out how long would Avi take to finish a cigarette.

Avantika returned and took her seat. As soon as she seated herself, the strong odour of Navy Cut told Shweta that her moody and at times even whimsical friend should have controlled her urge. But it was too late.

"I am sorry." Avantika tried to be at her courteous best.

"No no. It's the other way around. It's me who should be sorry." A note of apology coming from Mrs Khurana made everyone sit up as they sensed something terribly wrong, especially Sunny. Mrs Khurana's stare was transferred, from her nails to Avantika's eyes.

"As a considerate host, I should have known that creative souls like you are used to their quota of cigarette and booze and, therefore, should have offered you the same."

Avantika was flabbergasted. She did not know how to react. And the worst was yet to come.

"And if you don't mind, could you use a gum or something. The stench of your cheap tobacco is getting on my nerves." Mrs Khurana lightly touched her temples and grimaced.

"That's ok darling. All the cigarettes smell the same." Mr Khurana smiled, trying to play the good cop. "And for God's sake, she is not a kid. She is free to make her choices." He tried putting things in a proper perspective so as to avoid the embarrassment which was lurking just around the corner.

"Mama, Please. Don't create a scene." A visibly embarrassed Sunny seconded his father.

"So you think it's me who is the trouble maker? Your mother is creating a scene and it is making you so embarrassed?" Mrs Khurana hissed between her teeth. Shweta and Mr Khurana assumed that they were not a part of whatever was about to happen.

"It's not me, but your painter girlfriend who is creating the same; in your life and in our lives as well."

"But…" Avantika tried to interject.

"You dare not interrupt me." Mrs Khurana waved her finger menacingly at her and then turned to direct her outburst on Sunny.

"When you mentioned her for the first time, as a mother, something told me that someday things would get out of hands. Didn't I warn you?"

Sunny looked sheepish and had no clue.

"When you showed me her picture, I was shocked, not at her ugly duckling looks but at the pathetic choice of my son. I mean after all these years of having nothing but the best for him, how could he flip for someone with no looks, no class, not even decent family credentials." Mrs Khurana continued her anti-Avantika campaign.

"Suman, please stop this immediately. She is our guest and

aren't we decent and civilized people?" The host and the chivalrous man in Mr Khurana revolted against the brutal onslaught launched by his wife.

Sunny and Shweta had no clue as how to react.

They sat there as if hit by lightning. Avantika took a sip of Dom Periognon, and said, "No sir, that's perfectly fine by me. Please let Mrs Khurana share her feelings. After all, as she said this get-together is to know each other and what better way to know each other's true feelings than this candid, heart to heart conversation. Please carry on, Mrs Khurana. I am all ears."

Her confidence and strength to hold ground even under extreme provocation upset Mrs Khurana. Suddenly, she felt exposed and vulnerable; both, from a strategic as well as emotional point of view. She knew that her next move had to hit the bull's eye.

"Do you see her impudence?" Mrs Khurana complained to the jury.

"Mrs Khurana, you have every reason to thank my decent upbringing and grooming that stops me from slipping down any further. After that seething, personal and baseless attack of yours, my outburst could have been beyond your expectation." Avantika's tone was remarkably smooth and poised.

Shweta wondered about the source of Avantika's confidence and grit under the hostile environment. Till a few minutes back, under normal circumstances, she was the gullible one—lost and confused, searching for answers and acting like a teenage girl.

"Sunny, I have had enough of your girlfriend's nonsense." Mrs Khurana's voice rose and heads turned. She was trembling with rage, oblivious to pity mortal reactions.

"God, she is so crass in her thoughts and her lack of grooming just makes it worse. Even after *Panditji* told me that she is a *manglik*, I was ready to give in to your pestering. But her first visit to our place was such a disaster." Mrs Khurana was at her best theatre antics. "A loss of three million. And I am not even counting the money you spend on buying her trash paintings."

Mr Khurana got up with a start, his fingers tugging at his tie incessantly and his face set in infuriation. People sitting around were gently turning around to locate the source of commotion.

"I know there is no point in asking you to slow down," the sentence was aimed at his wife, Mrs Khurana, "so it's better that I leave. Avantika and Shweta, I am awfully sorry for whatever transpired today."

Avantika felt sorry for him. She never knew that even *Panjoos* had gentlemen amongst them.

"No sir, it's fine. Please don't embarrass us any further by apologizing. I guess it's just a bad day for all of us."

Avantika got up from her chair. She looked at Mrs Khurana right in her eyes and smiled. "Mrs Khurana, I am so grateful to you." Everyone was taken aback. Sunny blinked.

"You know, a few days back, I read a line." Avantika was in a contemplative mood. "It said if nothing changes, nothing changes. It was so right. Today, you initiated the change and now I shall take it forward." She turned towards Sunny who squirmed in his shoes as he had a vague notion of the inevitable bullet which was advancing towards him.

"Sunny, now you know what your mother exactly thinks of me. Having said that, let me clarify that I am not offended. Simply because she is not someone who figures in my list of people who really matter to me."

"Avi please, I am sorry." Sunny pleaded, stealing side glances to his mother.

Avantika stopped him. "I know you want to marry me, or at least, that's what you wanted till a few minutes back. But as things are placed now, you can clearly see that with such strong notions co-existing, it won't be possible. Having said that, let me also clarify that I respect her as your mom and that is why I took all this insult and injury. But then, Sunny there are times when you need to take a call and call a square a square. So, if you really think that whatever your mother said was misplaced and incorrect, if you really think that I am as pretty as you told me, if you think that I still am your lucky mascot and not a bad omen as your mom portrayed me, will you walk out with me, holding my hand, right away?"

A wave of shock hit Mrs Khurana's indignant face. Sunny looked at Avantika as if she was not being just by asking for an instant decision. Mr Khurana took a deep breath and adjusted his tie knot the tenth time. Shweta was dumbfounded.

"Avi, don't you think…" Sunny fumbled.

"Sunny, the time to think is over. It's the time to act." Avantika looked at Sunny, a deep stare. Their eyes met and she saw his eyes flinch.

"Shweta, let's go."

She looked at Mr Khurana and smiled. "Sir, after all this, do you think I am still working on your hotel project?"

Mr Khurana looked at her and walked towards her. To everyone's shock, he hugged her and smiled. A smile which a proud father reserves only for his daughter.

"Yes, you are and now more than ever. And if anyone, I mean anyone," his eyes darted in the direction of mother-son, "thinks otherwise and tries to act funny, don't hesitate to call me."

He pulled out his business card. "This has my direct number. All the best and God bless."

Avantika pulled out her earphones from her bag and put them on while she walked away to the door. Shweta blundered behind her friend. As Bob Dylan's 'It ain't me babe' filled her, a tear rolled down her cheek. A tear for having wasted her love and time for eight long years.

In God's Country

As she stepped out of the Jet Lite flight, she took in a deep breath, filling in her lungs with fresh air. Her effort to save money by not taking a direct flight to Cochin and instead taking an economy stop over flight had drained her of every single strand of energy and patience. It had been nine long hours since she had left her place and was not any closer to her final destination, the backwaters at Kumarakom. Every neck muscle ached and her limbs failed to move in unison. Slinging her small overnight cabin bag over her shoulder, she walked down the stairs while turning her neck sideways, on both the sides, to relieve the strain.

The small bus transported her to the arrival lounge. She was taken aback by the beauty of it. It looked like the foyer of a museum, not an arrival lounge of an airport by any stretch of imagination. Calm, quiet and clean, it was dotted with wooden sofa chairs with carvings on them. Their brown velvet upholstery, covered with beige coloured cotton cover, made them look so much more comforting and inviting. The liberal use of wood, from panels to door frames, ceiling to coun-

counters, gave the lounge an added warmth. Though it was her first visit, for some reason, it all seemed so familiar. The foyer was dotted with arches and pillars with ornate carving. The overall moisture-laden air was damp but fresh and seemed to make up for the frustration of those nine cramped up, claustrophobic hours. To her surprise, in the crowd, the ratio of foreigners to Indians was fairly high. The highest she had ever seen anywhere. Maybe even God and his land welcomed dollars more than INR. She mentally chided herself for getting into her Red flag mode. Minutes later, she strolled outside with the bright red backpack piled on her aching shoulders.

The hotel staff was waiting, holding a placard with her name. She noticed with a grimace. Her name was written as Miss Avantika Sengupta. She scowled, even though there was technically nothing wrong with the name, just associating her father's name with her own made her uncomfortable. And Miss? Her scowl gave way to a naughty smile as she wondered if the salutation of Miss had anything to do with the status of a girl's virginity? Miss for never done it, Ms for probably done it and Mrs for surely done it!

She was grinning to herself as the driver ushered her into the hotel car. The environment was already relaxing her. She made a mental note to call up Shweta and thank her for forcing to book the package with a luxury car pick and drop. As the car rolled out of the airport, she looked back to check if the airport building was a natural extension of its interiors. Yes it was! The top of the building was dotted with thatched, conical domes, made of red coloured bricks. The wall was lined with dark coloured window frames, with carvings on them. The round columns supporting the structure made the building look like a South Indian palace rather than an airport. She looked back again; where had she seen it earlier? Maybe in some picture or brochure, she told herself. After all, a picture of the Kochi airport was not classified information.

As the car hit the road, she could see the reason for claiming it to be God's own country. Wherever her eyes turned, things were a shade of green—bright and beautiful. She looked at the watch and realized that it was close to 6 pm. The sun was setting and so were her eyes.

"Hey babe, take a walk on the walk side; hey sugar, take a walk on the wild side." The unmistakable raspy vocals of Bob Dylan jolted her out of her sleep and hence the sleepy drawl. "Hello."

"Hi Avi, have you reached?" She took a few seconds to register the surroundings and the car movement, noticed the driver flashing a brilliant smile at her in the rearview mirror, and she realized that the caller was Shweta.

"I guess I should be close by." She ran her eyes across the panoramic view beyond the car window.

"Excuse me, how long before we hit the hotel?" She enquired the driver.

"Another 15 minutes Ma'am."

"Shwets, 15 minutes more. How are you doing? Hope you are comfortable there? I am feeling bad for leaving you there all alone." She was now feeling awake and fresh. The aching muscles seemed to have settled down.

"Don't be a fool. You have gone there for work. I hope you know how important this project is for you. Don't you?"

Avantika nodded. She knew it well that this was a make or break project for her. That was the reason why she wanted to give it her best shot. Even if it meant taking a loan from Shweta to travel some three thousand kms for the right inspirations.

"Listen, all the numbers you would need are in the small diary. The cabbie, the laundry, Pizza Hut, Dominos, Deez, general merchant, chemist..."

"Ok mommy, you stop worrying about me and concentrate on getting your inspiration right, before you get inspired by some local *Mallu* hunk. By the way, if you find one, look for two, now that we both are single."

Giggles and more of them.

"There goes my pervert queen! Not even a week away from your hubby and the need to be with some hunk, sweating it out, is getting on you." Avantika teased her. "Hey, why don't you call over Almost-Arnie, that personal trainer of your hubby? Now that you have a place, it ain't a bad deal babe."

"Shut up Avi. I am not as desperate as you." She laughed loud. "You take care and keep me posted. Bye."

After feasting on a sumptuous hearty meal of prawn curry, mutton stew and rice, in the comfort of her room, she felt exhausted but content. Gosh! It had been such a long day. A relay race since morning, except that she had been handing the baton to herself after each lap. From the early morning alarm, getting ready and rushing for the airport, boarding the flight to Mumbai, waiting at the Mumbai airport for the connecting flight, landing at the Kochi airport, the cab ride and now lying in a thatched roof hut, with banana leaves for ceiling, on a jute-filled mattress. She was listening to the silence.

Unlike the city silence, which echoed with the air conditioner, distant car honking, a dog's occasional yelp, pressure cooker whistle from the neighbour who worked late shifts, here silence assumed a different hue. The breeze whizzing through the coconut grooves, the soft waves lapping at some distance, a million variety of insects humming and creaking with various intensity, a dry leaf rustling at the door. She listened for more.

As she closed her eyes, all she could hear was the rhapsody that nature was doling out with its stillness overpowering her mind. She felt strange to the fact that when everything was right, sleep always eluded her only to hit her at the most odd hours—client meeting, while travelling, eating, even while making love. She smiled to herself and rolled towards the bedside table. In the dark, her hand groped for the cigarette pack. The hiss of the gas lighter broke the silence of darkness. Before the momentary flame died, leaving her in deeper darkness, she watched the thick white smoke curl up.

Life was so strange, she thought. When you have everything, it slips out of your hands, and when you think you've lost it, it snuggles up next to you. For all these years, she tried being a painter, but could never make it. And when she finally got her big break, it came to her, courtesy a *panjoo*, a tribe she had despised all her life. Was this compartmentalization of humans justified on her part? Probably not, as she knew that most of the Muslims went into a depression if India lost a cricket match. So, if all Muslims were not ISI agents, how could all Punjabis be uncouth, selfish, brash, loud mouthed and uncultured? Even *bongs*, her own father, was no less than a *panjoo*—crude, loud and debauch. Thank you Uncle, may God bless you. She thanked Mr

Khurana for his magnanimity and his confidence in her talent.

She was tired and needed sleep and stubbed the cigarette in the tastefully done ashtray made of coconut shell. Every piece on that property was so original, so creative and so simple. She would surely enquire about the architect and try to meet him and present her folio. Suddenly, she realized that a lot had been going on and at a very rapid pace in her normally boring, staid life. Rejections, dejections, new ways, appreciations; if one door closed, four new ones opened. The more she thought about the events, the more convinced she got that every step, every heart break was planned to pave way for something better.

Did the divine law of universe chart a plan for her life? To receive any kind of goodness, there needs to be a space created for the same. So to fill in her void of restlessness and no work, the universe blessed her with a prestigious project. If she missed her mother, the universe blessed her with a friend like Shweta. She stopped before her mind could process the next logic. No, she told herself, there was no need to go there. It was off limits, even for her mind. But being a mortal that she was, she lost. If there was a space after her breakup with Sunny, would it mean that some other person would step into her life? She shuddered. Not anymore; at least not as of now. She had enough of men and their ways, now she wanted a career first.

Mixed Day

"Hey babe, take a walk on the wild side, hey sugar take a walk on the walk side."

Having someone like Bob Dylan wake you up was indeed a value added service. The legendary singer tried another time, this time harder and succeeded.

A tiny hand with rosemary beads around the wrist searched for the phone on the side table and answered it. "Hello," the voice was sleep infested.

"Avi, sorry sorry sorry for disturbing you so early," Shweta's voice on the other end of the line was nervous and apologetic.

"What time is it?"

"7 am."

"All well Shwets? What happened? Everything fine?"

For some reason, beyond the realms of logic, a telegram or even a telephone call at a God-forsaken hour—early morning or late night—always ensured a panic attack, as it was perceived to bring some unfortunate news. The same thought had Avantika's eyes wide open.

For her, untimely call always transported her to the shrill phone in the middle of the night, when her drunken father had told her that her mother was no more! She took a second to realize that she was in Kumarakom, not Delhi.

"Yeah baby, everything is fine. I had gone for a morning walk. On my way back, I checked your letter box and guess what?"

"What?"

"Promise that you won't let this upset you and that you will keep a control over your favourite F words."

"Shwets, no games please, I am not in the mood", she spontaneously looked around for the lighter as she pulled a cigarette out of the case. "It's too early for me, you know." The grogginess was on gradual ebb.

"Take a guess Avi, pleaseeeeeee."

"Please Shwets. How on this earth would I know what was sitting in my letter box? Tell me before I hang up." The threat worked as Shweta knew very well that it would be carried out without any hesitation.

"Colonel Uncle, I mean your father is getting married."

"My what?" More than the question mark in her expression, it was the shock element that made her utterance so emphatic.

"Your presence is requested at a moment of transcendence. The mystery of two as one.

You will witness something more than ordinary life:

The transformation of two souls, into man and wife.

Date: 15th September,

Venue: DSOI, Dhaula Kuan, Delhi,

Time: 7.30 pm onwards."

Shweta read out the entire invite "and undersigned Col Sengupta, VSM, AVSM, and Simi."

There was silence. Shweta knew that thousands of miles away, now Avantika would be desperately looking for her cigarette pack. She was so right as Avantika already had one lit, in her hand, and was inhaling deep. Nicotine and twenty-six other chemical-infused smoke made her feel better to combat the onslaught of the most unexpected kind.

"Shweta, if this is your idea of some practical joke, let me warn you that it's a sick one."

"Avi, do you think I am this mean? Will I have a laugh at the expense of your father?" The silence assumed a gray shade to it, thick and heavy, spreading like a blanket. "Avi, you there?" No reply. "Avi?"

"What the fuck does this man think himself to be? Some Hollywood dude who can get married at 60? Is he out of his mind? Fuck, this is crazy man. I mean how can he… VSM, AVSM, my foot!"

"Don't get worked up Avi. I understand."

"No you don't. No one can. This man turned my mother's life into a living hell. God alone knows how many women he slept with after washing his hands off her. And now, when this VSM, AVSM can't get a fresh piece of ass everyday, he wants to get a permanent one."

"Avi, please. I did not intend to share this news as I knew it would affect your peace of mind and your work. But then, I realized that if I didn't tell you, you might feel more offended. I am sorry if I spoilt your day." Her voice was apologetic.

"Why should you be sorry when that horny son of a bitch is not?" She paused for a drag. Nicotine was already calming her. "It really doesn't matter any more. I really wish that bitch gets a taste of the same hell which she was instrumental in creating for my poor mother."

Shweta didn't know whether it was a good idea to sympathize or to just maintain silence. She chose the latter. The long silence on the other end made her realize that her friend was very upset and was already off the line. One glance at the phone screen told her that Avi had hung up and was now busy probably lighting her second cigarette.

As she looked at the red, single sheet card with golden cursive letters on it, she remembered how exciting it was selecting the card for her own marriage. Why do people get married? Maybe Avi was right. Just to have a permanent piece of ass in the house…for emergency.

A New Day

She slipped into her favourite pair of Levis, which last month, in a fit of creative designing spree, she had chopped to shorts and added strokes of colour to the jagged edges. To accompany the designer shorts, she had a chiffon shapeless shirt, her trusted loose flip-flops, which were secured by a bright red strap at the heels and the big bag with numerous boxes of crayons, charcoal, pencils, sheets and the paraphernalia.

As she walked from her room, towards the restaurant for breakfast, she could see that the corridor was flanked by glass windows across its full length. She could not help but notice the striking green colours outside. Being a coastal area, Kerala got an early monsoon. It was early August and the rains had washed and cleaned every strand of grass, every single leaf, every flower. Her eyes skimmed across the million shades of green the landscape had to offer. She was trying to remember the shades of green from her arts class, which Prof Barua had taught—Brunswick, Teal, Jade, Office, Kelly, Hunter, Celadon, Emerald, Sap, Moss, Pine green, all came cascading to her. The thought of how all pieces of memories get stacked neatly in the deep crevices of the mind which could be pulled out at any point in time made her smile. Of course, how could she forget the green she had grown up with, the army olive green!

The breakfast setting was almost picture perfect. Small benches dotted the green lawn set amidst a palm grove. She looked up to see a couple of young men perched on the nearest coconut tree and dislodging the green kernels, while their partners collected the same at the tree base. The waiter was placing the coconuts on a trolley and circulating them between the tables. Beyond the lawns, a water channel which seemed to have been diverted from the nearby canal was serene and reflected the deep colours of moss within and also the overhead trees and skies. She smiled at the young European couple, who were engrossed in the nimble finger movements of the young waitress, who was deftly slicing fruits for them at their table.

She lowered her painting bag on a bench and nodded to the waiter, when he offered her the filter coffee. Using a napkin to hold the steaming steel tumbler, Avantika walked towards the water channel. Every pore of her skin seemed to breathe in the moisture-laden air. A distance away, a large Gujarati family, of about twelve people, was seated around two benches. The children seemed overjoyed and were running around without any specific agenda, their mothers following with rolled *dosas* in their hands. The men hardly seemed bothered and were either immersed in the newspaper or just staring blankly into oblivion. The rest of the breakfast lawn was dotted with solitary honeymooners or elderly couples of non-Indian origin.

Avantika's senses seemed to be inundated with all the greens-blues of Kerala. She could not stop thinking about the next few days on the houseboat. Shweta had insisted her trip would not be complete, unless she spent a few days on a houseboat, and like all her other suggestions, she had given into this one too.

Later in the day, she was led for her massage appointment. The white wooden fence lined the walking track to the Ayurveda centre, flanked by thick shrubs on either side. She was led to a thatched enclosure which had no ceiling. In the centre of the 12×10 feet space, stood a deep oak wooden plank which had a sprinkling of some bright amber *Mukkutti* flowers. An invisible music player was playing a faint chant of *shlokas*. Another thatched table in the corner had a stack of green and yellow towels and an array of large stones and oils. Susan and Meena, the masseurs, smiled their warm welcome as she stepped into the enclosure.

As she lay on the wooden plank, staring at the overhead palm leaves and the blue sky beyond, her mind again was flooded with memories of her mother, father, and her father marrying someone else. She twisted on the plank, trying to get rid of the baggage. A dull ache plagued her, the aromatic candles were not making the heady feeling any better. Susan and Meena were working on her foot, her knees, abdomen, breasts and neck. After the initial rawness and embarrassment and holding back her breath, she gradually relaxed her muscles to the soft music, as the duo kneaded and chopped with their fingers. Avantika could feel the tension drifting away as the oil dripped into her hair. The massage made her eyelids heavy, and in spite of the beckoning blue sky above, which was laced with large bulbous clouds, she closed her eyelids. Faces, relevant and irrelevant, were swimming in the dusky clouds behind her eyelids. Sunny, his mother, Mr Lancolne, Shweta and her pumpkin-bottomed husband, Simi—there were so many of them and she was desperately swimming away till they remained a speck in the distance. All that remained with her was a quiet throb deep within, the faint music and the fragrance of God's own country.

Sunset Point

Amidst water infested with weeds, a small boat churned the water as the boatman paddled to get her to the Voyager—a forty-foot luxury houseboat. It was a fairly clear day. Unlike the previous day, the clouds were not threatening to collapse on the countryside. She used the rope stairs to get onto the boat. She looked around to see at least twenty of them, the houseboats, parked around. On each of the boats, which were getting ready to sail, she could see foreigners with their handycams, generally awed by the visual extravaganza. The young European couple from the resort was already on the deck of the next houseboat. The girl was sprawled on the deck, while a local was making a tattoo on her waist. The husband and the tattoo artiste seemed to be in an animated discussion over the choice of the motif and its colours.

As she stepped onto the Voyager, a man around 5'6, with dark tanned skin, milky white teeth, which formed the perfect contrast against his black skin, wearing shorts, a T-shirt and a warm smile came running towards her. He stood on the edge, waiting for her boatman to throw her red backpack. As it happened, in a perfect coordinated move, the Voyager guy snapped it with both hands. She looked around and was quite impressed with the arrangement. Plush sofa set, dining table, carpet, TV along with a DVD player inside. Not bad, she thought.

"Welcome aboard." A man in his early 50s came out of the adjacent corridor and greeted her. "I am Drego Verghesse, the owner and captain of this boat, and also your guide for the coming three days." The moment she caught his eyes, a vague feeling fluttered within her. Her mind told her that it was not their first meeting. She wanted to ask him if he felt the same but the woman in her told her that it would not be the best thing to do. His face was so familiar, especially those eyes; deep set, mystical, bright and full of life. She noticed that for his age, which would be close to 50, he was remarkably fit. Lean and straight with not even an ounce of extra fat. She tried to guess his height and decided on 5'10 or maybe 5'11, but not 6. Sunny was six feet and this man was definitely an inch or two shorter than him. Sporting a tattered jeans and a sleeveless black shirt, he was clean shaven. Only his salt and pepper hair—less of pepper more of salt—gave away his age. She noticed his eyes again. She couldn't be wrong in identifying them. She definitely knew them.

"This is my assistant Sudhakar," he pointed towards the man who had just collected her bag. "Sudhakar will show you around. In case you need anything which is beyond him, please feel free to let me know."

No wonder the resort guys had warned her. They told her she was booked on the Voyager only on her insistence, as all other contract houseboats were already full. They were not keen to sell bookings for the Voyager to their 'special' guests. The boat owner is strange, they told her. She realized within minutes of stepping onto the houseboat, how obsessed and full of himself Mr Drego Verghesse was. He had the aura of a superior being around himself.

"Come Madam, I will show you around." Sudhakar volunteered. "This is the living area," he said pointing towards the area where they were standing. "Here you can watch TV, and use the DVD player to watch a movie. We have a collection of both, Hollywood and Bollywood movies." He gave a simple and honest smile. "Breakfast, lunch, dinner will also be served here." She nodded as he walked towards the passage on to the left. On to the right, she could see a glass partition which led to the front of the boat where she could see a chair and the control wheel. Sudhakar followed her eyes and explained, "That's the captain's cockpit." Cockpit my foot, she shrugged her shoulders. As they took the passage to their left, the first door opened into a small room. "Your bedroom with attached toilet; it's western." Avantika stepped inside and was mighty surprised to find an air conditioner fitted onto one of the walls. "Does it work?" she enquired with suspicion. "Of course," replied the proud assistant pointing to the remote control lying next to the bed lamp. She peeped inside the toilet and was bowled over by the shower cubicle with dozens of nozzles and handles. "Hot and cold running water with Jacuzzi," came the explanation. As they came out of the room and walked down the narrow corridor, out of curiosity, she looked in the adjacent room.

Standing in stark contrast to the earlier room, this one was in a mess. With a bunk bed, a makeshift platform; which she guessed was used to cook, it screamed of disorder and mayhem. Also, she saw fire and ice coexisting for the first time, in the form of a dilapidated refrigerator and a gas stove placed right next to each other. The bed was littered with clothes. The whole scene made her miss her studio apartment. Sudhakar was visibly embarrassed and tried closing the door as quickly as possible. "That's his." He said pointing towards Drego. To take her mind off the sight, he offered something better. "Please come, let me show you the swimming pool." Swimming pool on a houseboat? She was intrigued.

Before she could ask Sudhakar, he had already taken the wooden stairs, which went up from the corridor towards the first floor of the boat. "Watch your head" he warned. As she climbed up, her eyes almost popped out. There was a blue coloured, big inflatable pool on the terrace. Why would someone come to the Backwaters and yet laze around in a pool? She placed the Red flag thought aside.

Standing there, she looked out. The landscape was nothing but green and its shades. Even the water was green. The huts on the side of the Backwaters were painted bright orange, yellow, even green. Small boats, ferrying passengers from the nearby resorts to the big houseboats were also painted in bright colours. Local womenfolk were cooking, washing or just chatting. The generators of the big houseboats were spewing enough smoke to make her feel nauseated. Was the Backwaters as beautiful as she had anticipated it to be? Too early to comment, she told herself.

Sudhakar asked, "Madam, for breakfast, I am making some *uttapam*, omelet and toast. What would you like to have for lunch?

Avantika was amused at the level of unparalleled and impeccable service being offered. Something in her said that all this was tailor-made to extort money from the gullible foreigners in the form of dollar tips. She enquired, "What choice do I have?"

"You can have prawn curry, or mutton stew or even fried fish with rice, *daal, chappati* or *Malabar parathas.*"

Food always confused her. But she knew that she had to come across as a client who knew it all, if she wanted top-of-the-line treatment. "Well, I would go for prawn curry and rice."

Sudhakar smiled. "Would you care for some beer or whisky?"

Damn. This was getting too good to be true. "Some beer would be fine. Kingfisher if you can find it."

The Voyager's engine sputtered to life as Drego took over the controls and steered the mammoth black boat towards the open water, the Vembanad lake.

Smoke On The Water

Two beers later, sitting cross-legged on the terrace, with the boat anchored in the middle of the largest salt water lake, the Vembanad, she was trying to absorb the magnificent sight. The monsoon sun was playing on the rippling waves. With just the sound of water slapping against the boat, for once she did not miss Bob Dylan, Dave Gilmour, Eric Clapton or any of her favourite sweet talkers. A puff here and there was keeping her alert and focussed.

"Why did you walk out of such a long relationship?" The abrupt question, which sprang out of nowhere, hit her like a 9 mm cartridge.

"Gosh, you scared me." She turned around, locating the source of question, Drego, who was standing there, squinting against the sun, dissecting her painting.

"By the way, what are you doing here? Aren't you supposed to be at the wheel?" The bluntness and the accuracy of the question had almost stripped her naked, though she was trying to play it down.

"You need not answer my question because I know the answer."

He smiled and his brown eyes crinkled.

His confidence and demeanour rattled her, and to muster support and courage for herself, she lit a cigarette again and took a deep puff. As she inhaled, she looked at him "What makes you so sure that your assumption is right?"

He walked towards the far end of the boat and then turned towards her. "Simple. I trust the inference of my observations."

"And may I ask what your observations are?"

"Yes, only if you pay me."

She was flabbergasted. "What? Haven't I paid you a fortune for this boat ride?"

He smiled again. "Ah... that? Well, that was for the boat ride, not for my observation."

Sudhakar's call, from the lower deck, interrupted the conversation.

"Sir, lunch is ready. Where should I serve it Madam?"

Drego looked at her, posing Sudhakar's question with his arched eyebrows.

"Not till I get my answer." The obstinate child in her was seeking attention.

"Not until I get paid." The seasoned sailor in him was not ready to give up. A naughty smile was playing in the depths of his eyes.

"What would it take for you to answer my question?" The child realized that the argument was not leading anywhere.

"Well, a formal introduction would do for now."

"What the f… You got to be crazy." She felt enraged. "This entire interlude just to know my name? Anyway, I am Avantika."

"Pleasure meeting you, Avantika. You have a pretty name."

"Tell me something I don't know. Can I have my answer please?" She was curt and business like.

He moved towards the painting. "What do you see in here?" He asked.

She was baffled by his highly moronic question. "Well, water, sun, birds." She looked at his face, trying to find if her answer did suffice.

"I am not asking you to list the objects. My question was more towards your point of view. If I may articulate, what point of view are you trying to present in this painting of yours?"

She felt cheated and retaliated. "Look Mister. I gave you what you asked for. So, rather than digging into my personal affairs, like a true gentleman, keep to your words and answer how you assumed that I have walked out of a long relationship."

He smiled again. "I was hoping that your own answer to my question would suffice, but anyway, I think I will have to explain."

He sat down and crossed his leg. "Can I borrow a cigarette?" And without even waiting for an answer, he nonchalantly picked the packet, pulled out one and lit it. The first puff sent him into a bout of cough. "Damn, I can never handle these Indian brands."

Avantika turned a shade of red; she was offended. The warning from the resort staff kept flooding back to her. She should have known about his mood swings and unhospitable ways.

Sudhakar came up and like a humble slave stated that the food was getting cold. His master did not even look at him. He took another drag; this time the coughing bout reduced. "Even someone like me gets used to junk and trash so fast." He laughed as he glanced at the cigarette in his hands in mock admiration.

"So coming to your question. Young lady, life is all about perspective and point of view, as we call it. Whatever we see forms an impression on us, and this impression affects our thoughts. And no wonder what we do—speak, write or paint—is nothing but an expression or manifestation of our own point of view which has been moulded by the past events and exposures." She knew that he had a profound thought going on, but her Bengali genes, for centuries, had not accepted superiority of any other race, let alone a sailor.

"I am still waiting for my answer." Her stare was direct and cold. However, she was already finding it difficult to hold his stare for a long time. He crushed the cigarette in the ashtray lying close to him. "This is the problem of your generation. You want to be spoon fed." He ran his hand in his curly hair and turned to look at Sudhakar. He smiled as if it was the only expression he knew.

"Sudhakar, you go and have your lunch, because I am sure that post our conversation, Miss Avantika would prefer to concentrate on things more meaningful than prawn curry."

He turned his glance back to her, the eyes were still smiling. She did not know if under the given circumstances, she should react like a client and ask for a refund or should she just be patient and focus her energies on absorbing the entire stimulus which was available. However, he was very clear that he wanted to play the mentor and nothing else.

"Look at this canvas—water, sun, sky and birds. Can you see something which strikes you?"

To prove that she was a painter and knew more about paintings than a sailor, she strained her eyes, real hard, but could not find anything which was out of place. He smiled and took a dry brush from the perforated blue pottery glass in which all her brushes were kept and pointed towards the birds in her painting. "Look at them."

Again, she tried finding an anomaly, but failed.

"This is Vembanad Lake. And I am sure like any other tourist, that is the only thing you know about it. Are you aware that the Vembanad wetland system covers an area of over 1512 km?"

She was pleasantly shocked and impressed. "The lake is bordered by Alappuzha, Kottayam, and Ernakulam districts. It lies at sea level, and is separated from the Arabian Sea by a narrow barrier island. Canals link the lake to other coastal lakes to the north and south. Several rivers flow into the lake, including the Achenkovil, Manimala, Meenachil, Muvattupuzha, Pamba and Periyar. The lake surrounds the islands of Pathiramanal, Perumbalam and Pallippuram. The Vembanad Lake is approximately 14-km wide at its widest point."

"My answer please."

"On its way. This lake also has a huge variety of birds. Waterfowl, Cuckoo, Wild Ducks, Brahminy Kites, Marsh Harries, Herons and more. During the migratory season, we get the Siberian Stork, Parrot, Egret, Darter, Teal, Flycatchers and Wood Beetle. Now, if you see the birds in your painting, you will see that their shapes are different." He was right.

"If you were a sharp observer, you would have noticed that birds, the ones I have named, only fly with their own likes or with their own flock." The *bong* genes were getting impressed.

"Now, about my inference part; remember, I told you that whatever we do is a reflection of our point of view which is affected by the events in our lives?"

She nodded in silent agreement.

"The birds in your painting clearly show that they are going their own separate ways. As per the nature of *Brahminy Kites*, when they fly that high, as high you have shown in your painting, they are in harmony, following one path. So even if after observing this, your mind perceived, processed and depicted it in a way which is opposite to the given fact, it goes on to tell that in your life, there is lack of harmony, especially with your partner and like your painting, both of you have gone your own ways."

"Damn, either this guy was a conman or a genius," she thought.

"You carry on with your work lady and sorry if I interrupted you. Your lunch is ready. Whenever you are ready, do let Sudhakar know. Have a good day."

He got up and stretched his back, looking at the clouds building on the horizon. She gauged his lean frame and deep eyes and asked, "I didn't get your name?" He smiled. "Drego. Drego Verghesse. You can call me DV."

With two beers down, beaten hands down some thirty seconds ago, she ached to prove her superiority. "What if I don't call you Drego or DV?" She challenged. "That would be fine by me, as long as you give me a new one." Challenge accepted and given back.

"What if I call you Captain?"

He laughed, loud and clear and it was carried miles away.

"That's a new one. Thank you for giving me a new name. I quite like it." She smiled, accepting his gratitude.

"Why don't you sit down Captain?" She smiled and requested.

"Even if the boat is being manned by God?" He cautioned her.

"Though I can't claim to be an expert like you, in observations, but whatever little I know of you, I am sure that you would never do anything foolish which could harm your boat or your reputation." She complimented him and one coming from her was a big thing.

"You got a nice boat here." She patted the railing on which she was lightly resting her back.

The Captain looked at the vast expanse and then at her. "You know Avantika, the authentic Kerala houseboats are called *Kettuvallam*. They are made entirely of jack wood planks and are tied together with strong coir rope to form a huge barge. The beauty is that in the construction of an entire boat, not even a single nail is used. The whole boat is coated with special resin obtained from boiling cashew kernels."

She lit another cigarette and pushed the packet towards him, "If you don't mind my cheap Indian brand, that is." Her tone was still caustic.

"You will be surprised to know that this brand of ITC uses better tobacco than most of the imported brands."

"Hmmm… as I can see, it's not only the lake, birds and observing people that catches your fancy. Are you an avid reader?"

"I was, during my college days. Habits picked then, generally last you a lifetime."

"Can I ask you something?" She hesitated while inhaling a full lung of nicotine and staring past Captain's shoulder to the distant shores.

"Sure. But please let me play the perfect host and save you the pain and effort of asking. I know you want suggestions on how to improve your paintings. Don't you?"

There were times when it was better to surrender, and she knew that for her own good, today was the day.

"What do you see when you see this unending stretch of water?" Captain asked. She had no clue but was confident that he had the perfect answer. And yes, she was right.

"To different people, it would mean different things. But to me, it's like an invitation. An invitation to surrender our acquisitions—success, failures, sins, shortcomings, apprehensions, defeats. To bury all of this deep under any one of these million waves. The waves will never complain and will silently hide these somewhere deep, so that we may come out clean and fresh, rejuvenated by the eternal source of life; water. So to put things in a context, if I were to paint this lake, I would paint a goblet, overflowing with beautiful bright light."

That would be an interesting depiction, Avantika thought. She pulled her big painting bag and unzipped it, and pulled out her folio.

"Here you are." She handed it over to him. "Could you please take a look and tell me about your impressions."

He looked at them, carefully, one by one, deliberating over some, flipping through the others, and pulled out another cigarette from her packet. "I like it now. The cigarette that is." A mischievous twinkle played in his eyes and lips. He lit the cigarette and looked intently at her. She got a little conscious and let out a defensive smile.

"What are you looking at?"

He took a couple of deep drags and stubbed the cigarette. "The reason for your failure."

She was taken aback by his honesty and felt a little awkward. "And you know what the reason is?" She just stood there.

"It's you." His tone was flat.

She was embarrassed and he continued. "You might hate me for saying this, but then am I not on a PR exercise, therefore it is not my job to please everyone around. Am I paid to make everyone around feel good? Damn no. Then how does it really matter if you like my viewpoint or not?"

He took another drag and tried to read the colours of her eyes. He could see the colours change with every word of his. Brown to grey, black to white. "If you are sane enough and if you see any merit in my advice, you will take it, otherwise you always have the option of walking out." His statement confused her further and he knew it.

"Avantika, all this while you have been trying too hard to please everyone. Your exhibitor, the critics, your friends, your boyfriend, your parents, your maid, your dog, the bird on the tree, I mean the entire world. Everyone, but the artist in you. You have never painted or expressed the way you wanted because you were too afraid and shaky to present your perspective. Your paintings were never an extension of your expressions but an effort to please the world around you. Haven't you heard the saying that if you are trying to please too many people, you end up displeasing all. And that is the precise problem with your paintings."

She could feel the bitter tears swell in her eyes.

"They lack a definitive point of view, a character of their own. They are so confused and fail to stand up for their own belief. When someone buys a Hussain, he pays a fortune to see Hussain's point of view on the canvas, not his own. When you read a story, a poetry or go to watch a movie, you do it because you want to know the poet's, writer's or the director's point of view. If you like it and share the same, you appreciate it, and if you don't, you criticize it. So either it evokes appreciation or hate, but never indifference. Unfortunately, your work evokes indifference because there is no point of view."

The sun was already touching the horizon in the west as the east sky was a murky orange, with the wild streaks of grey clouds and the immenseness of dusk spreading its tentacles. But only when the night sets, does it promise to bring in a new day.

Never Say Goodbye

"Have you always been a boatman, Captain?"

His smile faded, albeit only by few shades. "Well almost." The flicker in his eye stood a witness to the fact that he was lying. "Life as a boatman is quite monotonous and boring. Why don't you tell me about yours?" For his comfort, he put the ball in her court. It was so clear that even she realized and laughed. "Captain, not only are you wise but also smart. What skeletons are you hiding in your cupboard?"

The toddy was doing its bit. She could not refuse Sudhakar's offer earlier in the evening and had settled for the local toddy he presented along with the crisp fried prawns. As she swung her feet to the ground and tried to stand, it hit her, hard and straight, making her lose her balance. He was quick to move and hold her, by the shoulders first, then the waist, before she could land on the floor.

"Avantika, are you ok?" His voice had genuine concern and care. "Yeah. Thanks and I am sorry. I should have listened to you and gone a little slow." He was still holding her, as she swayed. She realized his grip was firm yet so tender, like being in total control without trying to overpower or hurt her. She looked at him, his face was less than six inches away. Damn, why did he appear so familiar? Where had she seen him? Where? She could not think of any common place and definitely his face was not in any brochure or on the Kerala tourism website. Where had she seen him? She blinked number of times, but her memory did not help, or maybe it did.

"As I count from five to zero, you will begin to go very deep in your mind. Your entire body will relax and your mind will become very calm. Five, four, three, two, one, zero. Deep sleep. Deeper and deeper with every breath, deep into your own quiet space where there is total peace and total light. Now, we will be inviting white light on top of your head. Like a waterfall, it will pour into each and every part of your being, releasing all stress and tension and filling you with divine healing energy. Your entire body seems to have become like a hollow cylinder now.

One… Two… Three… Four… Five…

You are as light a feather, free of all tensions and worries. With your permission, now I am going to take you into a life where your guides will show you the reason of your failures in this life. Imagine a beautiful door in front of you. This is a door through time and space, a door into your past lives. There is something for you to learn on the other side of this door… something that will help you in your present life. When you can see the door, nod."

Chauhan sir's voice was filling her senses. She could see a big, wooden gate, with metal door knobs.

"Counting backwards from five to one, you will now open the door and step in. Go to the door. On one, you will put your hand on the door

knob, on two, you will turn the door knob, three you will open the door half way, four you will step in, five you will close the door behind you. One, two, three, four and five."

"Can you see a beautiful light on the other side?" She nods.

"Go through the door and into the light. Go through the light and join the scene, the person, the experience, on the other side. It will come into complete focus on the count of one.

Five... you are going way back into your past lives.

Four... you can remember everything.

Three... you can see the scene, a person, an experience.

Two... coming into complete focus.

One... be there." The commands were getting more focussed, as if they were designed to channelize her journey.

"What do you see?"

She tried, but could not see anything.

"If you are in a body, look at your feet. Can you see your feet?" He asked. "I will light a torch which will let you see your feet. I have lit a torch. It is bright now. Can you see your feet now?"

She could see them, a pair of feet wearing Roman sandals.

"What do you see Avantika?"

"Roman sandals."

"Good work, now try to see people around you, try to see where you are, try to see what all is happening around you." She looked around and there was a lot happening. "What do you see, speak up."

"I see a woman, a pretty woman, big blue eyes, pale skin, blonde hair, wearing a long silk robe, standing in a huge hall with stone pillars."

"What place is it like? Where do you think it is?"

"It looks like Roman architecture. I see flashes of the Roman army, Roman generals and gladiators."

"What is this woman doing?"

"She is just watching all this."

"Who do you think this woman is? Someone you know? Look at her eyes. They will remind you of someone. Look at her eyes Avantika." He urged her.

"She is me. Yes, it's me. I am the Queen. People are coming and kneeling in front of me. I am sitting on a throne." Her narrative was sketchy. "They are kissing my hand. My finger has got a huge emerald ring."

"What more do you see there?"

"I see an elder man, dressed as a general, standing with me."

"Who is this man? Is he your brother, father...?"

"No, he is my lover. I am cheating on my husband as I love this man."

"Do you know this man in your present life? Look at him closely."

She tried looking at him. Weather-beaten face, rugged features and physique.

"Look at him, his eyes, closely. Do you think you know these eyes?"

She looked at his eye. Dark brown, deep, mystical and with an unparalleled shine in them.

"Do you know them Avantika?"

She did not, until she came to Kerala and met him.

Solving Questions

"Very nice. I love them." Captain looked at each painting with great interest, and with every new one coming up, his eyes got brighter. He glanced momentarily at Avantika, who was standing near the window of the boat's living room, her hands locked across her chest, head at a slight angle as if trying to read his expressions while he scrutinized her work.

An appreciation coming from him in particular gave her great pleasure and pride.

"Which one do you like the most?" She asked apprehensively, not wanting to sound like fishing for compliments. "And please, don't say all of them."

"That's a tough choice you are asking me to make." He started looking at the sheets again, slowly, appreciating each one of them. He was sprawled on the carpet with the entire spread in front of him. He slipped the sheets around, pushed some under the stack, pulled some away and finally pulled out two. He held both of them, weighing them against the light and finally waved her one. "This one is the

Rockstar, a winner! Of course, I am no painter or an art critic, but it is just my honest opinion."

He stacked all the sheets together and tucked them loosely inside her folder on the sofa. He then pulled out a black pack from his pocket and offered it to her. Her eyes scanned the black, glossy rectangular pack, which had YSL embossed in golden letters.

"It's a cigarette pack!" She exclaimed as her eye caught the statutory warning printed on it. She was amused and surprised, at the same time. "Gosh, I stayed in a metro for most of my life, smoked a lot, visited malls, stores, small shops, but till two minutes back, I never did see a pack of *Yves Saint Laurent* cigarettes. It's crazy. I mean why would the high priest of fashion even think of getting into retailing cigarettes?"

They both laughed as she pulled out the slim, long cigarette and lit it. Her fingers were playing with the cigarette, eyes roving on the golden embossed letters of YSL intertwined into each other in the logo, "Hmmm so this is your fine side. I am impressed."

The gracious Captain bowed and accepted her compliment.

"I am sure your girlfriend must have gifted it to you. It's got to be expensive. Isn't it?" Captain let out a feeble smile and his eyes got fogged with nostalgia. "Good old days," he smiled vaguely and turned to face the window and the water beyond.

"I know you have fond memories of your past and I also know that sharing it with anyone brings back the pain. Therefore, I won't even ask you about it."

He looked at her. "Well, it might sound strange and from my perspective, a little odd, but then I guess you have a right to know this. For all these years, I have been a recluse, a free bird and not very fond of people. I am sure before checking onboard the Voyager, your travel agent would have told you the same." She smiled and he continued. "When you came onboard, you were just a tourist who was drawn here by the government propaganda of God's own country, not even knowing what ecological havoc it plays to have you here. But then, something inside me told a different story this time. Please don't laugh at what I am going to tell you." He paused, waiting for her to respond. She was listening intently to him. "When I saw you, something inside me stirred. Something told me that I have known you. I felt a strange affinity towards you. A strange liking. I know, it is not right for me to tell you all this. After all, you are just a tourist who will go her own way, but don't know why I feel like sharing this with you. Like a fool, for the first time in my life, I am afraid that day after tomorrow you will leave."

He laughed, but it was bereft of any joy. Avantika was sitting still. She did not know what to say or how to react. Was it a coincidence that despite age, social and cultural difference, two people felt exactly the same about each other? Was the whole mumbo-jumbo of past life, karmic circle, unfulfilled dreams and desire more than fiction? She felt like sharing her past life experience with him, but then something stopped her.

"Would you like to have some cognac?" He enquired.

Without even waiting for her answer, he got up and walked towards his cabin only to return with a bottle of *Remy Martin*. By this time, she was well aware that he was a man of refined taste.

Out in the open, under a sky with dark clouds, she sat at the helm, on his chair. She felt so powerful and in control. Captain was standing behind her, sipping his cognac.

"Captain, do you think I am at the helm of affairs?" She tilted her head back and laughed the way she had not done in a long time.

"I come from a shipping family. We had liners, ships, fishing trailers and the works. Being the only son, my dad gave me everything he could. Best of toys, clothes, nannies, school, foreign travel. I guess, unknowingly he also passed on his vices; drinking and gambling. I went to the elitist boarding school, in London and then to Parson School of Design, New York. By this time, our fortunes were in bad shape. Business was going down. We had run into huge debts. Dad was diagnosed with cancer of the liver. I had to leave college and come back to Mumbai. Within no time, all my friends disappeared. I had no one. And then one day, Dad passed away. Various banks took over our house, ships, seized our accounts and I was broke. One of my Dad's friends was kind enough to lend me money, without any interest, which helped me get my darling." He patted the oak panel near the door where he was leaning.

It was getting dark as the sun hid behind the clouds. She looked at the green, palm dotted landscape and took a large sip of the *Remy*. Maybe it was Captain's narration or the cognac which made her realize that misfortune, pain, suffering were an integral part of life and not something exclusive to her. For some unknown reason, the thought made her feel better.

"You know Avantika…" the Captain's line was cut short.

"I am Avi, just Avi, for friends. So you can decide, whether I am Avantika or Avi for you." She was looking him in the eyes.

"That again is a tough one. Which one should I choose?" He moved in front of her, shades of melancholy got replaced with kid-like mischief. He absently flicked a loose strand of her hair, which had strayed outside the limits, the shine in his eyes intensified. "Ok, I guess Avi, just because it's simpler." They laughed.

"And you know what, for a change, I have seen a man who is a real tease. So may I propose to raise a toast for the long lasting friendship of the tease Captain and the coy Avi?' They both burst into laughter.

She got up from her seat and raised her glass. "Cheers" and the cognac went straight down to where it was supposed to do its job.

Goodbye Blue Sky

Time takes its own course, and the course its own sweet time.

When the going is tough, time seems to extend itself; making every day look like ages. On the contrary, when the going is good, it flies like a good night's sleep. Avantika's Kerala trip of six days was extended to ten days. The boat stay of three days turned into nine, and it all seemed just like yesterday. But ultimately, the moment of truth arrived—the time to say goodbye. The 'Voyager' was parked at Kumarakom, a small village on the backwaters.

"Avi, you need not do this." Captain was leaning by the door frame and smiling as he saw her tidying up his room yet again. "You would leave in another hour, so please don't spoil me."

Avantika acted as if she did not listen to his statement at all and carried on making his bed. It was surprising to see what a woman could do to a man's home. Captain's cabin, which earlier looked like a piggery, started resembling a bedroom, post Avantika's intervention. The bunk bed was neatly made with new bed sheet. A small wooden partition, which she insisted on picking up on their trip to a nearby town Alleppey, was put to divide the sleeping area from the cooking area. Three large plastic baskets were put on the side wall to house the vegetables. The refrigerator was moved to the far end of the room and the gas stove near the sink. The floor was scrubbed clean.

Sudhakar entered the room. "Madam, would you like to have some tea?"

Before Avantika could reply, Captain piped in. "Sudhakar, on a beautiful Saturday morning, don't you think serving tea is so very English and actually so boring?" Sudhakar smiled as he understood that his captain wished to have some beer. "Sudhakar," Avantika's voice with a stern tone stopped him. "Please tell your captain that morning is meant for tea only, which is very English and healthy, unlike beer which is American and not so healthy. And I will have mine without sugar, please."

Sudhakar looked at Captain with a slight raised shoulder to express his helplessness.

"Did you see that DV?" Captain talked to himself. "That humble slave of the boat refused to carry out your orders because he sold his heart to the Satan and traded his loyalty. Sudhakar, you wretched being, for all my love and affection, this is what I get?"

His theatrics amused Avantika. She rushed to him and hugged him tight. Even though Sudhakar had changed his clothes in moments of drunken stupor, his presence in the room now visibly embarrassed Captain. Not wanting to further mortify his master, Sudhakar excused himself. Captain patted her head and smiled, his eyes a little clouded.

"You know Avantika, it's not the destination but the journey which is most cherished. Unlike the destination, which is bereft of any story, the journey has its own sweet-tender moments, infallible charm, a zillion memories and excitement at every nook and corner. Therefore, a sane soul would choose to be a traveller forever, refusing to arrive."

Avantika remained in the embrace, inhaling his fragrancc which she knew was a mix of CK Aqua, tobacco and the residue of last night's scotch. "Captain, I'm a simple girl, not a philosopher like you. I don't know or rather don't care about this profound theory of yours called journey and the destination. But I know that if you are the father to this, it will surely have its own merit."

He let out a warm laughter, assuaging and comforting. He held her shoulders, tenderly, and pulled her away from himself. "What time is your flight?"

Avantika looked at him with pretentious anger. "As if it makes any difference to you. Does it?"

Captain looked out of the window, checking out the sun shimmer on the green water. "Avi, you know that goodbyes have never been my cup of tea. But having said that, it does not mean that I am insensitive. It's just that my perspective is different."

"Why can't you move to Delhi?" The question hit him out of the blue. He stood there, and within a fraction of a second, he realized that this innocuous companionship has assumed serious overtones, at least from her side. He lit a cigarette and from behind a veil of smoke, he delved into a monologue. "Avi, as we grow old, we become like this big banyan tree which has strong roots, running deep inside the crust of earth. Just due to the number of years, the tree becomes house to various life forms; birds, plants, organisms. After all this, even if it decides to shift, the same roots which nourished it act like shackles, making the movement impossible. So you see, I am this banyan tree. Have been here for too long. The mere thought of uprooting myself threatens and affects my being." Avantika listened to him patiently.

Captain took her hands and caressed them. "You know Avi, long before we are born, as souls, we are given a choice of bodies. Man or woman, fair or dark, thin or fat. Then we are given a choice of house and parents. Rich or poor, kind or cruel. As souls, we know what lessons we need to learn in our next life. And based on that, we choose a body and family which is the best to learn our lesson. And mind you, till the time we learn our individual lessons, we won't be able to break this circle. So as you see, in our own interest, it is important that we follow our destined paths and learn the lessons for which we are here."

Avantika nodded, more out of confusion than acceptance but surely out of admiration for Captain. "Do you think our choosing this life has anything to do with the desire to meet each other also?" Her question was sudden and caught him completely off guard.

He thought for a moment. "Avantika, there are some mysteries which a mortal can never answer."

She looked at him, her eyes glued to him but her mind, as if quizzing herself. "Then what is it that pulls me towards you?" Her question was simple, but the answer was mighty complex, even for someone like Captain. She continued, "Is it your wisdom, or your aura, or is it about your charm? Or is it some thing else, which even I am unaware of?"

Captain gave it a thought. "I think I know the answer. It's faith."

She looked a little confused. "Faith? What has faith got to do with my feelings for you?"

He looked at his watch and then turned his attention towards her. "It might sound a little weird to us, but every relationship is like a building, with various stages of completion. The foundation, the plinth and the consecutive floors. If you look around, people are drawn towards each other for different reasons. Some go for looks, some flip for intelligence, many for the money part, some even dig fame and glamour. So, if a relationship is based, say on looks, once the look factor wears away, it starts running into trouble. Or let's say if it's built on money, it will evaporate if some richer guy or girl steps in or if your own fortune dwindles." He paused to ensure if she was on the same platform. She nodded. "Then there are few relationships that are built on faith; where faith is the basis of all future conversations, interactions, liking and love. And as we know, it takes a lot to shake faith. With faith as the foundation, with every passing day, the relationship just keeps on getting stronger. And it is this faith that makes you surrender completely. When you surrender, the compartments of expectation, the difference between you and me, the class divide, the age conflict, the thought gap, all melt and you become one with your loved one. This oneness empowers and blesses you with a new identity, a new dimension and a new life. Am I making any sense?"

Life for her was getting clearer. In maybe two seconds, she could analyse the reason for all failing and falling relationships around her. Her father and mother, Shweta and Prashant, Sunny and her own. Now she could see that all of them never had any faith in them. All of them always wanted from the relationship, but never came forward to give.

"You know Avi, our interaction was based on faith. I don't know where this will lead us, but ours will always be a relationship to be cherished."

As the cab cruised on the serene, greenery dotted road, Avantika tried to analyse her relationship with Sunny. When she chanced to meet him for the first time, what attracted her towards him? Looks, money or something else? She could get no definitive answer. Then what made her stick to him for all these years? What blinded her to say and feel that she loved him? What compelled her to sleep with him? With every question, one more popped up. Her mind was getting flooded and choked. She decided to take the final litmus test. Did she ever have any faith in him? And the answer was a clear NO!

Late Night Drama

The scampering of heavy feet on the staircase led to loud thuds on the door, which were persistent and ascending in volume.

Knock, knock, knock, knock.

"Avi, get up." Shweta tried to shake her violently. Avantika was in a different world, sprawled on her queen bed, aboard the Voyager. Captain was watching her, smoking his YSL, smiling. Sudhakar was cleaning the window glass.

"Captain, don't wake me up. Please. You are such a spoilsport. Go away." She murmured.

"Avi, for God's sake get up. There is a whole team of cops at your doorstep." Shweta screamed. Avantika opened her eyes, still in a shock and not being able to sieve dream from reality. She looked around. Okay, she was not on the houseboat. So that part was a dream. So was the presence of Captain and Sudhakar. But Shweta trying to wake her up was not a dream as she was still there, crouched over her. "Avi, there are cops standing at your door. They have got a search warrant." She could not connect with her statement and it all sounded gibberish.

The three-hour drive from Kumarakom to the Cochin airport, the heaviness in her heart throughout the flight back to Delhi, memories flooding her eyes without any reason and braving the traffic snarls from the airport to her apartment in Defence Colony had her exhausted. To top it all, she had to deal with an overenthusiastic and inquisitive Shweta, who wanted to know everything then and there. She had no clue when she slipped into a semi-coma-like state, oblivious to the world around, oblivious to the fact that darkness and light, happiness and sadness, high and the low are two faces of the same coin.

Why would cops come over to her place with a search warrant? Someone knocked at the door again. "Madam, open the door. We don't have the entire night." She looked at Shweta with confused looks. Shweta's face had fear written all over it. She was trembling. Avantika got up and walked towards the door.

"Avi, please wear something decent before you let them in." Shweta warned her. She looked at herself in shorts and T-shirt and decided to put on a track pant. The knock at the door grew louder. She opened the door. On the stairs, there was a team of cops. A tall burly man, who looked like the seniormost accompanied by one man in plainclothes, two male and two female constables.

"Miss Avantika Sengupta?" the question was straight.

"Yes" she fumbled "but what is this all about?"

The tall, burly man handed her a paper. "I am Circle Officer Rajinder Sirohi, Defence Colony Police Station." He pointed towards another man, in plainclothes, "And he is Inspector V Reddy, the investigating officer from Guntur, Andhra Pradesh. In respect to the encounter of *Bengali Anna*, we have a warrant.

Avantika tried to read the paper which was handed over to her by Circle Officer Sirohi. But her lack of experience in deciphering any such document failed her miserably. She looked blankly at the cops standing there. The cop from Guntur, who looked kinder than his Delhi counterpart, spoke. "Madam, I would request you to co-operate in letting us carry out the search." She felt fear, the unknown kinds, crawl up.

"But Sir, I have not done anything. At least tell me what it is all about." The two women constables came forward and held her by her arms and pulled her aside. "What are you doing? Leave me, you are hurting me." She cried. "This is no way to treat a lady." To make it worse, one of the woman constables twisted her arm and pushed her towards the wall, letting her male counterparts enter her house. Avantika whimpered. Shweta came rushing to her rescue but the other woman constable intercepted her. While the women constables held them, their male counterpart started looking around. "Look for CDs, papers, bank passbooks, naxal literature or any arms and ammunition." The cop from Guntur instructed.

His order was taken seriously by the constables as one of them started looking in the kitchen and the other in the bedroom, turning bed upside down, pulling out the drawers and the cupboards. The humiliation was too much and Avantika broke down. Her tears had some effect on the woman constable and she relaxed her arm, though only a bit. Rajinder Sirohi looked at her. "If you want to call anyone, please go ahead."

Shweta pulled her hand free and rushed towards her mobile and dialled a number. Avantika straightened her arms and walked towards the table where her mobile was kept. As she stood there, holding it, she could not think of even one number which she could dial, but for one—Captain. But he was so far away. What would he do under such circumstance? Maybe maintain his cool because he always said that fortune and misfortune always come as a wave, and never last for long. God, she missed him so much. She turned towards Shweta who was already in middle of a conversation.

"Prashant, listen I know after whatever happened, I should not be calling you up and that too this late. But this is an emergency."

Avantika could not hear his reaction on the other end of the line, but whatever he said, kind words or hurting ones, made Shweta sob. "Yeah, I am at Avi's place and there are some cops with a search warrant. We are very scared. Please do something Prashant, please." She wiped her tears and handed over the phone to Rajinder. "Sir, my husband would like to speak with you."

He took the phone reluctantly. "Hello, this is Rajinder Sirohi, Circle Officer, Defence Colony Station." Avantika watched the cops ransacking her place with vengeance. Now they were joined by the women constables, who were having a gala time going through her wardrobe, especially her drawer where she kept her undergarments. She just shifted her gaze as she knew there was nothing she could do about it. In the meanwhile, Prashant had told the cop something which had sobered him down.

"*Janab*, I understand what you are saying. But we have a party from Guntur, Andhra Pradesh. They have procured this search warrant from the court of a judicial magistrate. I happen to be the local police station officer just assisting them."

Avantika could hear Prashant's voice, calm and composed, trying to explain something. "Prashant *Saheb*, I have heard about your family, but I am sorry, I can't do anything. This is some top naxalite investigation."

The voice on the other end of the line was pleading his case and it worked. "I am sorry. I did not know that she is your wife. What I will do is that I will wrap up the investigation for now. In any case, under the 160, the investigating officer will ask her to come to the police station for routine enquiry. No no, you need not to send Puri *Saheb* right now. You can ask him to come with madam tomorrow when she comes to the police station. I am sorry *Janab* but what to do. Earlier, it was terrorists who gave us sleepless nights, and now to make our life tougher, we have to battle the naxals also." He laughed. "Good night *janab*."

He handed over the phone to Shweta. His face was now softer. "Let's go." He ordered his team. He looked at Avantika. "I am sorry madam. I was just carrying out orders. Just to let you know, your brother, Partho Sengupta alias *Bengali Anna*, was shot a few days back in Guntur. Investigation led us to you and your father."

As the cops ascended the stairs, Avantika was baffled as she could not make head or tail out of the whole thing. Cops, naxals, search warrant, brother Partho Sengupta. She just stood there, frozen.

"Every night in my dream…" Celine Dion punctuated the silence and the illuminated screen announced that it was Prashant.

Thanks Prashant." Shweta answered the call. "Just a moment." She removed the phone from her ear and put it on the speaker mode.

"Yes, I have put you on the speakerphone." She walked towards Avantika who was still standing, confused, terrified, and all fuzzed up.

"Hi Avantika. Now listen to me carefully. I have spoken to my lawyer, Puri *Saheb*. He is a top high court lawyer and has been with our family for almost 20 years now. He will do whatever needs to be done on the legal end. You need not worry. As I speak with you now, he would be speaking with the Defence Colony cops to ensure that you are not harassed any further. I know, it is not the right time to ask, but I need to know if this naxal story is true."

Shweta took the charge, "Prashant, how can you be so mean? You know that Avantika has no brother. I have known her for almost sixteen years now. I can vouch for her. Why are you even asking this?"

Prashant's voice got curt. "Shweta, this is a police matter now. Therefore, let us stop vouching for people at random and assuming facts."

Shweta got the message loud and clear.

"Avantika, are you there?"

Avantika cleared her throat, "Yes Prashant. Thank you for all your help and I am really sorry for this inconvenience."

Shweta handed over the phone to her and walked away towards the kitchen. "Come on Avantika. You need not to thank me. After all, you are Shweta's best friend."

She smiled. "Avantika, I know it might upset you but I just want to share this with you so that you have time to prepare yourself for tomorrow's round of questioning." Her heart sank. She did not know what to expect in the next few minutes. "Puri *Saheb* spoke with the top cops and he was told that in the same context, your dad was also questioned yesterday and he did accept having a son named Partho Sengupta. However, he denied having any knowledge or information about his activities or whereabouts. Post his acceptance, they came to your place to cover all angles of their investigation." There was a silence. "Avantika, you there? Hello..."

Her legs felt like rubber bands and to support her fifty-three odd kilogram frame, she held the wall for support. Her lips quivered. She took a deep breath and pulled herself towards the side table, which lay upside down post the search storm. "Yes Prashant. I can hear you." With vacant eyes, she looked around, trying to locate something. "Just a moment Prashant."

Finally, she found what she was looking for: the white and red, Navy Cut pack. She opened it and pulled out one. Luckily, locating the lighter was not tough. She lit her cigarette and the nicotine made her feel so much better.

"Sorry Prashant. Yes, I am with you now." She took two or three long puffs. Shweta started putting her things back in the wardrobe.

"Avantika, tomorrow you will get a call from Puri *Saheb*. His car will come to pick you up. You will have to go to the Defence Colony police station. Don't you worry, Puri *Saheb* was kind enough to promise me that he will be there himself. And let me assure you that if the Defence Colony police station officers see you with him and if they know that he is on your case, from then on, no one will have the balls to walk into your house or harass you. At the station, Puri *Saheb* will brief you. As far as I know, he will ask you to say that you did not know about this guy called Partho Sengupta at all. And you don't worry at all. Trust me, this is just a routine enquiry. In any case, if you think you need any other help, you can always call me.

Avantika felt better. "Avantika, could you please switch back to normal headset mode?"

She handed over the set to Shweta to do the needful. She obliged and handed back the phone to her. "Avantika, I want to thank you for taking care of Shweta. I really appreciate whatever you have done." Avantika smiled, genuinely, after long.

Standing in her balcony, smoking her eighth or ninth cigarette, she tried to figure out the mystery of Partho Sengupta. Ever since Captain told her that anger was a habit, she had been trying to break it.

She looked at her watch. It was 12:30 am. Not late by Delhi standards. She checked herself out. T-shirt, track pants. Perfect, she thought, and came inside, slipped on her *jootis* and grabbed her satchel. Shweta was sleeping like a log. She wrote a small note and put it under her mobile.

As she walked down the staircase, she dialled 42424242. Someone had told her once that comparatively, radio cabs are safer.

Face To Face

Colonel Sengupta sat there, looking weak, guilty and shattered. Whatever little she had seen of him, weakness and guilt were feelings which were alien to his character. He was a man of strong likes and dislikes and always chose to live by rules set by him. Wearing a dark coloured T-shirt and shorts, he had stress written all over his face.

Finding his apartment in one of the high end condominiums in Gurgaon was easy. From Defence Colony to IIT, via Siri Fort, and from there a brief 20 minutes drive on the MG Road took her to a traffic cop in Gurgaon who guided her straight to Beverly Park 1. The pink coloured, high-rise apartments were swank. The uniformed guards at the entrance gate, in the lobby and the last one near the elevator made her remember her good old cantonment life. The only difference being that her past houses were guarded by gallant soldiers and her Dad's present quarters by poorly paid migrants from the nearby states.

When the guard called Colonel Gupta on the intercom, to seek his permission before sending her upstairs, Avantika was very surprised that without even a word, she was escorted to his apartment's door—almost as if he was expecting her. The scope for formal pleasantries were non-existent. As she sat on the cozy chair, she looked at him—her biological father. Simi came from the kitchen holding two mugs of coffee. The whole idea of having coffee in a mug with the word 'YOU' was not at all repulsive till she saw the other one, in Simi's hand with 'ME' printed on it. Simi was as garish as her usual self, attired in a leopard print night suit.

"So how is your painting going?" A bad ice breaker by the Colonel, but nevertheless it ensured a conversation.

"It's on." Simi was keenly observing Avantika and her track pant, T-shirt and *jooti* combo. Avantika caught her eyes. She got a little embarrassed and smiled. Colonel sipped his Black Label. "Dad, I want an answer. Rather, an explanation on whatever is going on."

Before Colonel could react, Simi jumped in, trying to play the protective lover and the would-be wife. "Avantika, he is your father and like any other father, he does not owe an explanation to his kid."

It was only after experiencing a surge of anger did Avantika realize that anger is a habit which she wanted to do away with. Therefore, she took a few deep breaths and thought of Captain's pleasing face, his bright eyes and smiled. She looked right into Simi's eye. "Surely Simi, I appreciate your point of view. But don't you think that after thirty years, if I'm told by Delhi Police cops, who raid my house in the middle of the night, that I have a brother, who got shot because he was a dreaded naxalite, I would demand an explanation?" She managed to control the pitch of her delivery. To her surprise, her calm tone unsettled Simi.

She continued. "I am sure Simi, if you were me, even you would ask for an explanation. Don't I have a right to know if I should mourn my brother's death who never existed for me or if I should feel relieved for not having known him as he was a naxalite?"

Colonel got up from the sofa and gestured Simi to keep quiet. Simi did not take it very well as she got up and strutted into another room. He motioned Avantika to follow her as he walked out of the drawing room, taking the long corridor to a balcony. On a normal day, Avantika would have been awed by the magnificent look from the fourteenth floor balcony, but today her mind was somewhere else. He looked at the stars, lost in them, and Avantika saw a tear trickle down his weather beaten face. Seeing Colonel Sengupta shed a tear was unbelievable. She wanted to hug him and console him, maybe cry with him as it would have made them feel better but she clutched the balcony rail tightly instead.

"I don't think that we need any prologue to this conversation." He looked at the skyline of Gurgaon and took a large sip of the scotch, bracing himself for the uphill task. "Well, whatever you have been told and have come here to validate is true."

"Dad, I don't want to leave any ambiguity here. So let me ask you this straight. Do you mean that for all these years, I had a brother named Partho Sengupta?"

He looked at her, gathered up all his might and strength and replied. "Yes."

There are times when extreme emotion and stress make us go numb. Avantika felt the same. She put her hand in her satchel and pulled out her cigarette pack. As she lit one and took a couple of deep drags, she felt like a living being. "So you mean, I had a brother and

I was not even aware of him? Illegitimate child?" Knowing her father well, it was the most obvious guess.

"You are now talking like a bloody civilian," his voice had a restrained thunder. "Avantika, assuming the role of a high moral priest, condemning everyone but onesef is the easiest thing, you know why? Because there are certain roads which take a great amount of courage to tread. And as your father, I know that you don't have the strength to face the truth. That was the reason I never told you about Partho. And for your information, he was your real brother, not a bastard as you did assume."

Avantika was deciphering each and every word of his patiently. When he finished speaking, she looked at him and moved a step closer, looking right in his eye. "Colonel Sengupta, though you might not think me worthy to be your daughter, but let me tell you that I have inherited your genes. And it gives me ample courage to stand and face anything. Remember, for ten long years, I watched my mom getting beaten mercilessly by you?" She took one last drag and without even bothering to stub the cigarette, threw it down the fourteenth floor.

His eyes tried to trail the falling cigarette butt. "I was posted with 3rd Cavalry in Andhra Pradesh. Your mother was pregnant. Ultrasounds revealed that the baby was deformed. I asked her to get the baby aborted. But knowing your mother, she did not give in. 31st December 1970: a baby boy was born, with deformed right hand and limb. I knew with his degree of handicap, surviving in this brutal, hard and competitive world would be impossible. And moreover, playing father to a handicap son, who would be the dart board of all ridicule, was not my idea of parenthood. I had always dreamt of a gallant son who would carry on our family tradition of joining the army, in the armoured core. Holding this crippled baby in my arms shattered my dreams. As your mom was reading the *Gita* those days, inspired by *Krishna's* address to Arjun, she named the baby boy, Parth. I could see that if I did not do something soon, parting Parth and your mother would be difficult. So the next morning, I took the baby and drove down about two hundred kilometres to this missionary in Guntur and handed him over there."

Avantika was listening to him but her mind was not ready to believe that a father, her father, could do such a thing. She was trembling with rage and hatred. With trembling fingers, she lit another cigarette. "And what did you tell mom?"

He was silent. He turned his head away from her and his voice dropped. "Told her that he died. I was in touch with the missionary sister for almost ten years. I kept on sending whatever I could: money, clothes, toys, chocolates. In 85 or maybe 86, the sister passed away. When I tried to enquire, I was told that post her demise, Parth fled the missionary and joined the local outlaws, the naxals. That was the last I heard of him."

Tears rushed to join Avantika in her grief. She made no effort to hide them, stop them or even wipe them.

"Avantika, if he was your brother, don't forget, he was also my son. Though he could not be a soldier that I wanted him to be, but what gives me great peace that at least he died like one, though on the wrong side of the line. I would have hated to see him rot and die in a bed, like a vegetable."

"I don't know if I should hate you more and if I should just stop emoting for you. I always heard stories of you and your bravery on the field. But if you ask me, you are the biggest coward that I have ever met. Would you ever leave your wounded men behind? I bet you won't. Then why did you have to leave your handicapped son?" She broke down. Colonel Sengupta made a gesture to console her but then decided against it. "Why did you have to do it Dad?" Her words were punctuated with sobs. "I don't know if mom forgave you for this; I don't even care if God will, but I will never forgive you for this. Till this time, I hated you for being a bad husband and a terrible father, but somewhere deep down I looked up to you as a man of principles, a brave soldier with an impeccable record. But from now on, you are just one of those petty *panjoo* shopkeepers who don't have any strength of character. You have failed me Colonel Sengupta, you have failed me terribly." Her voice was hysterical and her sobs were making it worse. Simi rushed in hearing the commotion. Colonel Sengupta shook his head and signalled her to leave. Simi banged the door and walked out of the balcony. Colonel Sengupta looked into Avantika's eyes. She was trembling with anger. Even on the semi-darkened balcony, Colonel could see that her face was flushed.

He wanted to speak but Avantika took the lead. "I, Avantika Sengupta, hereby disown you as my legal father. To ensure that you don't take it lightly, I will get the same published in newspapers, too. Neither do I pray nor do I believe in God, but if there is one, I will request him to give you the treatment that you have always doled out to your wife, your son and me. Goodbye Colonel Sengupta, have a happy married life."

Back To Her Roots

The cab stopped in front of the dilapidated gate of the big bunglow which housed Avantika's barsati apartment. Owing to a dispute between two brothers, the 500 yards kothi had been lying vacant for at least seven long years that she had been staying there. Though she always blamed luck for not being on her side, but on the same hand, she also thanked it for letting her have such a wonderful, peaceful home in the heart of Delhi and that too, for a paltry sum of ₹ 2,000. When she was shown the place, the property dealer had told her categorically that the owner of the house, an aging lady named Mrs Kalra, had made it clear that she will rent out her second floor barsati only to a single girl. So being single, not only did Avantika get the keys to the barsati, but also to Mrs Kalra's heart. At times, Mrs Kalra would invite her downstairs for a cup of tea or to have a bite of her special chole-bhature. Avantika still remembered the day when Mrs Kalra saw Sunny for the first time. That day, her interviewing skills could have put a seasoned HR professional to shame.

Unfortunately, Mrs Kalra, on one of her trips to Canberra, to be with her elder son, passed away. Within a week, both her sons landed in Delhi to claim the bunglow. It turned out that both of them had the original papers. So just like any other claimant, they filed a case. Each one of them posted a board, claiming that the property was under dispute, and to guard the disputed land, both of them posted their own guards, too. On Shweta's and Prashant's insistence, Avantika spoke with the brothers that she should not be disturbed till the case was settled. To make them take her request seriously, she threatened them with filing a case on them which could further complicate the right to ownership due to a pending tenancy suit. The NRIs bought her bluff. With time, the two guards posted by different masters, to guard the same properly became best of pals. And for ₹ 2,000, Avantika got a house with Z class security. Not bad at all.

As she paid the cabbie and started her journey up the long winding fleet of stairs, she wished for an elevator. Her left *jooti* hurt her toe. She got out of them, held them in her hands and started the climb barefoot. After a long day, this climb always reminded her of the *Vaishno Devi* climb and for the same reason, amongst her friends, her place was nicknamed '*Bhawan*'. She could see Shweta standing on the balcony. She was so tired that she did not have the energy even to smile at her. As she entered her place, she was surprised to see it spick and span, as if nothing had happened there. She looked at Shweta, with a 'thank you' and 'what was the need' in her eyes. As she scanned the room, her eyes caught Shweta's suitcase, all packed, and kept on the floor.

"Shwets, I had a very long and tiring day. I am in no mood for any more surprises. Please tell me that you are not planning to throw one at me."

Celine Dion crooned again, bringing Shweta's pink coloured MotoRazr to life. Avantika threw her hands up in despair and crashed on the bed.

"Prashant, just give me five minutes, please. Yes you can send the driver to get the luggage." As she disconnected the call, she looked at Avantika.

As if she felt her eyes burning a hole in her back, without even bothering to turn towards her, she said, "Close the door while you leave. And stop feeling guilty. I know no husband would like his wife to share an apartment with someone who has or had naxals for relatives. What if the media gets to know that Khemka's daughter-in-law is living with a girl who is related to a dreaded naxalite? I am sure Prashant would have given you this logic. Right Shwets?"

Avantika turned towards her. Shweta was standing there, tongue tied, with tears in her eyes. Avantika was in no mood to go soft that night, not after having the conversation with her dad. "Didn't you ask him if his getting caught by the media while humping his cab for hire in Mumbai and Bangalore would have made a bigger story?"

"Avi please. You have no right to insult him like this. He is my husband. And if anyone should have a problem with his sleeping around, it's only me."

Suddenly, Avantika felt lonely. First, it was Sunny and now Shweta.

"And how can you be so mean to him after he has helped you so much? Just to help his wife's friend, he put the most expensive lawyer on your case. Do you have any idea how much Puri uncle charges just for standing in the courtroom?" Avantika waited for the figure.

"Two lakh." She exclaimed while her fingers went up denoting the same sum. Avantika wanted to hug her innocent friend who could not even see that her mean, scheming and calculative hubby took this whole episode as an opportunity to win her over.

The uniformed driver entered the room and wished Shweta and Avantika. Shweta pointed over to the two suitcases. He diligently took them downstairs. Avantika felt her satchel, looking for her cigarette pack. She pulled out one and lit it. For a change, this time nicotine hurt her throat. She choked and coughed loudly and uncontrollably.

Celine Dion crackled again. "On my way. Just ten seconds." Shweta answered the call.

Avantika got into another fit of cough. Shweta looked at her with pity. "Bye Avantika, take care."

Avantika tried to control the bout and rushed to the washroom. As the bout subsided, she wiped her sweating face with her T-shirt sleeve. She turned on the light to wash her face and clear the basin, where she had spit. Tears rolled down her cheeks and gently landed in the basin, which already had traces of blood.

A Heady Mix

"Room number three please, Doctor Bakshi."

The receptionist politely guided Avantika towards the consulting physician. From her military base hospital days, surely healthcare had come a long way, especially for the super speciality hospitals like Max, Fortis, Apollo and the likes. These brands never ceased to surprise and amuse her for their antics, guised cleverly under the garb of words like 'patient comfort' and 'unmatched experience'. Not long ago, hospitals with a Barista or a Café Coffee Day outlet, a book or flower store were unimaginable. But now, practically every one of them had all this and more. Also, from the pristine white, over the years, they evolved to a more soothing aqua green. Even the snobbish and snooty doctors were replaced with more friendly and interesting faces. The other day she read an article which claimed that with its large number of competent surgeons and economical packages, India was emerging as the hot favourite in the health tourism sector. Health tourism? She almost freaked out. But despite all the cosmetic changes, for some reason, one thing still remained the same. The fear-struck faces of patients.

After all, how can death and suffering assume a softer context, even amidst five-star comfort or newly defined luxuries?

As she sat there, on the pleasant and comfortable beige chair, her face had fear inscribed all over. Her puffed eyes were a sure shot giveaway of the long and arduous last night. After the bout of prolonged cough attack, the moment she saw her white sink sport blood stains, her mind almost drew blank. For the first few seconds, she could not figure out the source of blood. When reality dawned upon her, instantly the statutory warning printed on every cigarette pack flashed in front of her. Her mind revolted at the thought of dying of cancer, and her body cringed with fear. God please, not now. Not when her life was just moving into a higher gear. Her effort to Google cancer symptoms threw up some 18,100,000 results. When she tried to narrow it down by rephrasing her search to 'lung cancer symptom', there were still 1,790,000 matches.

With all the information weighing on her mind, she reached a point where her mind just shut down due to fear and her eyes with sleep and tears.

She dreaded the thought of coping with cancer without any support system—parents, friends, well-wishers or even money. If nothing else, at least money could have ensured her a room and a nurse at a decent hospital. Why did she not opt for health insurance? She could not help but curse herself. Could she still opt for an insurance plan and get her illness covered?

Every question lead to more and the new ten ones branched off into an infinite number. Finally, when she thought she had enough, her fingers automatically dialled Captain. To her surprise, even around three, he was wide awake, and like always, his voice alone was enough to comfort her. In line with the fact that comfort breeds weakness and weakness becomes the source of many tears, she broke down and wept uncontrollably. Once tears flushed out her fear and pain, Captain got down to the constructive bit. He asked her to get a paper and pen. Like a child, she followed the same. Then he asked her to write down her biggest fear. Undoubtedly, it was the fear of death, the unknown. He went on to tell her though cigarette smoking increased the chances of mouth and lung cancer, but not consuming tobacco did not guarantee hundred per cent protection either. Therefore, like most of the dreaded diseases, even cancer was a karmic ailment. And like any other karmic ailment, if it has to happen, it will happen. When Avantika asked him as to what he was trying to say, he smiled and told her that the body was a slave of the mind and, therefore, by harbouring signs of fear or guilt, the mind starts passing off the same to the body and the body starts manifesting them on the physical front. Therefore, he concluded by telling her that to keep healthy, she should not lose control of her mind and should plant positive thoughts in there. For the same, he asked her to write down that she would not blame herself and feel guilty about anything.

The next thing she was asked to write down was to visit a good consulting physician to get herself examined. He enquired if she has ever taken a full body checkup. Her negative reply made him tell her the importance of a full body checkup as it was the only way to ascertain if everything was working well within the system. He also told her that she should not worry if even after a couple of tests, the doctor advised her to go for a biopsy.

Calling up an insurance agent and getting her basic health cover done for ten lakh was the next thing on agenda. Last but not the least, he asked her to promise him that she will quit smoking right then and there. He was sane enough to warn her of the palpable withdrawal symptoms forcing her to go back to it again. Therefore, he told her to think it over and make a conscious decision if she would like to live longer and enjoy the fruits of her labour, or if she would prefer going down as a loser. No wonder the choice was obvious. After she made her choice, he suggested her to make another choice as to whether she would like to live like a healthy individual, or rot in one of the government hospital wards. The choice again was obvious. To incentivize her, the Captain announced that he had also quit smoking. She smiled and said "me too".

"Ms Sengupta?" The attendant's enquiry brought Avantika back from her memories of last night. "The doctor wants to see you."

She knocked the door and waited for the customary 'come in'. When it didn't happen, she pushed the door a little and saw the doctor busy typing an SMS.

"May I?" She enquired politely. He looked up, got a little embarrassed and smiled. "Come in please. Please have a seat."

She took her seat and looked around the cabin. Neat and functional. The doctor put down his mobile and looked at her.

"Tell me what brings you here."

Avantika looked at the painting of two birds, on the wall to her right. What a waste of paint she thought.

"Ms Sen?" The doctor tried getting her attention.

"Well yes. I am here," it was her turn to get embarrassed. "Last evening, I had this prolonged bout of cough and I realized that there was blood coming out from my mouth."

She tried her best to stick close to facts.

"Do you smoke?" Without even looking at her, the doctor pulled out a paper and started taking her medical history. After twenty minutes of telling him things like if there is a history of cancer in her family, both on her father's as well as mother's side, the colour, consistency and texture of the blood, number of cigarettes she smoked every day, her smoking history, she walked out with a prescription with some dozen odd tests suggested on it.

She handed over the prescription at the reception. The receptionist, who was multi-tasking—handling two calls and attending to an enquiry punched a few keys on her keyboard, which was linked to a monitor concealed under her table and tore the paper that came out of it. "Nine thousand please." She told Avantika.

Without even looking in her satchel, she knew that she was not carrying that kind of money. After extending her Kerala trip by six extra days, for which she had procured a soft loan from Shweta, and with her impulsive shopping there, she had severely impacted her modest finances. The receptionist got tired of holding the printout for her and kept it on the counter. Avantika felt embarrassed and to hide the same, she opened her satchel and pretended to look for money. All of a sudden, she got this feeling that all eyes were on her, staring, watching her pretend looking for money which she did not have. While looking in her satchel, she came across Sunny's credit card, which he had given her just in case she ever needed it. She held it, weighing the pros and cons. She could still feel the eyes of people on her.

Suddenly, a young woman came and walked up to the receptionist, enquiring about her reports. Avantika took the opportunity to silently get away from there. While walking towards the door, her heart was beating fast, so loud that she felt that people around could hear its thumping. Her mind told her that the receptionist would shout her name, telling people that she did not pay the money for the test. As the glass door approached, her heart beat grew louder and feet got heavier. What would she tell if the guards stopped her? She prayed and walked faster, almost running. No she couldn't run, she told herself. People around might get suspicious and might apprehend her. She has to maintain her cool. She has to act normal. The door was hardly any distance now.

Maybe just fifteen steps. Faster baby, she urged her feet.

She inched towards the door. Her heart felt cramped. She could not breathe. The receptionist would be looking at her escaping and would be calling for the guards.

Eight steps or maybe nine to the exit.

She would give them Sunny's credit card if she was stopped. But what if they asked her who Sunny was? What would she say? She would say that he is her hubby, she thought.

Five steps only.

Three steps.

Two steps and she felt air rush in her lungs.

She almost choked on it as she filled her lungs with more and more of it. She was out of the door and no one stopped her. Her face was plastered with sweat, with her hair sticking to it. She was panting. Her hand immediately went into her satchel, looking for the Navy

Cut pack. She clutched it and pulled it out. While she pulled out a cigarette, her mobile immortalized the anthem once more. She looked at the screen. It was Captain.

"What did the Doctor say?" She was silent.

"Avi, you there?"

She did not know what to tell him. Should she tell him that she was broke and, therefore, can't get her tests done. She felt so small, humiliated and almost naked.

"Avi, talk to me. What's wrong?" Bordering on the verge of breaking down, she narrated the entire incident. There was a small pause.

"Avi, do you trust me?"

Without even seeing her nod, he knew the answer.

"Now listen to me carefully. Firstly, no one will catch you as you have not run away from there without paying. You got your consultation done, and for the same, you have paid them. Right?" She nodded again. "Don't nod your head Avi. I want to hear you say yes or no."

"Yes you are right," her words were weak and soft.

"So now you are going to walk up that door again, open it with confidence, look around to find the nearest water dispenser and have a glass of water..."

In the next few minutes, he assured her that everything was within her reach and control. She followed his instructions blindly.

"Well, I am sorry. I am not carrying this kind of cash with me right now. Do you mind if I give the same once I am here to collect my reports?" The doctor looked up at her and did not know how to react. "If you want, I can make an advance payment, say around two thousand." She offered a mid-term solution.

"No it's not like that. I did not mean it that way." She knew that she was caught on the wrong foot, without even intending to.

"I know you didn't. So the problem is that you don't have money. Right?"

"Yes Captain."

"Now the trick is not to think of not having money and not let it bother you. On the contrary, think of prosperity and abundance. How about thinking of a lavish meal tonight, celebrating with a bottle of some exquisite wine? Think of all the good things that you can. Do it for me, but do it with conviction. Believe as if you know that tonight you are going to have a ball of a time at the most fancy place. Think of it. Visualize the most expensive restaurant, a waiter wearing a tuxedo serving you sparkling champagne. Think of every little detail and see how beautifully it will work for you."

She overheard Sudhakar shouting that the air conditioner in the guest room was not working.

"I am sure you must have heard that I have a pressing business appointment; to fix the air conditioner." They laughed.

"All the best for your meeting, keep me posted and just in case my secret trick lets you down, let me know, I will transfer some money to your account." Before she could say anything he added "...as a loan of course."

As her cab pulled in the porch of Taj Palace, she checked herself in the rear view mirror. Not bad, she thought. Throughout her journey, from the porch to the elevator, elevator to room number 1401, she kept herself immersed in the thought of sparkling wine, expensive restaurant, caviar, cheese. Initially, about an hour back when she started off this exercise, she had a hearty laugh at her inability to think of expensive things. She looked at the brown teak doors on both the sides of the long, carpeted corridor. 1405, 1403, 1402 and there it was. The metal numerals 1401 were right in front of her. She knocked gently.

Dressed in a crisp white linen trouser, a pink cotton shirt, tan belt and shoes, Francois looked every bit of the much fashionable French. Donning his blue tooth mobile headset, he was probably on a conference call. He opened the door and silently gestured her to step in. While he was engrossed in the conversation, making interjections here and there, Avantika scanned his hotel room. His study table was in a mess, with various blue prints, drawings, pencils of various colours, strewn all over it. Maybe the room service staff was yet to do the needful. But for the study table, the room was impeccable. The bed was made, the side board clear. All this reflected that he had spent the night working and then got ready for his day ahead. In between, he also squeezed out time to see her. Avantika was nervous. She looked at her footwear, a shining pair of black stilettos. Meeting Captain had changed her for good. Though it even took him quite a while to convince her that meetings with clients meant business and no one likes to transact with someone dressed in shabby *khadi kurta*, shoulder bag and slippers. He had to also show her pictures of his batch mates at the Parsons College, where each one of the soon-to-be artists were nattily dressed in black jackets for the photo session. So, for this meeting, Avantika ensured that she was attired in a smart, formal suit and carried a more professional-looking folio.

As Francois ended his conversation, he turned towards her.

His eyes did notice the transformation in her and the gentle smile on his face made a statement that he was pleased with the change. "Hmmm, you look prettier and more professional." As he got in the beige upholstered chair opposite her, his eyes scanned her for good two seconds. "You know I am very impressed with your makeover. It clearly indicates that you are taking this project seriously, not riding solely on the recommendation of Mr Khurana."

Avantika smiled and thanked the Captain silently.

"Can I have a look at the first cut?"

She pulled up her new shining portfolio and unlocked the two gleaming black buckles on it. As they snapped, Francois smiled. She carefully took out the concept cards and put the deck on the table. Francois checked his watch.

"Mr Lancolne." She got into the groove of her speech which Captain had not only dictated to her but had also ensured that she rehearsed it at least ten times with him, over the phone. "As discussed and agreed upon during our last meeting, for the boutique property, *The Woods*, which is inspired by nature and will have the look and feel of log cabins, I was supposed to present some thematic representation for the wall paintings." Francois listened to her intently. "I am here to present the first cut, which will give you a fair idea of the concept, thematic representation, colour palette, medium to be used and the overall look and feel."

She pulled out the first 12 × 12 card which had a sketch of a wild flower. "While I was deliberating over the concept, I realized that the log cabin feel would be more in earthy colours. Brown, beiges, cream, mauves, etc. Also, the flooring and the walls would be made out of wood. Therefore, I thought that it would make sense to go the opposite way."

Francois sat up, getting interested. Avantika smiled and clarified her point. "I mean, instead of merging with the earthy colours, I would love to punctuate the monotony with a splash of vibrant colours by putting up pictures of wild birds, butterflies, flowers, all in bright colours. Not only will it add a touch of warmth to the interiors, but also go well with the theme."

Francois nodded. "Can I see a few renderings of the same?"

She knew that she was home and spread the deck across on the table, taking him through the cards one by one. With each card, Francois got more and more convinced. "Good work Ms Sengupta. I think I am quite convinced with your logic, though it's hard to find it amongst the creative lot." He laughed. "I buy your point and give my go ahead. After seeing what you have got, I don't think that we need to meet for the second cut. Go ahead with your final work. I will ask my colleague, Pooja, to get in touch with you for the exact numbers and sizes. In the meanwhile, you've got to see my finance guy, who sits out of our Connaught Place office. He will make you sign a bond, a legal contract which will state the terms and conditions."

Avantika had a surprised look.

Francois laughed. "Oh, nothing to be afraid of. Just standard company procedure. Once you sign the contract, you will be formally our painter for this project, and also, it will give you a signing amount to take care of your expenses during the project."

She could not believe her ears and had to pinch herself secretly.

"I will forward you the business card of this gentleman named Sandeep, who is our finance guy. The card will have my office address. I would suggest that you go and see him immediately and close this deal. I will put in a word so that he is ready with the papers once you are there."

"You were right." She shouted over her phone as she rushed out of the Taj lobby, like a kid who passed the exam by knowing all the questions beforehand. She still could not believe that she was all set to sign the contract and get the much-needed money and that too in advance.

"Congratulations." Captain sounded happy as well as relieved. His theory did stand the test of time.

The Swot Analysis

Since morning, Sunny was feeling terrible. Ever since he had seen pictures of Avantika and the boat guy, ever since he had seen Avantika's phone bill in which every other call was made to the boat guy, a strange feeling of jealousy and uneasiness was clouding him. He had cancelled his appointments for the day. He wanted to be with himself, to take stock of the situation and then decide on the course of action.

He took out a notepad from the drawer of his mahogany writing table and plonked on the small red coloured sofa, which was placed in one corner of his large room. Still in shorts and a tee, he put up his feet on the centre table and flipped open a fresh page. How good life would be if turning pages were so easy in it, he thought to himself.

AVANTIKA & SUNNY, he scribbled on the top of the white page. He looked at the two words. Somehow, he liked watching his name with Avantika's. He smiled. He drew a vertical line and then at the centre, crossed it with a horizontal one, making a big plus sign. Using his limited edition Mont Blanc, he named the top two grids as STRENGTH and WEAKNESS and the bottom ones as OPPORTU-

NITY and THREAT. Like a true management graduate, he planned to do a SWOT analysis of his relationship with Avantika.

He looked at the strength column. For the first time, he realized that it was hard to list down even one strong point. But how can an eight-year long relationship have no strength, he thought to himself. With each passing moment, he got more and more uneasy as he could not find even one strength to put it down there, in black and white. Forcefully, he scribbled 'Sunny's love for Avantika'; 'long-term association'; 'stable future with Sunny'; 'Sunny's financial stability'; 'Sunny's family reputation and social standing'; and finally, 'Sunny's ability to take her tantrums.' As he checked the points, he knew that he was not being fair, as he was cheating, no one else, but himself.

But then, he also knew that there was no problem that could not be fixed. For the WEAKNESS section, he did not have to strain himself as points kept on flowing. 'Lack of compatibility'; 'too different family backgrounds'; 'no common interest or hobby'; 'different intelligence and emotional quotient'; 'Sunny's family resistance towards her'; 'Avi's indifference towards him'; 'growing distance between them'; 'lack of physical compatibility,' and the list seemed exhaustive.

In the OPPORTUNITY section, like a business strategist, for nearly forty minutes, he racked his brains, covering every single aspect from every angle. Though he hated doing it, but he had no other option but to put a big question mark there.

Figuring out the THREAT part was easier. Especially after the photograph and the phone bills provided by the private eyes. It just had one entry in big and bold. THE BOAT GUY.

He looked at the white sheet of paper which had the facts plotted before him strained hard to find a solution. Maybe a smoke would help, or so he thought. He lit a Marlboro Lights. As the smoke curled up towards the ceiling and slithered down his lungs, he felt better.

But after a few drags, the more he inhaled, the more it clouded his logic and judgment. Disgusted with himself, or maybe the cigarette, he went inside the washroom and dropped the half-lit cigarette in the WC and flushed it. The gurgle and surge of water took it away. He watched the swirling water and was quite fascinated with the small ripples that it created. He shifted his focus from the abyss of the WC to the mirror. As he checked himself, he concluded that he was definitely a good looking man. His sharp features, fair skin, well built and toned body made him look younger than his actual thirty-two years.

Something crossed his mind. He hurried out of the washroom and walked towards his drawer. As he fumbled inside it, he finally found what he was looking for. A big manila envelope. He opened it and pulled out its content. He flipped through them till he reached one which he was looking for—close-up of a man. Maybe in his early 50s. He had curly, salt and pepper hair. The deep creases on his forehead and around his eye made him look older. His lips were dark due to the harsh sun. The only thing remarkable about him was his sparkling eyes. Full of mischief and child-like innocence, they stood out like bright polar stars.

Damn this boat guy from the backwaters, he cursed him. As he looked again at the picture. He consoled himself that he was definitely better than him. What he could not figure out was the reason which made Avantika flip for this oldie. Should he use Shweta to dissuade Avantika from seeing the boat guy? But within a second, he decided against it as he knew Avantika too well.

Surely, there would be some way to get her back into his life? He missed her for whatever reason. Did he love her? He had no clue and did not even want to figure it out. The only thing he knew was that getting dumped, that too in front of his parents, had terribly hurt his male ego. Come what may, he wanted to restore his male pride. Even if that meant seeking help from his father. After all, it was his father who always fixed things for him. Right from getting him a seat in the most coveted school and college to gifting him his dream car, setting up his small business empire, everything was given by him. As he walked towards Mr Khurana's room, he was sure that he would help him in getting back his dream girl, too.

Reconciliation, If Any

Though the dimly-lit interiors made it almost impossible for her to be certain, but she guessed that the man sitting at the far end of the hall would be Sunny. Walking towards him, looking at the interiors, she tried to figure out the thought process of the designer who had designed this high end restaurant—'Elements'. With its blood red painted walls, which looked more garish and outright appalling with the bold, gold motifs on them, the place looked more like an orgy room of some middle-east billionaire. The black colour, thick carpet planted in patches, imparted the place a sinister aura. Big candles planted on huge wrought iron stands, with icicles of wax hanging were straight out of some Dracula movie. Even the seating arrangement was very unlike any other restaurant she had been to so far. The large, red coloured velvet couches were paired with high back chairs, wrapped in gold colour, patent leather, making them look like the prized throne of some kinky medieval duke. The lounge music was adding more horror and gore to the already unbearable ambience.

As her eyes got accustomed to the low intensity lighting, she could see Sunny seated there, punching his Blackberry keys deftly. He was attired in a crisp sky blue linen suit. Knowing his penchant for brands, she knew that it ought to be either from Hugo Boss, CK or Armani. As he sensed her, he looked up and smiled. She smiled back and sat on the red couch only to realize that having a conversation seated uncomfortably on the couch would be a tough task. Sunny looked at her, almost checking her out. She got embarrassed and as an involuntary reaction, her eyes moved around to check the restaurant only to find it almost deserted.

"You are looking good." Sunny posted his first comment after the long observation.

"Thanks," she smiled back.

"Your face is glowing and your eyes have got their spark back," Sunny commented. She shifted her gaze to the golden coloured wall motif.

"It's good to see you Avi." He adjusted himself on the oversized, badly designed and completely out of place throne styled chair. "Dad was asking about you. He was telling me that your painting project with Mr Lancolne is shaping up well. Also, he did mention that Mr Lancolne is very impressed with your pragmatic thinking and radical approach."

She blushed profusely. She knew that to her untrained ears, it would take some time to get accustomed to kind words. "Your Dad is a very nice and kind man. Please convey my regards to him. How is your mom doing?" Just the thought of her made her squirm.

"Oh she is doing great. She has gone to Milan to attend a seminar."

Without even Sunny elaborating upon the content of the seminar, she knew that this high-flying, overseas conference ought to do with either poverty or poor kids. And she was correct.

"Considering her impeccable credentials on rural sanitation and women's health, for this Milan conference, she was appointed by the Ministry of Health to represent India."

Avantika could never reason out why the socialites were always drawn to depressing issues like unsafe abortion, child prostitution, rural health and sanitation, just to name a few. Was it out of sheer concern or…

Sunny exclaimed, "Hey Avi, you have changed for the better!"

She could not get the source of his sudden exuberance and looked at him, seeking an explanation. He laughed at her reaction.

"I don't see those parasites sticking to your ears anymore."

It took her a few seconds to figure out that he was referring to her earphones. She laughed out loud. She was amused to learn that he had started noticing even small things, like her missing iPod. "Well, I decided to give it a miss as there is already so much on my mind."

His face suddenly assumed a different hue, of curtness.

"That I am aware of."

"Sorry, I didn't get you." She was slightly puzzled at his expression and statement.

He looked at her cynically and let out an 'I know all' smile.

"Sunny, I know there is something going on in your mind. You can share it without sounding sarcastic or bitchy about it."

The old Avantika got the better of the new one and made her presence felt emphatically, making Sunny a little nervous.

"You care for a drink?"

She looked at him with a little apprehension as knowing him for long had made her realize that he ordered drink, especially on a bright afternoon, only if he had to make the liquor his alibi, while he spoke his mind.

"Thanks. Some water would be fine."

As Sunny interacted with the waiter, ordering his variety of *Rusty Nails*, Avantika's mind raced to decipher the objective of this meeting. Whatever it was, she thought, bring it on fast. The music was getting to her nerves.

"Sunny, could you please request the man on the consoles to turn down the music a little?"

Her wish was granted but with a twist. Seeing a young couple, the DJ assumed that it would be better to play some romantic music. Damn, she should have just avoided getting into the music part as the romantic piano sonata was taking her to the Voyager.

It took him three large gulps of *Rusty Nail* to get all fired up. "That day, when you walked out on me in front of my parents, I felt so small, so humiliated. But even then I told myself that your reaction was also my fault. Maybe, I could not understand you, or figure out what was going on in your mind. For eight years, I tried too hard to understand you, mould myself as per you, do things to please you. But whatever I did, you were never appreciative of anything."

Avantika was listening and was waiting for the real reason behind his uneasiness.

"Fine, we were seeing each other, we liked each other, we even had our share of fun, but never were you truly mine. Your mind belonged to someone else. Even when we made love, you never participated. You were there with me in bed, but just physically, and it confused me. Remember, when on my birthday, Dad gifted me a car? You were so hurt and offended as you wanted to be the one who gifted me the most precious thing. I still recall that night in your apartment, you told me that I was the most precious thing you had. And just to beat my Dad, you gifted me something which no one could ever match, your virginity. I also know that for a girl like you, it meant a lot. But the same girl, who let me enter her body, never really let me anywhere close to her heart. I was never your partner, your soulmate. To make matters worse, with each passing year, with your growing failures and my rising success, you drifted further apart. I did try my best to be there for you, help you, even with something as obscure as painting, but..."

She shifted on the couch, adjusting her frame. He looked at her, deep in her eyes, while feeling the inside of his cheek with his tongue. After swirling the *Rusty Nail* in the glass, he took a large sip and a bite of the chicken tikka. Listening to what he just said, Avantika felt a little sorry for him. Somewhere deep down, she liked him as a man, but not as a lover. Maybe when they had met, times were different, their aspirations, needs, desires and perspectives were different. Over the years, things evolved and changed, for better or for worse, she had no clue.

During her initial years, when she had met Sunny, she was a lonely girl, looking for company. No doubt, Sunny was a good one. He took her to fancy pubs and bars, places, gatherings, parties, showed her around and even cared for her. He gave her whatever she needed at that point in time—care, strength, company, financial help and a support system. Since the past few years, her needs changed. She wanted someone to be her mentor, guide, friend and her man. More than a companion, she wanted an anchor, an intellectual support and that too a strong one, to keep her secured and grounded, yet to let her go on expeditions that she always dreamt of.

She gathered herself and her thoughts and tried to articulate.

"Why don't you tell me what's on your mind? Look Sunny, we have gone our own ways. If you remember, during our last meeting, I had made it very clear, without any ambiguity, that if you wanted me as your companion, it was then or never, and you chose the latter. It's over from my side. Why are you starting this all over again? She sounded a little agitated.

He placed a large manila envelope on the table.

"When you dumped me…"

She interrupted, "I never dumped you Sunny. For God's sake, if you cannot respect me, at least use better words to describe our parting."

Her voice assumed a vitriolic tone. While her temples throbbed, she could feel her pulse racing. She could not lose her temper now, she told herself. She took a deep breath and closed her eyes. She wanted to focus on the issue and not dissipate her energy by going for an ugly outburst.

"Yes, you did. Ms Avantika Sengupta, you did dump me."

He patted the manila envelope. She had never heard Sunny say her full name and that too with a definitive, emphatic tone. She knew that the envelope was the source of his assumptions and heartache.

Therefore, without wasting much time, she took it and opened it. As she looked inside, she could see some pictures. She pulled them out. As she leafed through them, her guts churned. How can this man, with whom she spent eight years, stoop so low?

Sunny calling out her name, clicking sound of her stilettos against the wooden floor, the soft piano sonata—everything blended in her ear to form one eerie soundtrack. She rushed out of the grotesque place, with tears doing their best to match her speed. She could not believe that Sunny actually put a detective on her trail to follow her to Kerala.

Doctor-Doctor

"There is a good news and then there is a bad one." Doctor Bakshi smiled. For some odd reason, the sight of a smiling doctor always looked phony to her, both on and off television.

Ever since she got her check up and tests done, which was almost a week ago, her life had been a roller-coaster ride. Meeting Sunny to waking up to the fact that he had actually put a detective on her trail to working towards meeting the deadline for the hotel project, there was a lot happening around. So much so that she had almost forgotten about the reports till one morning, she saw blood in her washbasin again.

"Ms Sengupta, contrary to your own symptomatic diagnosis validated by Dr Google, you don't have cancer."

There are times when joy exceeds expectation by an unimaginable stretch, making it hard to either smile or laugh. Avantika experienced the same. She sighed and uncrossed her fingers, which were tucked under the table. Now, she was braced for the bad one.

"Thank you Doctor." She muttered.

"Not so soon. The bad news is yet to come." Doctor Bakshi smiled.

As she walked out of his cabin, she could not wait to get out of the front door and dial Captain.

"Guess what?" she exclaimed as Captain answered the call, "I am not going to die. I don't have cancer." She burst out laughing. Captain was amused as well a little skeptical as he knew that blood coming out of body was not a good sign.

"That's good. What did the doctor say?"

Avantika was finding it hard to hide her excitement and in this celebration of life she had almost forgotten that she was suffering from an ailment, though not as serious as cancer but, nevertheless, not a minor one too.

"Nothing much. It's peptic ulcer," she chirped.

Captain sighed as he knew that it was her wrong and erratic eating habits, stress, litres of coffee and cigarettes which had led her to this juncture. He also knew that telling her all of this would be futile.

"Can I smoke a cigarette? Just one?" she requested.

"You know my answer. Don't you Avi?" He was stern.

"You are so boring. Why can't I have one? Just for old times' sake." Avantika should have known better that acting like a little girl would have no positive effect on the hard boiled Captain.

"Because peptic ulcers are quite serious and they tend to aggravate with smoke, spices and liquor. Therefore, from now on, you are completely off cigarettes, coffee, Old Monk or spicy food. Masala prawn included." His tone was gentle yet firm.

"You are such a bore. I should have nicknamed you Granpa,

instead of Captain," she protested.

"Even if I were your Granpa, I would have told you the same thing," he responded with ease.

She stepped out of the clinic and put on her glares. The world around her turned orange. She pulled up her glares, a little and the world came to its normal colour. She put the glares back and again the world changed colour. She was quite amused. Though it was not a new phenomenon, but she noticed it for the first time and was able to understand its significance.

Dark Cloud

"I am sorry Ms Sen but I am sure I can help you feel better."

Francois looked at Avantika, who was dabbing her handkerchief into her moist eyes. "Please be seated," he requested.

He was in far more casual attire than usual. A white turtleneck tee with a blue *chakra* and the word INDIA dabbed in amber. The black double stitched jeans gave him a leaner look. As an afterthought, Avantika thought that his dressing was probably intentional so as to make the situation casual and easier. She looked around the coffee shop. But for two fair, well built and rustic looking characters, whom she assumed would be property dealers waiting for their client, it was deserted. She again dabbed her eyes, cautious enough not to soil her liner.

"Ms Sen, I am sure that my office would have told you that the boutique hotel project, 'The Woods', for which you were commissioned to do the paintings, has been stalled by the government due to certain environmental issues." She nodded

"The reason I wanted to explain this whole thing to you in person was because being a creative person myself, though of a different kind and medium, I understand how you might feel. Therefore, to make you feel better, I thought it would be appropriate to present you with another point of view."

He stopped and looked at her, as if he expected her to interject.

Francois opened the bottle and poured some water for her.

"Have some. Water is a great stress buster as it keeps your system hydrated."

She smiled and followed his tip.

"Let me give you a new perspective which will help you in the times to come. For any commercial project, like this hotel one, the artist and the client share a very special relationship, that of a man and woman. They, as a couple, mutually decide to create a baby. The client assumes the role of a father and takes care of the financial part and the artist that of a mother and takes care of the creative part."

Avantika was amused at the unique simile.

The waiter appeared and smiled.

"Would you like to order anything in particular?"

She shook her head. He looked at the waiter and gave him one of his patent warm smiles.

"Could you please get us some coffee with oatmeal cookies?" She watched the confident aura of Francois.

"Would that be all Sir?" the waiter enquired.

Francois smiled and nodded shifting his gaze back to her.

"Sorry for the interruption. So then, like any other couple, the client and the artist go through the inception, conception, and if all go well, the delivery. But there are times when, due to certain reasons, the delivery is not possible. What does the couple do?"

Avantika had no answer to the big question mark on his face as her attention was more on observing him animate his conversation, using his face and hands.

"They abort the foetus." Francois answered his own question. The reply was cold and matter of fact.

Now, she could see a glimpse of his viewpoint, but still a long way to go.

"Ms Sen, this abortion happens not because the couple, in our context the artist and the client, did not want to have the baby. But they take this cruel decision in the long-term interest of the baby and their own relationship."

He paused.

"In my long career, I have played both these roles; of a father as well that of a mother. Even as I speak with you right now, I am playing both the roles. For Mr Khurana, I am the mother, and for you, I am the father. During each of my roles, I have been forced to abort the baby many a time. But do you know, as a proud human being, a good soul, what I have always maintained?"

She raised her eyebrows quizzically.

"The relationship," he answered. "And I take great pride in the fact that I have delivered many successful babies; post-abortion, with the same artists or companies."

As she toyed with an oatmeal cookie, her mind could still not come to terms with the fact that her first big break, the big opportunity, got shelved because of some freak environmental clearance from the government. Why was it always her? Out of so many projects—hotels, commercial and residential—why did the government single this one out?

Francois placed the bright red coffee mug on the table, glanced at the watch.

"Aren't you feeling devastated?"

She did not know how to respond.

"Do you know that every incident, every happening, has two sides to it; the positive and the negative?"

She wondered if there could still be any positive side to this fiasco but she also knew that he was building up his argument towards tackling her apprehension.

"Let me state the obvious, the negative first. This was your first big project and just when it was about to go live, it got stalled due to no fault of yours. I won't give you any false hope by saying that it's just a matter of time as I know that any laxity on the environmental compliance front, especially in environmental sensitive areas like hills etc., never see the light of the day once the media starts advocating and rallying around it. So from your point, this project is dead. And so are your hopes of showcasing this project to get more of them." He shrugged his shoulder.

"Now, let's look at the positive side. Please don't get me wrong when I try to put a figure to your creativity. But purely, from a discussion point of view, you have been paid an advance for your efforts. If you would have gone through the contract, which I am sure you would not have, you would have noticed that clause 13, sub-section 2 states that in case of termination of the contract for any other reason than competence by the company, the company is bound to pay you fifty per cent of the contractual money. Also, the same clause, sub-section three states that in case of withdrawal, the company will lose all intellectual property right."

She could not make out anything and her eyes had too many question marks floating in them.

"Confused?" he laughed. She nodded.

"In simple terms, you get paid and you don't even give us your paintings. Isn't this a win-win for you? I know as an artist, you would have loved to see your work go live but then given the situation..."

Avantika was experiencing the sight of a lifejacket while drowning in deep sea. She was still staring blankly at the table cutlery, trying to fathom the reality check. Not too good but not that bad either, she thought and looked at Francois. Her heart was full of gratitude and she did not have enough words to thank him for empowering her with a new ray of light and hope. His acute and precise comprehension of the problem, in no time, helped her to come out of her depression mode. Though she was pathetic when it came to arithmetic, especially mental calculation, but on the basis of his inputs, she was able to calculate that after all the heartache, she would still be a woman richer by close to three lakh rupees. Not bad at all, she smiled.

"Mr Lancolne, I am very grateful to you for counselling me. I understand that a man like you was not required to do this. I am really indebted to you for your time and for showing me a completely new viewpoint."

He raised his hand and gestured her to stop the unending adulation.

"You are embarrassing me Ms Sen. Whatever I did was my moral duty. I like your work, and moreover, I like your spirit. So you need not thank me for anything. And if you insist on doing the same then you could pay me back, in some other way."

She could not get his last line and was completely taken aback, wondering which unknown bullet was about to hit her.

"Can I have the pleasure of your company on the fifteenth of this month, eight pm at the Hyatt Ballroom?"

Avantika was caught off balance by the sudden change of role and request and did not know how to respond.

"Ah, I am in no hurry, you can think it over and drop me a text to let me know. I can assure you that your company will be my pleasure. Also, you will need to run along to my office, sign some papers and collect your cheque. Have a good day Ms Sen."

The Darkest Hour Is Just Before The Dawn

As the cab stopped in the brightly lit porch, a burly Sikh, seven feet plus, rushed to use his body mass to perform a task which least required it—to open the door. His body-hugging dark blue *angrakha,* kind of long coat, with brass buttons, further highlighted his tall and burly frame. His neatly tied turban added a few more inches to his imposing frame. Avantika looked at him and wondered why most of these guys sported such intimidating, gelled and twirled moustaches. She always pitied them, as she felt that for someone as genetically blessed as them, carving out their livelihood on tips doled out by patrons was such a waste of God's splendid creation.

She hurriedly glanced at her watch, then at the rearview mirror and finally the cab meter. All of them told her a different story, giving her a different reason to feel differently about. Her watch announced that she was just on time and to maintain the same needed to hurry up. The rearview mirror clearly reflected the positive results of her abstinence from tobacco and alcohol and the cab meter made her feel exasperated as she realized that her short trip from Defence Colony to Hyatt had set her back by ₹ 300. Damn this Captain who got her into this bad habit of cabs. She controlled her swaying thoughts as she knew that during the past few weeks, following his 'think of abundance and you shall have it' principle has been showing positive results. Comforting her miserly self, she paid the cabbie and stepped out. As she walked towards the door, she felt a little conscious and desperately wanted to have a good look at herself before she stepped towards the rendezvous point—the Ballroom.

The overhead chandelier in the lobby lit up the streaks of the cherry-black hue in her hair. She was slightly unsure of her gait as she looked around for the ladies room. From the corner of her eyes, she noticed a couple of appreciating looks and suddenly she straightened the base of her spine and the unsure steps had the little spring of confidence. Once inside the restroom, she tossed her pearl coloured bag on the couch. She looked at herself standing in front of the big, well-lit mirror. Her face was glowing and eyes sparkled, coupled with lustrous hair and a younger looking skin. She adjusted the neckline of her deep grey black dress, which was accentuated by the large grey pearls which Shweta had gifted her on her last birthday. She twisted her lips in a mock pensive pout at the neckline, which she thought was a little too revealing. The lips twisted to a naughty smile, while she adjusted the important straps of elastic. She was pleased with her overall look and picked a stray turquoise orchid from the bowl for 'good luck' and dropped it in her clutch as she walked out, looking for directions to the Ballroom.

"Ms Sen, I am overwhelmed that you finally accepted my invitation." Francois, the gentleman that he was, greeted her with unabashed warmth.

As she entered the hall, walking beside him, she could not help but notice that he was quite tall and had a strange energy in his steps. She looked around the carpeted and chandelier-lit hall. It was full of faces she could recognize; courtesy television and her page three scanning.

"Ms Sen," Francois looked at her and quipped, "what does the painter see in here?"

She looked around. Her cursory glance was enough to capture the essence. She looked at Francois, a small unsure cough adding to her articulation. "Clearly three groups."

He was amused. "Could you please elaborate?"

"Sure. The first one is the corporate group. Well groomed and heeled, in dark suits, sipping scotch, on the rocks or wine. Their spouses are decked in expensive dresses or saris and are largely having red wine."

She casually twirled her eyes, scanning the hall once more, picking up vital clues while Francois's eyes followed her gaze trying to corroborate her theory. "I am listening," he muttered, seeming to be quite interested in the next part of her explanation.

"The second group, in ill-fitting bush shirts, safari suits, outdated suits, largely not accompanied by their spouses, is the business class. Most of them are enjoying their scotch with soda. The third and the last group is the political group. If I can spot them correctly, there are four of them. Dressed in *bandgalas* and *jawahar* jackets, they are accompanied by security personnel and are standing in large circles."

Francois looked around again to validate her observation. "Good work Ms Sen. Now I understand the secret to the intricate colour replication in the flowers and birds that you paint; they surely are a manifestation of your unique observation."

She blushed slightly and with a tender bow of her head at an angle, accepted the compliment graciously.

"What can I get for you?" Francois asked her and looked around to locate one of the waiters.

"Some orange juice should be fine."

He turned towards her sharply. "No creative person I have met so far thrives on juices, and definitely not on orange juice of all," he insisted.

"Mr Lancolne, I really don't want to have anything but orange juice."

Francois still could not believe and insisted, "How about some full-bodied vintage wine, I believe the bar has some excellent collection.

Avantika moved close to him with the twinkle playing in her eyes and whispered, "Just some of that drab orange juice would be good for me, thank you."

Sipping on orange juice, which was served in a tall glass and a fancy decorative dressing, she looked at Francois. He was dressed immaculately to suit the formal occasion—smart black suit, white shirt and a wine coloured tie.

While refusing a waiter his offering of a canapé, she playfully twisted her fingers around the glass and asked with quiet nonchalance, "Mr Lancolne, though I accepted your invitation, I am curious to know who is sponsoring my orange juice? I am sure it's not you."

Her humour caught him off guard as laughter hit him while he was sipping on the golden champagne, making him choke on it. He pulled out his handkerchief and covered his mouth. She did not know what to do. Depending on her instincts, she patted his back, as he coughed uncontrollably. A few deep breaths and the pat helped him to recover.

"Thank you so much for your help. I am feeling better now." He wiped his face. The fair tone on his cheeks was now red and flushed due to the exertion.

"Sorry for my clumsy behaviour. It is just that I witnessed your sense of humour for the first time and could not help but burst into laughter."

She was still worried for him but seeing him regain his composure, she smiled.

"I will be more careful the next time my humour tries to break loose, as I now see it may affect people adversely."

He laughed and raised his long stem glass, "Cheers, to your sense of humour and long live our host, Mr Khurana."

Bewilderment was written over her face and as blank as she was, she asked, equally blankly, "You mean I am here attending a party hosted by Mr Khurana! Sunny's father?"

He moved closer and whispered, his voice laced with sinister black humour, "Surely, he is Sunny's dad, though I cannot guarantee the biological part of the story."

She wondered if the golden liquid was getting the better of him as she had never seen the child in the worldwide CEO of Lancolne and Crafts—the largest interior design firm.

"On a more serious note, let us walk out of this claustrophobic place teeming with just the three kinds of people. By the way, lady, did you consider which group we belong to? Maybe, we should go to the pool side and discuss it further. Care for a refill?" His monologue made her smile and throw up her hands.

Undoubtedly, the pool side was more peaceful. The late evening's glistening ripples of the pool did not have swimming enthusiasts and the blue pattern on the pool floor gleamed enticingly in the subdued lighting. The vines hung loosely from the canopy overhead. Francois walked over to the garden chair and unconsciously pulled a chair and offered her. They both seemed to be lost in the tranquil moment. He sat there in an introspective mood, while Avantika crossed her legs and placed her chin firmly on the laced fingers watching the ripples play, assuming various shades of the colour, depending on the ray of light that they could catch.

"What would be your best guess as to why I invited you over?"

Before she could react to his question, he dialled a number. His face had a naughty smile and his eyes, a glint.

"Sorry to disturb you. Yes, she is here. We are at the pool side. Sure. Not a problem. Take your time. See you."

He disconnected the call and looked at her. She was a bit overwhelmed by the alacrity of events—his question, the phone call, her reference. The twinkle in her eyes was now replaced with a million questions. Francois seemed to enjoy the mystery and the aura which was being created.

"Have you ever seen a falling star?" His unexpected question caught her off guard. Her chin still placed on the flat of her laced fingers, her eyes shifted to him.

"Well, can't remember seeing one. Though I have seen enough Hindi movies to know about them."

He looked at her intently, shaking away the slight jeer or humour which may have been there in her statement.

"If a star or two fall, or maybe even hundreds of them, do you think this sky would be any less beautiful?"

Her obvious reply of "No" was long and accentuated.

He nodded. "You see those stars," he asked, pointing towards the sky.

"They are like dreams in our eyes. Millions of them—small and big, short lived and permanent, bright and not so bright. Just like them, our dreams also keep on failing and falling at regular interval. Some fade, others disappear, some even get replaced with passing time. But just like the sky, even eyes should never get short of dreams. And it is this power to see new dreams that keeps us going."

Avantika had lifted her chin off her fingers and was watching him in animated and intense silence. The philosopher in Francois had caught her attention.

"Hey Francois, didn't I warn you that your French charm would never work on Indian women. They are way too intelligent to fall for your boring cheese and wine ritual."

The voice of Mr Khurana pierced through the tranquility. Both Francois and Avantika turned to see his robust frame hurriedly walking towards them. Francois got up from his chair and reciprocated his banter.

"Don't we know that soldiers and flirts never quit, they just fade away?"

Avantika giggled as she felt a little embarrassed witnessing two grown up respected citizens, exchange their thoughts so candidly. Mr Khurana came and wrapped his arms around her.

"How have you been doing?"

She smiled coyly as she never expected such warmth from her ex-boyfriend's dad and was overwhelmed.

"Niceties over, people, I come straight to the point." The business leader in Francois was back. He looked at both of them, Mr Khurana and Avantika.

"Before I start off, I want to put this on record that my proposal is based purely on merit and have nothing to do with any personal relationships." He placed his glass on the centre table. Both Mr Khurana and Avantika looked at each other and smiled as they knew how Francois loved to use his hands to animate his presentations.

"Mr Khurana, I know that you are planning to take your construction business to Europe soon. The projects there will be more of a commercial nature, along with high-end luxury residential projects. Your target audience would be largely restricted to the corporate honchos—the CEO variety for the commercial ventures, rich and powerful individuals who will invest in expensive homes, chalets or villas and the top government officials who would play the licensing role. To impact them and their decision, surely you would need to create a positive brand image. Though it will be taken care of by your advertising and PR agency, as and when you launch your projects, but getting into the sub-conscious minds of your target audience of tomorrow, today, would be a great idea if the cost justifies this action. To give you a casing point in Indian context, Audi, as a brand, was well entrenched in the minds of Indians long before their formal launch in India, courtesy the same brand car won as a trophy by a famous Indian cricketer.

"Yes, it was Ravi Shastri," Mr Khurana filled in. Francois gave him a 'thank you' smile.

"So, we can see that it makes sense to sponsor events with a high interest and recall value for your target audience."

Mr Khurana nodded.

"Now what could be the medium through which we can reach out to your target audience—the business decision-makers, the rich and the famous and the top government officials?" Francois's question was directed towards his audience. He looked at the faces of Mr Khurana and Avantika. Mr Khurana was searching for the answer and Avantika was lost in his charm and knowledge-driven oratory. Finding none of them up to his expectation, he guided them towards the expected answer. "Surely that brings us to a medium that caters exclusively to your target audience. Something meant for the evolved souls, accessible only to the rich and the famous. A medium that is as priceless as time..."

Mr Khurana interrupted "...Something like art?" His interjection was more of a question.

"Bang on, Mr Khurana," Francois exclaimed. In the midst of the animated discussion, he waved off a waiter who had trailed Khurana with a serving of prawn satay. "There you go," he brought down his hand on the table for emphasis. "It is undoubtedly art, painting to be precise. Loved, discussed and collected by the rich and the powerful.

Visit any art exhibition, at a top end gallery and be ready to bump into the who's who of Indian business, politics and page three crowd. It is the same in every other part of the world. No wonder, the bigger corporate houses have started showing interest in sponsoring art. Take the case of your home grown brands—Tata, Jindal, Reliance or even global brands like HSBC, ABN Amro, Cartier. The list is endless."

He looked at his audience, breathed deep and smiled. "Now, the question is even if we know of the right medium, how do we identify the media—the gallery and the artist? Let me start off with the gallery first. I know of this gentleman named Dimitr Roche. An artist himself, he has branched into the business side of art. He owns the biggest and the most renowned art galleries across Europe and America. An exhibition at any of his gallery is a sure shot way to generate mega publicity and the required footfall. Needless to say, he is very finicky in signing up artists. For the past few years, purely from an investment point of view, he is promoting new talent. He feels that they are easy to handle, negotiate and also have the spark which is required to break the clutter." As his hands moved in sync with his lips and articulated thoughts, the Frenchman continued to mesmerize his audience—Mr Khurana by his business brilliance and Avantika, by the grandeur of it.

"Dimitr's art galleries being the most renowned in Europe also attract the media. Pardon my use of a cliché, they either love him or hate him for his picky behaviour; but surely cannot afford to ignore him. Therefore, sponsoring art exhibition at his galleries would surely give you sticky eye balls, thus ensuring top of mind recall for your brand at a fraction of the cost of running a full-fledged brand campaign."

"I buy your point." Mr Khurana shared his point of view.

"Thank you Mr Khurana. Now the next logical question would be, if Dimitr's gallery is the place of exhibition, which artist would your brand associate with?"

An instant rush of divine intervention told Avantika that the artist ought to be her. But her shaky and pessimistic side stopped her. Mr Khurana looked at Francois and then rolled his eyes under the crooked brow at Avantika. He took a large one from his glass.

"No guesses. You tell me." He left his cards open.

"Mr Khurana, you are an Indian, your company is Indian, your brand is Indian. Therefore, the artist has to be from India as well. Bigger artists have their own whims and fancies. They are also hard to manage. Therefore, we need an artist who is young, talented and has got a repertoire."

Avantika felt her heart pounding. For some odd reason, she was feeling embarrassed.

Mr Khurana looked at Avantika and smiled before returning his gaze to Francois. "All right Mr Lancolne, if you think Avantika should be the artist, she will be. I trust your judgment."

She was dumbstruck. The simplicity of the whole thing was not letting her believe that she was the one, the chosen one, to hold her own exhibitions across Europe, at leading galleries. She wanted to step on her toes, with the black stilettos, to be sure that this was not any kind of a wild dream.

"Ms Sen, won't you like to thank your sponsor for giving you this wonderful opportunity and also for the orange juice which you have been cradling for the last hour or so?

While Khurana was picking his next drink, Francois laughed and Avantika blushed.

Knock-Knock

The rolling green valley extended itself as far as the eyes could see the horizon. Flanked by snowcapped peaks on either side, the distant horizon was dotted with healthy, silent pine trees, all in a solemn row, faintly dusted by snow, as if guarding the peace and the serenity of the valley.

The vast expanse echoed and reverberated with laughter and the voice of a family that seemed straight out of a picture postcard—happy, content and together. The man, dressed in army green, ran towards the pretty and doe-eyed woman and hugged her tight. The woman gave out a laughter which throbbed with happiness and joy. The man lifted the woman in his strong arms and swung her around, the sky blue skirt danced in a wild billow. The entire sequence seemed staged, in a soft slow motion. A pretty girl, aged eight or nine, ran towards the couple, holding a peach coloured lily in her hands. Her hair bounced with her rising and falling steps, her little locks and cheeks seemed to capture the afternoon glow and joy.

Suddenly, from the cracks of the mountains on either side, tanks and mounted artillery started descending the slope. The valley, which echoed with laughter till few seconds ago, now reverberated with the thunderous roar of the fire-spewing iron monsters. The slow motion frame snapped and the thundering machines seemed closer and louder than reality. The little girl stood there, almost frozen, terror struck, with her angelic face smeared with tears. She looked around, searching for the man who was there with the woman. But he was nowhere to be seen.

She reached out for the woman, who held her closely, trying to comfort her and seek the same. While they huddled to crush the terror, the peach lily was squeezed between their hands, a parched petal just floated away, the limp flower lay at their feet. To their horror, one of the tanks stopped and the turret slowly moved towards them. The woman held the girl closer, trying to shield her from the expected sharpnel. As the moment froze, the top of the tank opened and the man, who was with the woman a few moments earlier, emerged, smiling menacingly. This time the little girl could recognize his face. He was her father, Major Sengupta, and the woman was undoubtedly her mother. Major Sengupta looked at them with disdain and contempt and his lips moved… FIRE. The tank recoiled as it fired. The thunderous noise of the shells and the rattle of the machine guns almost ruptured their ear drums. Both, Avantika and her mother, stood there and howled. The incredible noise was increased by the shrill sound of a ringing telephone.

Boom… Rat…Rat…Rat…Rat…Tring Tring…Boom…Tring… Tring

The sound of the ringing telephone kept on getting louder.

Avantika sat up startled, sweating, shivering. Even in December, her sheet was soaked. Her feet were entangled in a mass of the blanket and the bed sheet. She had no clue as to what was going on. She looked at her mobile which was resting peacefully. The bell must have been just a part of her nightmare, she thought, still trying to wriggle out her bound feet. As she glanced at the daylight peeping from the crack of the door, and fiddled with her phone, coming to realize that she just had a nightmare, the shrill doorbell jolted her out of her introspection. Puzzled at the unexpected caller at this hour, she got out of her bed and conscious of her skimpy dress when the morning chill hit her, picked a scarf and plodded towards the door. As she unbolted the three-lever bolt lock, undid the safety chain and opened the door, she thought that she was still in some dream. Dressed in a thick, Himalayan expedition jacket, holding a bag, Captain stood there. Avantika's eyes just froze and she did not know what to say or how to react.

"Good morning Ms Sen." He greeted her playfully and lightly touched her cheek.

She did not respond or move as she found accepting the reality so tough that it almost looked surreal. She had not gotten over the experience of the past five minutes, and now started doubting her mental robustness.

"I know you are surprised but I just hope that it's a pleasant one. Do you mind if I step in? Delhi is freezing outside your door." Captain requested.

Without even saying a word, she stepped back from the door, allowing him to step in. As she closed the door, she still could not believe that it was him. Captain took a cursory look around her apartment. Her gaze followed his and she felt embarrassed. Somewhere, the woman inside nudged her that the man in Captain would never like a woman who was a lousy homemaker.

The bed was in a mess. The soggy blanket a mess on the floor, covered with a faded bed sheet and a pile of quilt strewn on it. The bed side table, which was barely a feet-and-a-half, had quite an assortment—a broken lamp balanced on one and a half leg like a trapeze artist, jam bottles converted into pencil stands, an alarm clock which had long forgotten its function, some odd bills rolled and held together by variously coloured rubber band, a jar of calcium tablets with the blue lid undone, some strips of random medicine and a vodka bottle acting as a money plant holder. The far end of the room had an aisle with a half finished canvas perched atop and nearly one odd dozen of them stacked untidily against the wall. This was accompanied by umpteen numbers of paint cans, tubes, thinner bottles and an assortment of brushes strewn all around. The wall around this area was dotted with streaks of multicoloured paint. On the opposite corner, a small refrigerator acted less of what it was and more of a shelf, with a million things on its top. The cane chairs were buried deep under heaps of clothes, magazines and newspapers.

Gosh! She almost cowed at the sight of her own living space. If she had her way, she would have put a big bed sheet to cover her entire apartment. Captain, as he could read her mind, smiled.

"I am impressed. Your place truly looks like an artist's pad."

"You mean it?" Her apprehension was evident.

"Of course I do."

She smiled and hugged him tight. "This is one of the biggest surprises I've ever had. But what made you come over?"

Captain hugged her back.

"You," he whispered.

"But you have a business to take care of. You are not a teenager anymore who can just pack his bags and scoot whenever and wherever he wants to." She chided him affectionately.

"Never too late to feel and act like a teenager again." As he replied, his arms hugged her tighter, and made a mock effort to get warmth as he rubbed his palms against her arms.

She cuddled up against him. Something about him was so comforting and so nice. Her head rested on his chest. Everything in her life settled down. Both of them were unaware of the fact that this was their first hug which was not induced by intoxication but purely by inexplicable warmth.

"But you could have at least told me. At least I would have tidied up my place." They laughed.

"When I got your panic ulcer call from the hospital, I instantly decided that I needed to be there with you. I need to ensure that you get into a regular regime of diet and self-care."

"Did I ever tell you that you are a darling?" Her voice was bubbling with love for him.

"Never too late." His reply was casual, with the unmistakable twinkle.

Over numerous cups of early morning green tea, biscuits and the warmth of the quilt, Captain explained to her what he had in his mind. His boat was booked by a wildlife photographer and his two assistants who planned to stay afloat for eight to ten weeks, as they were shooting a documentary on migratory birds. For the same, he had handed over the boat to his deputy, Sudhakar, who would take care of the guests. For his Delhi trip, he had checked himself into a nearby guest house for having the flexibility to spend most of his time with her and then getting back to his guest house to catch a wink. Though Avantika was tempted to ask him to stay with her, but she stopped herself short, knowing very well the wagging tongues around her in Delhi. Blabbering neighbours was the last thing she wanted in her life.

As Captain opened his bag, he pulled out numerous books on healthy cooking, eating, yoga, bottles of massage oils, cornflakes, dried bananas, roasted chips, small knick-knacks and something which made both of them burst into laughter when they saw it—a typical Kerala style *lungi*.

Blessed Life

Everything changed in Avantika's life. Her routine, diet, health, fitness, perspective, mood, approach towards life, shine in her eyes, glow on her face, her room, just about everything. And to bring about this metamorphosis in a structured way, it took someone as focussed, systematic and knowledgeable as Captain.

From his guest house, which was just a few minutes walk away from Avantika's apartment, every morning at 5.30 he called her. Being a late riser all her life, for the first few days, she found it impossible to answer his calls, or eventually slept off after mumbling the customary, "Morning, I am awake now." She tried all the tricks of burying herself in the layers of quilts or just ignoring his calls, but the persistent Captain would be knocking at her door in no time. Any legitimate or feigned excuses would not make him budge. In the dark, cold, winter morning of Delhi, he would literally pull her out of her warm quilt, throw the jacket on her shoulder and push her out in freezing cold for a three-kilometre walk. Though Avantika initially slept through the routine, gradually, even though she hated to admit it, she started loving the razor sharp crisp fresh air on her face along with the all-day energy and bounce which the early start gave her. She enjoyed the way the Delhi chill settled on her nose and made it red. The walk made her whole routine fall in place—getting up on time, eating on time and hitting the bed like clockwork.

After the walk, they returned to her apartment and Captain served her warm water with honey and lemon to boost her metabolism and detoxify her system. She had a wry smile on her lips when she first saw the diet chart stuck next to the light switch in the kitchen.

Breakfast

Monday: Milk, muesli, one fruit and a boiled egg.

Tuesday: Two boiled eggs, toast with peanut butter and fresh fruit salad.

Wednesday: Porridge, fruits, milk and two digestive biscuits.

Thursday: Milk, cornflakes, cottage cheese salad and fruits.

Friday: Milk shake, oatmeal and fresh fruits.

Saturday and Sunday: *Idli, dosa, poha, appam.*

Their regular shopping now had to cater in advance for the next day's meal. Every evening, he soaked four to five almonds in a small bowl and left it by the kitchen window, to be consumed the next day. By the time she got ready for the day ahead after the brisk walk, Captain laid the table as per the pre-charted breakfast schedule. He made sure the fruits and milk were fresh. At times, he would keep a few flowers picked during the morning walk in a glass bowl on the table; at times it was replaced by a lone unique twig or green fern which he found attractive.

Post-breakfast, she would sit down to paint; with a glass of green tea while the Captain took a short break. During this time, he would go to his guest house, scan the newspaper, grab a shower, a short nap and then come back, all charged up, for his second round. He shopped for the vegetables himself, everyday, and would mostly boil or steam them for their lunch. At times, she would throw tantrums but the Captain was experienced enough to handle her. Pampering, cajoling, requesting, incentivizing, chiding and finally threatening—he did whatever it took him to keep her on track. Dinner was usually soup with some steamed fish or boiled chicken.

The result of all this hard work was not only evident in her looks and in her energy levels but also in her medical reports.

It was not only her diet but also her apartment which Captain turned around. He repainted the entire apartment in light pistachio green with foliage green highlights. When she saw the final result, she thought it was nothing less than a miracle as she was always skeptical of the green colour when he chose it. The newly-painted apartment also got a new mattress, bright coloured sheets and matching cushion covers. The old ones were ripped to replace dusters and the rest were laid to rest in the dustbin. Two small terracotta stools were placed as bed side tables. Things which were not working or not needed—alarm clock, dried tubes of paint, brushes, cans, toothpaste tubes, broken mugs and jaded carpets were discarded. The kitchen was more organized with new containers and crockery. Even the bathroom got a new lease of life—the shower now spewed a uniform spray of water, the innumerable pieces of soap which had shrunk in size yet hung around and plastic shampoo bottles bereft of any content were all loaded in a plastic bag and dumped in the garbage. The refrigerator, the wardrobe, the chest of drawer, everything was rearranged.

Avantika was surprised to notice the soothing impact of a de-cluttered house on her mind, work and her whole being. Her paintings reflected the same—confident with clean strokes. Not only did it make them look more vibrant, more contemporary, but it also gave them a definite positive aura.

At times, when she watched the Captain cook or rearrange her wardrobe or even do little things like arranging the magazine rack or clean her brushes, it often made her wonder the relation that they shared. What were they? Lovers? Friends? Soulmates? Or maybe something more? But the common thing was that whenever she thought of the relationship, it made her feel very nice, warm and loved. She knew beyond any doubt that in her entire lifespan, no one had ever bothered to manage her life as unselfishly as he did. His unflinching devotion towards her made him look like a man with a definite purpose, a goal in life—a mission to better her life, to make her a better woman, a better painter, and moreover, a better human.

Was Sunny capable of doing all this? She did not even attempt answering this one. Even being an atheist, she folded her hands, closed her eyes and thanked God or the Supreme Power for blessing her with someone as special and as precious as Captain. When she opened her eyes, she saw twin red hibiscus floating in a glass bowl on the terracotta table and smiled.

Hot On Trail

If cities were assigned zodiac signs, undoubtedly Delhi would wear the crown of the Gemini twins. After all, only few cities in the world can boast of versatility, adaptability and extremes—all peculiar twin traits. Playing host to five dynasties—the Slave, Khilji, Tughlaq, Sayyid, Lodhi and finally a British Queen, this city imbibed the best from every era, picking and retaining unique architectural features from each age. No wonder, the congested lanes of Dariba Kalan, where it is not possible to cross a lane without rubbing against the bystander on the brick-lined wall, to the Gulmohar tree lined, impeccable Shanti Path, co-exist in the same city. Even the weather Gods displayed their extreme side; fifty degrees in the month of May to two degrees in December to complement the diversity of this city. They say it is possible to survive in this city in ₹ 500 a month to providing ample avenues for people who earned a million times over.

For the same reasons and more, Delhi never ceased to surprise Captain. Every day for him was like a day in a new city. A clearly defined population with distinct culture, mannerism, clothes, even food habits. Muslims with decades of legacy staying in the Walled City to the Punjabis of Karol Bagh, from the colonial architecture of Lutyen's Delhi to the confused new-age architecture of the swank malls of South Delhi. It was a city where inhabitants swore by the culinary delights—be it the *nihari* at the Jama Masjid or *chaat* at Sundarnagar, *kebabs* at Gole Market or Giani's *lassi* at Chandni Chowk. From BMWs to tongas, Captain loved every bit of the juxtaposed, chaotic confusion. Maybe staying in the backwaters for too long had parched his eyes and soul of all the action, different colours and levels of energy.

Though Avantika was not an avid shopper or an outdoor person, but showing Captain around gave her immense joy and pleasure. It could be due to the reason that it was the only time for a role reversal for her—telling and showing Captain something he did not know earlier. It was not so much for returning the favour, but more about enjoying his company and discovering parts of the city in a completely new light. She tried her best to take him out to at least one new place every other day. Though the Captain insisted that she needed to concentrate on her paintings and also get the much-needed rest, but her hectic schedule rejuvenated her for another day of a marathon painting session.

With Paris exhibition just around the corner, to be followed by four more, at Vienna, Stockholm, London and Rome, all within a time span of two months, there was a lot to be done. Paper work, visa, shopping, selecting the frames, meeting with the packers and sending the paintings in advance, sitting with the advertising agency for finalizing the content and design for the website and the invites. Gosh, the list was endless.

Captain and Avantika were out since seven o' clock for their Schengen visa interview. As Paris was their first city, they had to apply for the visa at the French embassy. They had an appointment at nine in the morning at the VFS office, behind Nehru Place. The guard nodded in the direction of the office, when they asked for the VFS section in the large building. The queue outside the office was manageable and Avantika noticed most of them were burly Sikhs and Jats, surely from the neighbouring states of Haryana and Punjab or boring business executives. None of them looked to be the kinds who would be interested in renaissance, culture, or even French cuisine. By the time the VFS officials went through their paperwork, asked them pertinent questions and finally deposited their paperwork, they were famished. Though Avantika was tempted to take Captain to the 'O Calcutta' restaurant in the vicinity to introduce him to the flavours of her kind of cuisine, it seemed too early to have a full Bangla lunch buffet. So she suggested an early Chinese lunch at Connaught Place, where they had plans to pick up essential winter clothing later in the day followed by walking him down Janpath to show him the street market frequented by Delhi's rich and foreign tourists.

It was a rich sunny January day. Standing in front of the gate, she was in animated explanation of her shopping, Captain nodded while watching out for the radio taxi which they had booked 10 minutes ago. Knowing the Delhi rush hour well, she knew that the taxi would take well over 20 minutes at this time of the day.

The Captain moved across the road to check if the waiting taxi was for them. Avantika was disinterested in Captain's enthusiasm which had just discovered the unique experience of radio taxis in India. She looked on towards the multiplex across the road and noticed that she had completely severed her ties with Bollywood. She scanned the posters for the new movies and the new actors which were now showing. Her line of vision caught a purple coloured Zen car parked across the street. It was not the car, but its occupants which attracted her attention. Though she kept looking at the posters, she could not help but notice the two rough looking guys on the front seat, watching her. Though the back-seat window was rolled up and was slightly tinted, she could make out the guys on the back seat. What was the car doing there? Surely, there was no movie show at this time in the morning. Her eyes met the eyes of the guy in the driver's seat. He was in his early 20s, unshaven, scruffy face, crew cut hair, heavy round face, wearing a brown sweat shirt; he looked like one of those wrestlers who later joins the lucrative profession of land grabbing and extortion. She also managed to have a look at the guy in the passenger seat. Middle aged, he was surely not of a noble pedigree either.

She reprimanded herself for the strange unsettling feeling. Her logical self told her that in all probability, they were accompanying some visa aspirant from the neighbouring state of either Haryana or Punjab. She looked around again for the cab and decided to call the agency again to check the time she could expect the taxi. Captain was strolling towards a cigarette kiosk to probably pick up a mint pack. While calling the number, she glanced at the occupants of the purple Zen again. Surely, they were discussing her. But why should they? Definitely, it must be her mind which was playing up. But her notion was proved false the moment she saw them pointing a finger towards Captain. What was wrong? Her mind tried to figure out. She the shrill voice of the agent from the taxi agency who was at the other end of her call. Her instincts told her that something was just not right. She looked at Captain. He was walking away from her, towards the kiosk on the other side of the road. Then she quickly scanned around to check the car and noticed that it was slowly rolling towards Captain. She wanted to scream out his name and warn him. But she was blank as she opened her mouth; she was not sure what to warn him of. Her eyes darted towards the car again, which had accelerated to a higher speed and the occupants were focussed on Captain, who was about twenty metres ahead.

She looked at Captain and tried to scream, but her voice was choked out of fear. She could see the car wobble sinisterly towards him. Sheer helplessness and fright enveloped her, moving from her spine and spreading towards her heart. She could see the car speeding up towards him. Don't hit him, please, she pleaded, in her mind. Her throat felt as if it had no power, no life. She looked around like a woman possessed, trying to locate the nearby guards in a wild frenzy.

As the car swaggered dangerously towards him, she just broke down. Her legs lost all strength and unable to prop her body weight, she landed on the pavement. Brakes screeched and drew nonchalant attention of the passersby. Lying on the pavement, with her face smeared with tears and her hand still outstretched to reach out to Captain, she saw the heavyset guy get out of the car holding a hockey stick. The screeching sound of brakes made Captain turn to locate its source. Before Captain's mind could decipher the situation and react, the hockey stick landed on his right thigh. She heard his grunt, loud and clear and saw him crash on road, writhing in pain. The back door of the car opened and two more guys sprinted towards him. With tears blurring her vision, she could see their outlines pounce upon Captain, kicking him in his stomach, back and face as he tried to shield himself with folded arms.

God, please protect him, please. She spoke with God only for the second time in her life.

A Friend In Need

"I am positive. The number was HR 26 AS 6604. Also, I overheard one of them being addressed as Satinder." Captain was ready to bet anything on his memory, instinct and presence of mind.

Avantika turned her attention to the guy on the other end of the line.

"Prashant, he is positive about the car number and the name."

"Ok, give me some time to figure this out. You might receive a call from Nehru Place Police Station. Just tell them whatever happened today. Also, whosoever calls you from the police station, tell them that advocate Khanna is handling the case. Tell them that he is your lawyer and they should get in touch with him for any further clarification. I have already briefed Khanna about your case, so no worries. I have also forwarded you his business card, just save it. In case of any further assistance, don't hesitate to call him."

"Thanks Prashant. Yes, I have received the business card."

Avantika felt small for having to call up Prashant for favours. Earlier, with Shweta being her best buddy, it was still acceptable. But after the distance creeping between them, it was just like telling them that she was an orphan in the city and would constantly cling on to them for any support.

"Stop thanking me Avantika. It's the least that I can do."

"You are being modest but I am really sorry for being a source of constant inconvenience."

"Please stop it Avantika. You are embarrassing me now. Instead of thanking me, you should be thanking your lucky stars that nothing much happened." After a quiet break, he added softly, "Trust me, it could have gone real bad." She knew that he was right.

"By the way, do you have any idea, what could have provoked them to attack your friend? I mean, any personal enmity, feud or..."

"It baffles me too." She expressed the truth. "My friend runs a tourist boat in Kerala. There is no way that he could have even known those ruffians, leave alone having anything to do with them."

"You don't get worked up. We will do whatever can be done to nab the culprits." Prashant assured her.

"Can I speak with Shweta for a moment?"

"Sure, she misses you a lot and often talks about you."

Avantika felt ashamed of herself for being so rude to her.

"Hey Avi, I guess Prashant has sorted out your mess." A light chirpy voice cooed on the other end. For some reason, Shweta's voice and presence always had a soothing and comforting effect on Avantika.

"Yes he did, thanks and tell him that he is a darling."

"And you are a super idiot." Shweta laughed. "You silly woman, you do not need to get so overwhelmed. Arre, it's me, your college friend with whom you had made a pact to share everything, husband included. Remember?" Shweta laughed. Avantika blushed, remembering her stupid promise and seeing Shweta so normal, as if nothing was ever wrong between them. They both laughed and when laughter is mixed with silent tears, it cleanses the soul of every strain and heaviness.

"Hey, tell me, is he the same guy, the boat guy from Kerala?" The chirpy, gossipy and inquisitive Shweta took over.

Avantika turned and saw the Captain sprawled on her bed. He was covered in multiple bandages and dressings. He had a thick dressing on his forehead, from which the red spot had now disappeared after two dressings, few random stitches on his arms and leg. The doctor, who attended him at the nursing home, was relieved when his fear of any internal injury was ruled out after an ultrasound and a couple of X-rays.

"Well, yes and he is just a friend." She tried to underplay it.

"My darling Avi, I think even I qualify as your friend. Then how come it's him and not me who is travelling to Europe with you?" Shweta teased her.

"Because I am not interested in women, PQ!"

A huge round of laughter again. In no time, friendship regained the lost ground and also acquired new territory. That's why someone said that a true friend is someone who scolds like a father, cares like a mother, teases like a sister, irritates like a brother and loves like a lover.

The Truth Emerges

As her hand searched for the incessantly ringing mobile, her eyes tried to adjust to the semi darkened and sleepy room, which was waking up to the first rays of the winter sun. Since her morning walks had been temporarily suspended, after the assault episode and advocate Khanna's advice, she spent every possible extra cosy minute under the blanket, in Captain's arms. The screen displayed the name 'Shwets'. Avantika's heavy pupil shifted from the name to the small clock counter on the right hand corner of the screen. It was exactly seven am. By any standards early for Delhi winter mornings. The commotion on the bed had woken up Captain also. His body was not taking very kindly to the torturous Delhi winter. He curled inside the three layers of quilt and blanket.

"Hey Shwets. All well?" Her voice was drenched in sleep, but looking at the time of the call, her mind was alert, ready to anticipate and react to the news.

"Good morning Avi. I am sorry for calling you up so early. I know you are a late riser but I have been waiting all night to speak with you and I don't know if the news would be a good or a bad one."

Her long sentence had made it clear that something big was about to be revealed.

"I hope everything is well Shwets?"

By now, Captain was wide awake. He could hear the conversation. His hand moved under the labyrinth of quilts and it held Avantika's waist. She snuggled close to him. Captain kissed her shoulder; a friendly comforting kiss.

"Well Avi, please don't overreact to this one. With all your exhibitions lined up, you ought to focus on them."

"Shwets, please don't kill me with curiosity. Please."

"Well, the cops managed to nab the three assaulters."

"That's good. Wow. Never knew the Delhi Police force was so efficient."

She turned towards Captain and squeezed his hands, "Did you hear that? The cops have got those three bastards. I feel like killing those motherfuckers." She was in a confused mood, a mix of happiness, hatred and anger.

"Ah, I guess your friend is with you now?" Shweta had the slight playful lilt in her voice, but quickly moved on. "But that was the good part of the news."

Avantika held her breath and something told her that the bad part would shatter her.

"Avi, when the cops interrogated the three culprits, they confessed to the crime and told that the attack was carried on the behest of Sham Sunder Rathi, a contractor. Based on the confession, Sham Sunder was arrested and the cops found out that he was a contractor with the residential construction division of Mr Khurana."

Avantika prayed that her worst nightmare should not come true. But then, there are certain prayers that always go unanswered.

"This Rathi chap told the cops that he was just a middle man, who on the behest of Sunny Khurana had hired mercenaries to attack Captain to break his limbs. As the cops had no conclusive proof, and then, as you know that the Khurana family enjoys quite some clout in this city, so the matter was hushed up."

Her heart stopped for a moment and her ear, which had the proximity of the mobile, turned like hot coal. The simmering heat made its way to her cheek, her complete face and travelled the other side, to her other ear too.

Paris Perspective

BA 316's gentle touchdown nudged Avantika from the light sleep on Captain's shoulder, who was looking at her heavy eyelids from as close as the economy seats squeezed them. He leaned across her sleepy face to welcome the early evening sun on his face.

Charles De Gaulle seemed like a city in itself. Avantika was light on her steps and her eyes quick to register the foreign colours and texture as they snaked through the immigration. The official behind the desk, in his crisp shirt and question laden eyes was going through the pages of her passport, her hotel reservations, letter from the curator, agency, reference letter from Lancolne, for what seemed like an eternity. Captain had already cleared his turn with the immigration and was on his way to pick the luggage.

"How long do you intend to stay in Paris, Ma'am?"

"A week." Her response was followed by a click and a thud of stamp on her passport as he pushed the blue booklet towards her. The thud of the stamp rang an imaginary "Welcome to France Mademoiselle". Even though there was no reason or apprehension to not clear the immigration, she felt a surge of relief rushing through her. The trip was too important for her.

Ah, Paris at last, she thought to herself.

Every artist's dream, every romantic fool's destination. For years, in her dreams, she had lived in the French capital, and today, the ground beneath her was breathing French. The signage, the conversation, the commercials on the overhead television monitors, all this was in an alien language. But she felt as if she had known the language from a past life. The adrenalin was constantly pushing at her veins and the desire to burst out of the airport and smell the French air was stifling her.

Captain and Avantika located Claude, who was holding a placard with AVANTIKA posted on it. Claude's head was a cluster of unruly golden curls and his brown T-shirt offset against the golden skin gave him a Cupid-like look. She smiled to herself, it was probably Paris; everything seemed to have a romantic correlation.

"Claude, glad to meet you, finally. Thanks for all the coordination for our trip."

"Ah, I do as Jules says; glad to be of help Mademoiselle." He made a large sweep of his hands and rested it on his heart, in an opera like movement, to show his pleasure. Clearly, English language was not his forte.

Captain, while following Avantika and Claude through the elevator in the parking lot, was silent, as if trying to relive old memories. They were cruising at a reasonable speed listening to some vague French music along the motorway. "Oh dear, it's almost the last light." She sighed, "I don't want to lose Paris in the last golden ray."

Her quick glance at Captain did not indicate whether this was a question or just a plain statement. Then, with a sudden change in tone she was back to being the self-assured Avantika.

"Claude, can you do us a favour? Please drop us off at a central place and can you please have the bags dropped off at the hotel. We will find our way to the hotel." After a pause to let the request seep in, "Do you think we can do that?"

Captain was already smiling indulgently and nodding his head to "Si si."

"I drop you to Arc de Triomphe, a good walk down the road and further ahead will get you to the hotel. I tell Jules and the hotel your arrival, and I pick you at 8 morning tomorrow."

Claude's acceptance of her offer made her feel that it was perfectly normal for any visitor to request the same after arriving in Paris. No wonder he gallantly obliged to drop off their bags at the hotel.

The car stopped after an intersection. Avi was almost floating as she glided from the car to the sidewalk, still groping for words mentally, trying to encapsulate the life around her. Captain was stuffing the business cards of the hotel and some other numbers from Claude into his pocket and waving him away.

"My *bong* bomb at a loss of words?" a soft whisper caught Avantika in her trance-like state.

"Uh, yes, isn't this so incredible?" She was not actually expecting an answer as she stared at the magnificent Arc de Triomphe. "A lot like our own India Gate? Do we have enough time to visit this place? How do people cross this street to reach the monument?"

She finally turned around to see Captain staring at her intently.

Her quizzical look only drew a naughty smile.

In the last rays of the setting sun, her black cherry dyed hair were radiating burnt coal amber; she pulled her burgundy cap over her ears; clearly she had underestimated the February chill in Paris. The casual black jacket was accompanied by a crushed tussar skirt. It fell straight till her knees and then flared the crushed pleats till her ankles. The wooden bead necklace hung low till her navel and the matching wooden crescent moon pair earrings played hide and seek between her locks. "Hey Avi, let's visit the monument later this week. I have a better idea. Do you want to feel Paris?"

His voice was soft, never leading, always suggesting, with a hint of mischief and intrigue. He casually wrapped his arms around her shoulder and drew her away from the monument along the sidewalk.

"Avi, the perspective is always important. Whatever you are observing becomes as important or not, in light of what is around it. I have been in Paris for years, yet I have discovered it in a new light every time, because I wanted to experiment with my own sensibilities. The brick and mortar buildings remain exactly the same over the years, but the way you look at them will determine your own impression."

"Here let us have a cup of coffee," he indicated to a small roadside café.

They snaked between a few tables and reached a free table, which offered a clear view. He guided her to a chair. She tossed her orange embroidered satchel in the next chair, a Janpath purchase for her trip.

"Now if you give me a minute, I will just run around the corner and pull some Euros from the cash machine."

She nodded silently. The lights in the café suddenly came on and bathed her in yellow. The orange satchel with the Rajasthani embroidery glittered in the dusk. An unexpected thought, like a bolt from the blue, made her smile. She remembered the unfinished painting at home—*Krishna* and his herd of cows returning amidst *godhuli*, his fingers dancing on the flute. She suddenly saw behind *Krishna* and his herd, the Arc de Triomphe, hazed by the dust. Her heart skipped a beat at the unimaginable thought.

She thought how right Captain was when he explained to her that the images which they form were very dependent on the perspective. She knew that probably whenever she would try to imagine Arc de Triomphe, it would always be a backdrop to her *Krishna*!

Her smile and reverie broke as Captain sank into the next chair. A pretty girl placed two cups of coffee on the table and he placed a few stalks of lavender tulips on Avantika's lap.

Although right from the vegetables to the bed sheet, fruits to the table lamp, snacks to paints, whatever she had in her life was all bought by him, but this was probably the first time when he had gifted her something in a formal way. She held the flowers close to herself and held her nose against them.

"Most tulips don't have fragrance."

She nodded and held on to the flowers. Those few stalks seemed to convey the most genuine emotion she had ever felt. For a few seconds, her eyes moistened as blurred faces of her mother, Shweta, her primary school teacher, Mrs David, Sunny… all rose in unison and as quickly as they appeared, they disappeared, as she looked up at the Arc de Triomphe, now lit and conveying a completely different perspective to its ever-stunning beauty.

She pushed the chair, got up, left the flowers on the table and turned to Captain. She clasped his hands and sat on her heels, at his knees. The sight was truly a compelling one.

"Captain, thanks for accompanying me. What would I have done without you?"

"Oh look at the great *bong* bomb! Is she getting carried away? No, you are not Avi, it's just that you are too overwhelmed by the day."

"Could be. I know Captain, yes, probably yes. But I feel so close to you right now. I have never felt this warmth for anyone before."

He gently held her hand and lifted her. He picked the satchel from the chair, and the flowers from the table, and left the money on the table and held her elbow and started walking.

"Do you see the Arc de Triomphe?"

"Yes."

"Can you see the two pillars stand apart?"

She strained her eyes.

"Listen to these lines by Khalil Gibran, from The Prophet, on marriage." He went on to recite the lines, in his rich baritone, while they walked matching stride by stride,

"You were born together, and together you shall be
forevermore.
You shall be together when white wings of death
scatter your days.
Aye, you shall be together even in the silent memory of God.
But let there be spaces in your togetherness,

And let the winds of the heavens dance between you.
Love one another but make not a bond of love:
Let it rather be a moving sea between the shores of your souls.
Fill each other's cup but drink not from one cup.
Give one another of your bread but eat not from the same loaf.
Sing and dance together and be joyous, but let each one of you be alone,
Even as the strings of a lute are alone though they quiver with the same music.
Give your hearts, but not into each other's keeping.
For only the hand of life can contain your hearts.
And stand together, yet not too near together:
For the pillars of the temple stand apart,
And the oak tree and the cypress grow not in each other's shadow."

She felt so lost, so romantic, so confused, so grounded, so much of everything.

"Avi, to flourish, it is important to stand apart, and to give strength to the drowning, it is important that you remain on firm ground."

Her eyes remain transfixed on the monument as she breathed in every moment of its light-washed grandeur. The line 'and stand together, yet not too near together, for the pillars of the temple stand apart' still echoed in her ear. She smiled to nothing in particular and squeezed his arms.

They walked down the Avenue des Champs-Élysées. The giggle was back on her lips. They sauntered into a wine store and she picked a vintage bottle as a gift for him. She was not sure why, but it just seemed right. The grey stone buildings, the slate roofs, the carved entrance facade was spiced with contemporary designs in the stores within.

"The Avenue des Champs-Élysées is one of the most famous and beautiful streets in the world. Of course, it has a matching price tag as well." Captain kept filling her with trivia about the history and the culture.

They walked with the tourists, the locals, completely oblivious to the people. But what mattered to her was the contentment she felt. Blending in with the moving crowd without even making an effort, they realized that they stood there, facing the Eiffel Tower. They held hands and stood in silence watching the gigantic structure in Champs De Mars. Standing under the Tower, she remarked, "So much of metal. Doesn't it look grotesque in the daylight?"

"Avi, I told you, it is the perspective; yes, it is a mass of metal and hardcore engineering which stands tall in a city which centres on art and creativity. It has developed a personality of its own, even though made from pieces of cold metal but the end result is a masterpiece, which speaks a different language—the sum is greater than its parts.

They sat under the tower as tourists flirted with the evening. Children scampered with balloons, lovers kissed passionately, groups posed for pictures as memorabilia, some waited patiently in the queue to board the elevator and a lone musician played the violin near the South Pillar. They both felt like a tiny speck of existence that was absorbing the warmth of life and which was ready to devour every stimulus the skyscraper had to offer.

Avantika and Captain walked further into the left recess of the park. She took off her boots and placed her bare feet on the grass. On a sudden spurt of imaginary music, she twirled her crushed silk skirt and turned on her toe. Captain took her satchel as if to give her the complete freedom from any bondage.

His frantic glances at the watch caught her attention and she asked, "Isn't the hotel close by? Do we need to go?"

"No, but I have a surprise for you."

She was still barefoot on the grass, now moist. He held her hand and turned her back towards him, and made her stand on his shoes.

"Captain, we are not doing a Titanic here, are we?"

He held her from her back and placed his palms on her eyes.

"Just stand still for a minute."

She felt as if everything had frozen. Feeling his breath rise and fall with her, she could feel its warmth on her nape, and she closed her eyes.

"Now," he whispered into her ear, and gradually removed his hands from her face. She was facing the Eiffel Tower, which had now completely metamorphosed into a sparkling giant. The entire Tower was saddled with a million small sparking bulbs which twinkled like millions of diamonds studded on it.

Avi leaned back on him as he hugged her lightly.

"I understand Captain. I have seen beauty in a different perspective today."

The Price Of Success

Money is a powerful animal; if not well domesticated, it can get wild and play havoc. Strangely, this beast has the power to impact and change the basic fabric, the whole essence and existence of any human. As a cardinal rule, it never comes alone. Success, power and pride are an essential part of the coterie. Like any other bad company, this one also plays truant with the sense of right-wrong and good-bad, stealthily turning self-confidence into overconfidence, self-pride into false ego, friends into suckers, and sycophants into friends. In the long list of casualty, well-wishers and friends always find a place at the top. No wonder, for the same reason, it has always been referred to as the root of all evil. This held good for Avantika as well.

In no time, the art circle of Europe warmed up to Avantika's paintings and her artistic sensibilities. Amidst the clinical precision of European brush strokes, her heartfelt renderings, of nature and humans made everyone sit up. Her use of colours and strokes had the flavour of Van Gogh, yet juxtaposed with the contemporary and untamed. Francois was very right in banking heavily on the goodwill, clientele and clout of Dimitr and his art galleries. Just owing to the fact that his galleries were profiling an upcoming and promising Indian artist had got the media abuzz. *Courrier International, Equipe, L' International Herald Tribune, L' Humanite, Le Figaro* and many other publications carried full-fledged write-ups on Avantika and her work. *Les Echos* went on to profile her as 'Artist of the Year'. The PR agency also released her photograph as part of the press release. A wild-eyed Avantika in a red tie and dye *kurti*, the neckline plunging provocatively offset by a sheer white silk skirt, the blue and green tassel dangling casually by her side. After the major media blitz, no wonder, Avantika's work was lapped up by art lovers and connoisseurs, critics and the art investors alike.

Just a few months ago, when she had landed at Charles De Gaulle for the first time, she had no clue about the success which she was all set to experience. Like a virgin to success, she had only heard stories about how good it gets and how good it could be. She had also read how instant success catapults people from a 'nobody' to an 'instant celebrity' overnight. But she had always taken all these stories with a pinch of salt, till the time she was sitting there, in a small room, sweating and trembling, with two dozen media eyes glued to her face and the same number of ears tracking every word, every whisper of her. Unfortunately, despite her wish and pleading, Captain was not by her side. After all, it was not his press conference. Like a true friend, mentor and guide, he played his role and part to perfection. He pre-empted, planned and rehearsed every single thing—coaching her tirelessly for the unexpected questions, rehearsing every phrase of her introduction, spending hours selecting the perfect outfit, accessories and hairdo, drafting and redrafting the press release.

Due to her lack of experience, the first press conference was a little awkward, terrifying and nerve-wrecking. She stammered at every question and looked at Captain, or the organizer for the right clue to answer the paparazzi. However, as these conferences went on, her confidence level soared; with each encounter, she got better, more confident and more adventurous. Her wild smile, wit and unruly hair caught the attention of the Press. So much so that one of the journalists termed her as a 'wild thing from the East'. But everyone knew that even this left-handed compliment was doing her image real good. After all, no one was interested in a drab painter or her work.

Even after years of experience in the art circle and after having launched more than four dozen new artists, Dimitr was pleasantly shocked and surprised at the response which Avantika and her work generated. In no time, she was the darling of the media and the critics alike. Her work was fetching unimaginable prices. Some part of her success story was due to the huge PR and media machinery deployed by Mr Khurana. She, of course, was not oblivious to the fact that her initial paintings were bought at an astronomical price by his company, of course, under a pseudo name to give her market a push. The move created the right ripples in the right places, to set the stage for the approaching storm. And a storm it did create.

While Avantika swept up the accolades and hogged the arc lights with aplomb, Captain was having a tough time multitasking as her manager, friend, guide, mentor and a bit of boyfriend. With each passing day, juggling his feelings, emotions and the role was becoming tougher. When he acted as the manager, he knew that he wasn't being true to her as a friend, and while acting the other way, there would be a clear clash with her professional interests. The friend and the mentor in him were worried about her health more than anything else. But as a manager, he knew that he had to push her harder and live by the proverb—make hay while the sun shines. Also, the hectic tour and a demanding lifestyle ransacked her regime. Right from caviar to wine, cheese to champagne, every thing was flowing on the house. Rushed mornings, fast food lunches, too much coffee and late night parties were clearly showing their dark side on her face.

After an intensive showdown, it was mutually agreed upon that she would be allowed to smoke during her Europe tour. Knowing her, Captain did not bother to discuss and put a cap on the number of cigarettes she could smoke. Gradually, success, name, fame, with their associated accompaniments, smoking and drinking, became her best buddies and anyone who objected to this coterie, turned into her worst enemy. No wonder, now Captain was just her business manager, a role he never envisaged for himself.

Mr Khurana was going gaga over Francois's selection of both, the artist and the gallery. With just four exhibitions spread over 90 days, Mr Khurana ensured that every single person who mattered to him, knew of his company's name—The Orchid. As all the leading glossy magazines covered the exhibitions, and by the virtue of being its sole sponsor, the brand got its due mileage. At every exhibition, the PR agency was shrewd enough to club Orchid's profile along with Avantika's. On its website, in the 'coming soon' section, the group announced its ambitious project in Europe. Courtesy the immense goodwill, which the brand had managed to create, enquiries were pouring in.

Sunny started calling up Avantka again. Initially, his calls were just formal ones—to congratulate her, wish her, etc. But with time, the frequency and the duration of the calls kept on increasing. During the initial phase, Avantika despised taking his calls and avoided them under some pretext or the other. After all, with the scar of the attack on Captain etched on her memory, her reaction was not unexpected. But then, time is the best healer. Gradually, her resistance started to decrease. Sunny, on the other hand, ensured that during every conversation, he dropped the name of his father and made her realize, in some way or the other, that his dad was sponsoring her indulgence in art. During his calls, Captain always excused himself as he never wanted to embarrass Avantika. Somewhere deep down, he felt a little jealous and his heart warned him of her fickle and waning loyalty. But isn't love all about selfless dedication rather than expecting loyalty or commitment, he consoled himself.

The Final Blow

"See Chow, I really appreciate your effort in putting together an itinerary for my show, but my calendar is blocked for the coming fourteen months." She smiled, more at her fingers, checking if the colour on them were nicotine stains or signs of proximity to turpentine oil and paint.

"Ms Sen, when I planned this eight-city exhibition for you, I was aware of your prior commitments." He let out a 'know it all' grin, while tapping his black Mont Blanc on the mahogany table.

"Now, if you see my plan," he said, turning the laptop screen towards her and pointing to the green row on a complex MS excel grid, "it would take just about 28 days to hold a series of eight exclusive exhibitions. This will also give you your much-needed footprint in the emerging art capitals of Asia—Shanghai and Hong Kong. After Europe and India, these two cities should be your next destination. I understand that you have a pre-planned Middle East, Far East and America commitment but..."

"Chow, I really don't know how to put it across, but I am really in no mood for this. I am sure you know that I am contractually bound. I have to work exclusively for Mr Khurana and his company Orchid, and I will never do anything which might hurt this arrangement."

Captain heaved a slight sigh of relief and settled an extra inch into the chair. He felt smug to still see the flash in the pan—he could still see the nice and honest girl alive in her. But he should have known that the unscrupulous demons were out there, looking for every single soul, to cast their evil shadow upon.

"Ahh... you need not worry about any hassle with Mr Khurana. I have spoken to him and his legal aide. We will make some arrangement which will keep the contract between you and him intact. We can work out something in parallel." The tone in his voice was just on the edge; he was the hunter, delicately holding the bow and balancing the arrow, trying his best not to alert the prey.

Captain got a little uncomfortable as he knew that Chow was going for his kill.

"The new drafted contract between me and Orchid will just introduce me as a third party where I will be employed as your talent manager, employed by Orchid."

Avantika was a little confused. She quickly glanced at Chow and then towards Captain, with her lips puckered. Captain tried keeping a straight face but instinctively he knew that his role just got over.

"See Ms Sen, let us face the facts," Chow explained.

"Your friend," he pointed towards Captain, "was kind enough to be your manager during the initial days. And I must congratulate him on his wonderful work." Even his sly hunter's tone failed miserably to camouflage his evil intentions. "But now your stature has changed.

From a new painter on the block, you have turned into a hot selling painter. This changes the market and the marketing dynamics. Now you are riding on big bucks. Therefore, you ought to have a professional manager who knows these rough waters. Let me warn you Ms Sen, the placid sea is not as calm as it looks." He waved his arms around dramatically. "Someone like you needs to be steered clear of the sharks. One wrong move and the sharks win." The soliloquy over, with the subtle hint of threat in his dialogue, his eyes had a strange smile.

"Mr Chow is absolutely right, Avantika." Captain knew that there were times when it was better to cave. "Now you are a full-fledged, successful painter. Now is the time for you to be with people who know this business. In any case, I have been too long away from my own business and it's time I go back to what I do the best, captain a boat." He smiled. Though their relation had gone through a lot in the past couple of months, lot of water had flown between Captain and Avantika, but the mere thought of his leaving and going back to Kerala came as a rude shock to her. For some inexplicable reason, probably she had assumed that he would always be there by her side, irrespective of her treatment. For a moment, she shuddered at the thought and a guilt wrench hit her guts hard. She looked at him. Did she see his eyes moist? She hated herself for being mean to the guy who was the reason for everything which she had now. But wasn't he the one to make her realize that success was a result of one's own talent, luck and perseverance?

Her thoughts were interrupted by Chow's never-ending sales pitch.

"Captain sir is so right. And, moreover, I will take care of everything. Booking, travel, invites, logistics, PR. Let me assure that you will be covered by all leading national dailies of India and, of course, China." Avantika gave Chow a nice look, wondering what success can do to a person. Introspecting, what did success do to her? Now, after tasting some amount of it, she knew that it changes people who experienced it and also people around successful people.

"Ms Sen, if you allow me, I have one more submission."

She was enjoying the power play and Captain despised her for enjoying this trivial game.

"Though I have spoken with Mr Khurana about the whole thing, but it would be nice if you could do me a favour by recommending my name as your manager."

Avantika looked at his face and experienced a bitter taste in her mouth. Maybe her system did not really take kindly to Chow's look. His immaculate cut tweed jacket, his well-fed, shaved and groomed face, his expensive watch, everything about him looked so plastic and reeked of filth, stench and greed. Too bad for him! She looked through his eyes and her stare was cold.

"Instead of your standard thirty per cent commission on the paintings sold, I will only pay you fifteen and you will foot the bill of this entire series. This will include the airfare, my stay, shopping and all other trivias."

She got up and casually picked her bag as if she had all the time on this earth, as Chow looked on in awe. She pushed back the chair and turned and kept walking to the door and suddenly stopped midway. "And if you are ok with my proposal, please make sure that the contract papers are ready by no later than tomorrow evening for the signatures."

Captain dragged himself behind her, admiring her new found confidence and conviction, yet hating her ruthless ways. His heart whispered to him that before the maxim 'proximity breeds contempt' comes true, it was best if he could just leave.

Bridge Over Troubled Water

"Avi, I know whatever happened was not in our best interest, but then there are times when destiny takes control of the situation and forces you into taking decisions, which you regret later."

Sunny paused, hoping to read and decipher the impact of his opening line. She was listening to him and, to some extent, was pleasantly surprised by his philosophical narration. To her, Sunny was always a logical guy, the number cruncher, so to say—the right brain types. Though at times, he would sit with her, holding her hands, looking into her eyes and telling her sweet nothings. It was only now, after sharing and exploring so much with Captain, with her new found perspective, she could see that those sweet nothings were nothing but just rehashed version of some Bollywood-Hollywood lines.

She clearly remembered the times when Sunny would try to make her all mushy-mushy, by trying to take her down the nostalgic lane and how irritated she would get at her inability to feel any emotion. Was it due to her poor articulation or was she way too removed from all the so-called 'good times together'?

Unlike Captain, he was not the one who knew about every thing and had a point of view on them. He was a simple, focussed guy who only cared to know about things which mattered to him. Fortunately or unfortunately, she was one of them. Now on hindsight, she wondered that maybe it was his focus that made him so successful, unlike Captain.

She focussed her attention back on Sunny's face. Short cropped, black curly hair deep set, dark brown eyes, high forehead, perfect aquiline nose, bow-shaped full lips, clean shaven face which radiated with good health and a cute dimple on his chin. She found him to be very handsome. Maybe distance made her heart grow fonder. Her painter mind tried to sketch Captain's face. On the wrong side of 50, maybe in his early 50s, with messy salt and pepper hair, eyes set amidst deep creases, dark lips and post his Europe tour, a slight paunch.

Set and match to Sunny!

"Avi, for all these months, I missed you and I loved it." She was getting uncomfortable.

"I realized that every little space in my life was filled with your memories. Yes, I accept playing the jealous and possessive lover and putting a detective on your trail. But it was only because you meant everything to me. I did not want to lose you. When I saw your pictures with that wretched boat guy, I was infuriated. When I was told that you were travelling with him to Paris, I felt this stab in my heart. It made me realize what you meant to me and that I would like to spend the rest of my life with you, irrespective of what anyone thinks of you, my mother included."

For some odd reason, even after splitting up with Captain,

Avantika did not like him being referred to as the 'wretched boat guy'. No wonder, her expression fluctuated. The swing was so remarkable that Sunny noticed it. He immediately held her hand and looked into her eyes.

"Avi, I love you and will always do."

She felt clueless. Should she say the three magic words or should she just maintain silence. One part of her wanted to reciprocate Sunny's feeling by telling him that she loved him too, but the other part still pulled her towards Captain. His old but bright eyes were there, right in front of her. Shining like two stars with an air of serenity around them. Tears swelled in her eyes.

"That's ok Avi. I know you have missed me too. You need not say it. We all have our own journeys and weak moments. But I am glad that for our sake, you realized that our paths and journey are the same."

What was she doing with Sunny? If she loved him, why did she go away from him in the first place? If she did not, why was she back with him discussing life and future? Suddenly, she got up. Sunny got baffled and looked at her, expecting the most unexpected.

"Don't worry I'm just going to the washroom."

Colour returned to his face and he took a deep breath. He watched her as she walked away towards the washroom. She had changed a lot. From her Fabindia *kurtis*, tattered denim and *jooti* days to white Polo shirt, navy blue denim and pumps, she had surely come a long way. Also, her streaked hair gave her an air of glamour. How did she change so much in such a short time? He wondered. Surely that boat guy would be something to impact her so much. His eyes slid from her back to her rear which seemed so much ripe and full. Images of naked Avantika and the boat guy making love flashed in front of his eyes. He was appalled at the thought and shrugged it away.

Avantika looked at herself in the big mirror. The lights all around it made her see her face clearly. She felt like crying out loud. But why? She had no reason to cry. She was getting back with the guy she loved, and wanted to get married to. Following her heart, she tried living on her own only to realize that somewhere deep down, she was still attached to him. She adored Captain but he was too strong a guy for her—too articulate, too knowledgeable and almost too good for her. But then was she looking for a man who towed her line, who looked up to her for everything and to whom she could dictate her whims and fancies as and when she pleased?

She chided herself. Sunny was cute and nice. He was the ideal husband material. And to top it all, he loved her immensely. He would give her a comfortable future; a nice home, a big fancy car but would the woman in her be able to detach herself from the unblemished love, the all giving Captain?

Her face had confusion written all over it. Also, the bright light made her notice the fine crow feet near side of her eyes. They weren't there till a few days back? But then, with age getting them was just a matter of time.

She pulled up herself and gave one last look. Finally, the time to face the truth had arrived. She opened the door and walked towards Sunny.

Everybody Needs To Change Sometime

It's easier being a Kabir than trying to be a Buddha.

This profound thought draws truth from the fact that taking to simple life without experiencing the finer side of it is easier than the other way round. If given a choice, would Kabir have chosen abject poverty over the comforts of life? The answer is as illusive as the question itself.

But for Avantika, the choice was straight and simple. After years of struggle and frustration, when a twist of fate changed everything for her, she quickly shelved her austere lifestyle to embrace the chic, flashy and desirable one; much to the dismay and chagrin of Captain. Overthinning long distance calls, Captain knew it well that after all it was her success, her money, and her life and there was nothing much he could do to stop it from impacting her.

So, in the long list of makeovers, change of address topped the list, even if it meant shifting from her residence of eight years, which Captain had painted and refurbished himself so painstakingly. But not wasting energy or time on emotions, like a true high flier, she went for a fully-furnished apartment in an upmarket condominium in Gurgaon. From the 'low maintenance, painter types,' in no time, she graduated to a 'no-nonsense, luxury brand diva'. Fabindia, Mojri and Timex became history as now nothing less than Gucci, Chanel, Elizabeth Arden, Mango, DKNY caught her attention. This list got more exclusive with every single canvas of hers finding a new home. Her phone, satchels, footwear, wardrobe, makeup kit, everything changed, sadly even her friends. The Chows of the world were now her advisers, friends and lifeline. The yesteryear firebrand and intellectual *bong* lady now felt more comfortable in the company of 'pseudo and slimy' Delhi *panjoos.* Riding the success chariot, it was only natural for her to like people who could help her earn more and transact better.

Sunny was back in her life. Now, as they shared the same mindset; of more money and success, she started enjoying his company. Even his conversations, which she earlier found to be too constipated and inane, now made her giggle and laugh like crazy. Within the cocoon of her new-found success, she had no qualms in accepting the fact that considering everything—love, age, family, money and future security—he was indeed the best bet. Also, without any evident reason, she started finding him more caring and compassionate. After all, to celebrate the success of her exhibitions in Europe and India, he gifted her an exclusive studio. Situated on the twenty-second floor of an exclusive condominium, it offered a breathtaking view of the Gurgaon skyline. From being a painter, who celebrated when her 3 × 3 canvases were taken for ₹ 15,000, now she sulked if the same went for anything less than ₹ 20 lakh. With Sunny's cocktail circuit clout, within no time she became a page three regular. Top socialites were the ones with whom she hobnobbed, as most of her work adorned their walls.

No wonder, Captain did not figure in her new scheme of things. He was asked to take a back seat long ago. The calls got occasional, just to update him of any of the latest exciting happenings. Never during the calls did she ever enquire about his boat, Sudhakar, or even his health. In her new world, Captain's honest advice and support was needed as much as a cup of coffee during a marathon walk on a sultry day! So was his love. After all, with lady luck on her side, the small little bird had grown up to be a pretty, confident one now. Ready to pursue her destiny, she had to leave the nest, which she did.

But being her friend, well wisher and more, Captain, in his new found yet limited capacity, did try to bring her back. But unfortunately, the conversation to bring her back on track proved to be their last one.

"Avantika, don't you think that you are rushing into things too soon?"

Her cold stare into nothingness was obvious as they were on a phone call. She vehemently opposed even the genesis of his thought. He continued with his straight advice. "I mean, this is the time when you should put your head down and paint."

The cold stare was substituted with an indifferent silence.

"Avantika, you should treat this time as your real investment. If you ask me, these years should be as important and crucial to you as your formative years. Instead of dissipating energy on trivia like finding a better house or a dress, you should look at exploring different facets of life."

"And what makes you think that I am not doing the same?"

"Because I don't see you doing it."

Honesty always was not the best policy.

"You know Captain what your problem is?"

He knew that a confrontation was inevitable. "No, I don't. But what I know of is this brewing contempt and a deep seated irritation towards me. Why don't you let it out? It's time Avantika," he urged. "Tell me. Speak up your mind."

"Yes, you are right. Even I was thinking of having a conversation with you for a very long time now." Suddenly, every thing in the brightly painted apartment started looking saturated and bereft of any energy. The green walls lost their freshness. The bright orange bedcover started looking pale. The whole apartment made her feel so claustrophobic that she had to get up from the mattress and open the window. Captain softly cradled the receiver and said, "Look Avantika, I have been always honest with you in my criticism. For once, I expect the same."

She looked around, restlessly, maybe searching for the right expression. But finally, she aborted the thought and decided to go ahead with the flow.

"Captain, you are a good guy. I really mean it. But you know, maybe you are just too sweet and too right."

He was listening to her, expecting her to unleash the real part, the bitter part.

"The world of your thoughts or maybe of your dreams and the real world out there are diagonally opposite. Being righteous is not bad, but then, life is not about the black and the white. Most of it exists in shades of grey. We all exist in the same shade. A mixture of good and bad, a blend of the right and the wrong."

"Avantika, I appreciate your perspective and as someone close to you, I fully respect it. But my point was that at this stage, you should be concentrating on your work rather than shifting house, going shopping and indulging in abortive page three PR exercise."

Something snapped.

"Just because I don't heed your advice anymore, you are trying to portray me as a blabbering idiot? Don't you think I know what I am doing? Do you think without any IQ, my paintings are selling at eighty thousand square feet?"

"Avantika, you are getting me wrong."

"No, I am getting you absolutely loud and clear. I had got you wrong earlier," she hissed.

"What did you say? Come again," he could not believe his ears but his mind knew that there was no ambiguity in her statement.

"You heard me right. You are nothing but a control freak who wants to exercise his power over lives just to satiate your king-sized ego. It gives you a sense of accomplishment. It lets you play the God. Even being away, long distance, you want to hold the strings to this puppet of yours.

He was stunned by the baseless, acerbic attack and did not know how to react. She continued, "A God who can control my life, to whom I look up to for advice and opinion. Doesn't it make you feel omnipotent?" More venom was spewed and some more was on its way.

"Do you have any clue how hard I have tried to have all this? I have spent all my life dreaming of this moment, wishing it to come true and now when it's here, you want me to abort it? Why? You were the one to tell me to think of all the good things, prosperity, the best of wine and dine, expensive restaurants, swank cars. Didn't you? Now when I have it, why are you asking me to step back? Tell me? Am I wrong in doing what I am?"

He tried to be as rational as possible. "Avantika, whatever I did was out of love, not for some control, and you know it. Don't you? When it comes to the abundance part, yes I did ask you to think of it. But then there has to be some balance in life. Abundance without a concrete base is a myth, a falsehood, a mirage. Environment was kind to bless you with all the abundance it had. But after accepting it, you have to create good *karma* to ensure a regular flow of the same. The day it starts breeding greed, the environment would stop giving you any more. I am sorry if I misled you, but that was never my intention. I really want to see you going places. Please don't insult my good intentions." He almost pleaded, not for himself, but for the sake of his love.

"Could be. But if what you say is right, then why did my success perturb you?"

"Please don't blame me for things which even you know are not true. I think I can expect at least this from you?" He had tears in his eyes.

"So you are telling me that I am a liar? Aren't you?"

"What is wrong with you Avi? Why are you doing this to me? Do I have to tell you that I came to Delhi just for you? Just to see you happy, I left everything without even thinking twice."

"Did I tell you to leave anything for me? Tell me. Tell me now," her whip like voice hit him hard. While he was trying to deal with the blow, like a true whip master, she delivered another, more fatal this time. "And please Captain. Don't give me that sacrifice story because I am not going to buy it. By the way, back there, from where you come from, I don't think that you had anything to lose as you were already a certified loser. Your business was in red. Resort owners were not ready to send tourists to you. Your boat was as old as you. So don't try to give me that crap that you gave up everything for me."

He was stunned.

"And if it has come to this level, let me tell you that for whatever you did, or claim to have done, I have paid you back handsomely, more than you actually deserved. Didn't I take you to Europe, showed you around, put you up at the most expensive hotels, treated you to the best of the food and wine? Do you think a boat owner back in Kerala can afford all this?"

With great difficulty, he managed to pull himself up from the chair on the deck of his boat. He crumpled the Kochi-Delhi air ticket which was delivered earlier this afternoon. He had wanted to surprise her with another visit. His face was flushed red and his lips and legs trembled. His cheeks were streaked with tears.

"Thank you Avantika for paying me so handsomely for all my love and affection," his voice, now almost a whisper, quivered dangerously as he managed to walk away from his life's blunder.

It All Came Back To Me

Sitting in the lobby of the Taj Palace hotel, Avantika wondered if she could term her life as fair. Well, she had her own share of nightmares, bad patches, good times, fond memories, failures and now, success too; though it started quite late. She felt a little cold and realized that it was already November. Was she early? She looked at her Longines and it told her that she was on time. Maybe Shweta had got stuck somewhere in traffic. The mere thought of Shweta always made her feel so loved and cared for. She felt a little bad for not being able to take her calls during the last fortnight or maybe more than that. But she couldn't help it. Post her mega success of the six-city exhibition, everyone who was anyone wanted to interview her, talk to her, be seen with her and book her next painting. Gosh! She could not believe that all this was happening to her. A new house, a plush studio, new found success and a new guy, well almost new, as he was back after a break. She was happy to be back with Sunny. To her surprise, now he was more mature and compassionate. Maybe, during the separation spree, he worked on his shortcomings and towards changing himself so that they could have a future together.

Throughout her life, the face of her prince charming kept on changing. From Tom Cruise to Bon Jovi, Rahul Dravid to Captain. The last name shocked her. She could not believe that at some point in time, she was actually in love with Captain. Thankfully for her, he never proposed or else without any second thoughts, she would have said a 'yes' and would have ended up making prawn curry and rice at his houseboat, for his sporadic clientele. Bad idea, she thought. But how did she fall for him in the first place?

He was surely not her type. Also, he was definitely old, with no style, class or bank balance. To give the devil his due, he was well read and travelled, and his logic and deep-seated philosophical theories could have put the most profound thinker to shame. What did she like in him? Was it just an infatuation or maybe just a temporary crush to ease the turbulent memories of her parting with Sunny? Thinking of him made her feel a little melancholic. She knew that she was trying to pull him down as she did not want Sunny to lose his place in her heart yet again. But deep down, her soul knew that no one was capable of loving her the way Captain did. He had so much of conviction and care. But then what went wrong? Her success or his growing interference? His old school of thoughts or her new found ways to succeed?

She brushed the thoughts aside as it was all over now. The good part was that she felt so much better without him; with so much more freedom and space. But if love was all about sharing everything, then how could one think of having his or her own space. Wasn't the term 'own space' more aligned to ego and its satisfaction?

Did she really love Sunny? Well, she liked him a lot, that much was for sure. But were liking and love interchangeable words or did they exist on their own, in isolation? Did love translate into going out with someone to pubs, parties, on drives, movies and then to bed? But to go out to these places and to have a good time, in bed included, did one really need to be in love? She knew the answer instinctively. She looked at her Longines again.

She decided on calling Shweta.

Her effort landed her listening to the automated voice of the operator telling her that the number was switched off. She wondered as to how her number could be switched off. While she prolonged over this thought, her phone came to life. An unknown number. She debated if she should take the call, as she hated the obtrusive bank and credit card callers, not to mention stray buyers and journalists. Finally, she decided to go for it.

"Yeah."

"Is that Avantika?" The voice on the other side was cold. Avantika sat up. "Avantika, I am calling from Max Hospital, Panchsheel Park. Do you know anyone named Shweta?" Thoughts rushed to her mind and none of them were too comforting.

"Why do you ask this?"

"Well, she has been brought here in a critical condition, and on her phone, we found that the last number dialled was yours."

She could not figure out how to handle the sudden change in her life. She felt her hands and legs go numb.

"You there?"

"What has happened to her?"

As the caller explained to her Shweta's critical medical condition, it made her stomach churn and the Taj lobby swirl. Long after the call was disconnected, she was trembling like a leaf, with tears silently pouring.

She gathered up all the strength and dialled a number. "Sunny, there is an emergency. Meet me at Max, Panchsheel, as soon as you can. Don't worry. I am fine."

***

"In which room is Mrs Khemka please?"

The station nurse, a young girl with pleasant features but cold eyes, punched a few keys on the keyboard and murmured. "She is still in the OT. You can wait outside. Second floor, first left after the cafeteria."

As Avantika rushed towards the OT, she was panting and sweating profusely and her lungs were under tremendous strain. All the late nights and page three partying and binging were surely not doing her any good. Severely out of breath, to catch a few, she had to stop mid way in the long corridor. Her eyes could clearly see the OT signage at the far end of the corridor, but her legs were in no position to carry her there any sooner.

As she dragged herself towards the OT, from nowhere she saw two cops emerge from the adjacent turn. Like any other respectable citizen, the sight of cops made her a little nervous. She looked around the operation theatre, looking around to find someone who could guide her to Shweta. As she stood there, feeling helpless, one of the cops approached her. She looked around to see if there was anyone in the corridor.

"Are you with Mrs Khemka?"

"Well, yes... I mean I am her friend... I just got a call from the hospital that she has been brought here." She was frightened, which led to her confusion and speaking far more than what was required.

"Madam, my name is Inspector Dalal. I am from Saket Police Station. May I know your name?"

"I am Avantika, Avantika Sen."

"Avantikaji, do you know anything about this suicide attempt?"

While Inspector Dalal was interrogating her, the other one, who was maybe a rank junior to him, started taking notes.

"What is he writing? I don't know anything about the suicide attempt. I am just here as her friend."

"You need not to be frightened Avantikaji. This is just a routine investigation."

"But why are you asking me? I don't know anything."

"That is what we are trying to find." Inspector Dalal smiled.

Suddenly, the door of the OT opened and a middle-aged man, wearing a green gown, walked out. His point of entry and the green gown told everyone that he was the doctor. He looked at the motley gathering—two cops and Avantika. His eyes stopped at her.

"Are you with the deceased?"

She could not decipher whatever the doctor said or implied. Or maybe, she was not ready to believe his statement.

"How is she?" was all that she could murmur.

"Well, I am sorry but we could not save her. The blood loss was too acute which led to a cardiac arrest. I am really sorry."

Avantika could not believe her ears. She was devoid of all emotions—grief, pain, everything. The cops walked away, silently.

Once the cops were out of sight, the doctor pulled out an envelope from his pocket. "You said you are Avantika, right?"

She pulled herself up, tied her hair back and nodded.

"When she was brought here, your friend I mean, she was still breathing. Just before slipping into coma, she handed over this envelope." He handed the long sealed, white envelope to Avantika which bore her name.

"She had specially instructed me to deliver this to you only. I don't know what is in there, but I do know that the cops would have loved to lay their hands on this. So be a little careful."

Seeing Shweta's handwriting on the envelope, she broke down again. When her mother passed away, she was too scared to react. When her brother was gone, she was not even aware. This was the first time when death dawned upon someone so close to her. Her sobs were silent but the copious tears told the doctor that the deceased was very close to her.

Without any attempt to comfort her, as a matter of fact, he stated his belief.

"You know Avantika, I think your friend was under a lot of stress. She chose to commit suicide the day when there was no one at her house. It's only when she realized that life was slipping away, did she call us. But by the time the ambulance reached her, it was too late. Sleeping pills with slashed wrists is always fatal."

Avantika wiped her tears and looked at him.

"But she was a happy woman."

The OT door opened again. A stretcher wheeled out the dead body of Shweta. She was there, lying under a white sheet. Avantika wanted to stop the stretcher and have a look at her but she could not muster up the courage.

The doctor looked at Avantika and folded her stethoscope. "I also found something very strange while I was checking her phone to inform her near and dear ones. Her phone had only one number, yours."

Still shocked, she dialled Prashant's number. After all, he was the deceased's husband. She also called up Sunny to check his status and was told that he was stuck in a bad traffic jam somewhere near Khan Market.

***

'*Dear Avantika,*

I am sure you know that to me a newspaper means only the Delhi Times supplement, with all its page 3 gossip. Today, when I got up and opened the newspaper, I was so happy to see you there. Long live my PQ. Hahahahahaha. You were looking ultra hot in your off-shoulder, black dress. (By the way, who was the hot dude next to you in the pic? Hahahahahaha.)

You know Avi, when someone close to you, rather a part of you, your own children, your kid brother, your darling sister or your closest friend does well, it feels so good. It almost feels like it's you who is doing it. When I see you going places, I feel so happy for you. You've always dreamt of being a painter with name and fame. With the blessings of Mata Rani and your hard work, finally you achieved what you always wanted and deserved. As I write to you, your painting titled 'Krishna in love' is right here in front of me. (Prashant always teases me that you are no good a friend if even I have to buy your paintings at full price. HAHAHAHAHA)

You know Avi, you paint so well. The Krishna and Radha in the painting look so real, so divine. The peacock feather looks so alive, as if it is throbbing with life, all set to grace the mukut of Krishna. I am sure, if Krishna saw it, he would have congratulated you for capturing the serenity, the maya, the love and tranquility of Vrindavan, Mathura and Dwarka, all in one painting. I have booked another one of yours, titled 'Nidra', the one which was at your Delhi exhibition. I was thinking if I should put it in the living room or the guest room. But I guess with its dark blue background, it will go well with the off white walls of the living room.

But you know Avi, and please don't get me wrong, with every success of yours, I feel that you are drifting away. I know, your life has changed. Now, you have too many commitments to honour; both on the personal as well as on the professional front. But I miss my 'cocky lil' PQ'. I suddenly realized that without you, there isn't a single soul with whom I can connect. You know Avi, if you were still with me, around me, my life would never be what it is today, in a complete mess that is. A short stay with you would have made me feel better; at least, it would have given me more strength to face the truth.

Remember the night when after your brother's news, I went back with Prashant? It took me a while to realize that it was one of my life's biggest blunders. If I would have stayed away from him, though I would have stayed in a mode of denial, but at least I would have lived a happy life. After all, ignorance is bliss. But stepping back into his house turned into a nightmare. I had accepted the fact that in this life, all my life, I will have to accept and live with a womanizer as my husband. But I can never live with the fact that my husband, the father of my child, is a pedophile.

I can imagine the surprise, scorn, hate and disbelief at your face right now. But trust me, it gives the chill even to write this to you. I had no clue when during our regular shopping trips, at every store, I would find him checking out frocks and dresses for kids, slippers, sandals, friendship bands, toys. I assumed that it was for his friend's children or maybe he wanted to keep a tab on these things as his kids were also growing up. Never in the wildest of dreams, I could have ever imagined anything on this trajectory. But then, knowing the fool that I am, I could not even guess something amiss when I found a school tie, with an elastic band, in his car.

Finally, the act itself revealed the macabre saga. I saw him in the act with the eight-year old son of our maid servant. I cried all night. Avi, can you see what a fool I am? Even after seeing it with my own eyes, for some reason, I was not ready to believe it. I called up every suspicious number on his mobile. City after city; Delhi, Bangalore, Ahmedabad, Surat, Vishakhapatnam, it was proved beyond any doubt that my husband was a certified pedophile.

Then I confronted him. First, like any other culprit, he resisted, gave excuses. But then after I gave him all the conclusive proofs—names, numbers, etc., he was cornered. Do you know what his reaction was? He told me that every man has a vice and young children were his. No big deal.

While all this was…'

Words got blinded by tears. "Sorry Shwets, I really am. If there was the slightest clue that success to me would mean losing you, trust me, I would never have bargained for it. Sorry baby, please forgive me."

Avantika got up from her chair and walked out.

Are You Lonesome Tonight

Avantika walked in and threw her Chanel handbag on the couch.

"Sunita," she hollered, "get me some *nimbu paani*."

It had been a long and hectic week. Last Tuesday, the PR agency had launched a coffee table book which featured some of her work, along with the work of some other contemporary Indian artists. Though focussed more at an international community, it was also kept at all the leading book stores in India. She had hopped across eight cities in the past week, spending time at the bookstore, meeting people and personally signing the books. By the time she was over with her last appointment at the Oxford Book store at Connaught Place, she was completely dead. Every bone in her body ached and she desperately needed a warm bath.

She kicked off her boots and sank into the beige couch, toying with her new toy—the home automation panel. She could never get used to all these fancy gizmos. If it did not come with the apartment, she would have never got it installed herself. She brushed her thumb to switch on the water heating and to dim the lights overhead.

"Good evening Madam, *nimbu paani*," Sunita was a smart new generation housekeeper supplied by the housekeeping agency. She spoke a reasonable smattering of English and could handle the home automation gizmo better than her.

"Yeah thanks, can you leave some clothes for me on the bed, and fill in the bath, I need a shower desperately." She looked up finally to see Sunita, who was dressed primly in a white *salwar-kameez*.

"Did you use Sugar Free in this?"

"Yes Madam."

Avantika glanced around. The house was really looking smug. The far wall on the left was done in red terracotta designer tiles, in the centre hung a mask she had picked from Vienna, she smiled at it, remembering her reaction on seeing the masks at Sunny's house for the first time. The couches were from the best designers in the city, one of her favourite paintings hung above the single couch. It was a grey evening dissolving into a darker shade of night and she loved the whole essence of metamorphosis.

From the painting, her eyes fell on the side table and she could not help but react. "Sunita! What have you done to the candles? Why are they red? Oh my God, they look so terrible; the entire colour scheme in the room has gone so wonky."

Sunita sheepishly replied, "Madam, the morning helper had knocked off the candle stand today morning and the candles broke."

"So? So what? Why are they red?" Now she was almost screaming.

"Sorry, well I did not have more white candles so I used the red ones, I will get a new set tomorrow."

"You better do Ms Sunita. Please only have white candles in this room and red in the lounge. Remember, I do the planning stuff here. Rubbish! I am away from home for a week and you guys turn it into a garage." Avantika was infuriated and was breathing heavily. She went back to the panel in her hand, brushing various switches and playing with the volumes, speed, and then she pressed the bottom button to swing the curtains.

"Sunita." Another holler. "Why on earth have you left the terrace door open?"

"Madam, Sir is in the balcony. He has been waiting for you."

"What, when did he… oh where?"

Avantika peered through the open door. Sunny was lounging on a beach chair next to the pool, intently peering into the laptop. She walked out slowly.

"Hey Sunny, surprise-surprise. When did you get in? You didn't tell me you would be coming."

"So do I now need to inform you before I come over?" Sunny winked at her while he continued playing the game on his laptop.

Avantika placed the glass on the table and walked across to him. Sunny placed the laptop on the table and pulled her to his lap.

"Come here sweets, we have not spent more than a couple of hours put together in the past week. I have missed you so much."

"Baby let me go, I need a bath and to freshen up, I really am very tired."

"Ok. Sure thing honey." He was a little dejected. "Come on quickly. See I have already placed the sparkling in the ice tub. We have to celebrate tonight, what say?" He squeezed her thighs and gave her a naughty look.

"Yes sure… but Sunny, I really need to unwind, and I need to complete the painting I left unfinished. And we did… err meet earlier this week. Didn't we?" She pleaded.

"Ah my baby, come to me, I will give you as much time as you need. Do you even understand how much I ache for you? All your sensibilities you use to make your paintings, I wish if you would use them to understand me as well." The earlier sarcasm was raising its head.

"I am sorry honey; I will be back in a while."

She was turning cold inside; the smile on her face was not the least inviting. It was then that she noticed the little tea lights which were lit on the terrace, the bunch of lavender orchids stood in a bunch on the hanging vase next to the broad terrace swing.

"Hey Avi, also check out the gift package I have kept for you on your bed. Love you darling." His voice wafted inside the apartment while she trudged inside her bedroom.

A silver bag lay on her satin bedspread; she dipped her fingers inside to pull the black camisole that lay within. She did not even bother to pullout the lacy stuff to check the brand, design. Right now she was just not interested. She picked the simple white linen tunic which Sunita had laid on the bed and walked inside for her bath.

It was already nine pm when finally Avantika walked out to the terrace. She wore a simple white tunic, a thin platinum chain with a heart pendant and Amarige by Givenchy. Her freshly washed hair sparkled at odd angles in the scant, candle-lit terrace.

"Madam, what shall I make for dinner?" Sunita posed a soft question behind her. "Just keep the ingredients for a Caesar salad ready, I will toss them before we want to eat and probably some bread. Would that do for you Sunny?"

"No way, tonight we have to celebrate your first coffee-table publication baby. We will go out later tonight, after... well... err." He winked at her and then he turned to Sunita, "You can pack up for the day, I will make sure that I take your Madam out and feed her well."

Avantika chipped in as calmly as possible, "Sunny, please let's stay at home tonight, I have been eating crazy stuff for the past few days. Let's eat something light and healthy at home?" Healthy food made her think of Captain for a second. At times, she did miss him and all his care. But why was she missing him now? Wasn't everything over?

Sunny seemed to be in full control of the cockpit and ignored her completely. "Don't worry about anything darling. What you need is some good music, food and my company. You will be absolutely fine in a while. Sunita, good night."

Avantika helplessly sat and stared through the glass windows as Sunita packed for the day and left to retire to her quarters in the basement, which housed the support staff of the residents.

He walked up to her with glasses of champagne.

"Hey baby, what is making you so edgy? Don't you love me anymore?" He smiled questioningly. She could only mumble a reply, which the wind just swept away. He clinked his glass with hers and walked behind her and started massaging her neck. In spite of everything, it did seem to relax her and she was getting slowly lost in depth of her thoughts.

"Dear, did you not like the gift I got for you? I was hoping you would wear it?"

"I will, but maybe another day. I will save it for a special day." She muttered a nondescript answer.

"I thought today was special. Wasn't it? Oh, why do I love you so much? I swear, I just love it when you wear the Amarige, you smell so heavenly, my tigress." He scooped her in his arms and laid her on the lounger next to the pool.

It was a strange night; she was getting split into two. She was not sure what was it that her body and mind were craving for? Even though she was longing for a warm touch, a cosy moment, which Sunny was dedicating to her, she was far from fulfilled. While she lay under the March stars, maybe the dry night had sapped her. Sunny gave everything she wanted and asked for; yet her heart was where the stars were. She stared wide eyed into the skies searching for answers for her strange behaviour.

Her cold demeanour did prompt Sunny to ask in moments of drunken stupor. "Is there anyone else?" But she ignored his question as he slumped back to sleep. She was facing a strange urge within, which the physical intimacy was not fulfilling. Finally, when she heard his steady breathing, she swung her bare feet onto the ground. She set up the easel next to the pool and loaded the table with colours. The sky was then a strange shade of grey, when the moon was taking its last bow, the faint breeze was weaving knots in her hair. She was battling the surge within to reach fulfillment. At a complete loss, she stared into the blank canvas with the brush in her hand for a while, and then in a fit of ache, she threw her brush away and dipped the right hand into the oil colour. With her fingers dripping with paint, her lines found their way across the canvas. It was a mad rush of colours. She moved her fingers slowly first then at a certain speed. Her entire body moved in rhythm with her fingers, till she was breathless.

When her eyes were closed and she could only feel the dry paint on her fingers, strangely she had a vision of blue waters, a coconut tree on the horizon and a houseboat.

Heartaches And Heartbreaks

Hundreds of miles away, on a houseboat, for someone on it the night was still. The loneliness within him was making it even more depressing. He looked out in the darkness, straining his eyes, hoping to see at least a flicker of light, if not hope. But maybe both, light and hope co-existed, as none of them were to be seen.

The air was humid and heavy. He felt a rising heaviness in his heart. Ever since he stepped out of Avantika's Defence Colony residence, this heaviness had been growing, steadily. He took a few deep breaths, filling his lungs with the damp and humid air. It made him feel somewhat better. The Vembanad Lake was as silent as ever, discounting the chatter of waves, the creepy sounds of the insects and the far cry of some lost solitary bird, seeking directions.

After a very long time, he again started feeling lonely and depressed. He had experienced this similar feeling of hopelessness and gloom while he held the limp hand of his dead father. Some thirty years back, in the sterile ward of JJ Hospital, Mumbai, when he watched the lifeless frail body of his father, he immediately deciphered that he was more than his biological source. That body under the white sheet was his passport to a good, carefree life—the exorbitant tuition fee of Parson's College, his fancy apartment's rent, sponsoring his lavish parties and lifestyle and maintaining the never-ending queue of swooning beauties in love with his style, intellect and talent. Sitting there, alone, in the hospital ward, he knew that with his father's last breath, everything was history. But today, on his houseboat, alone, he knew it well that his present state was more intense and suffocating.

He lit a cigarette. As smoke filled his lungs, the long abstinence made his body revolt. He coughed. He could not believe that in just a few months, his long companion of almost thirty-five years, cigarette, now almost seemed like a stranger to him. He took another puff, a deep one. Against the pitch dark background and the most sweetened cacophony of the waves, the thick curling, white smoke assumed a new proportion, manifesting itself in new shapes and forms.

He scrambled his mind, searching for the original string of thought. Ah! There it was—Avantika and him. Her mere thought made his whole system get into an overdrive, with diagonally opposite emotions confronting him. Undoubtedly, the bitterness of the split was imprinted on his soul. But why should he feel dejected or sad? She was leading her own life and so was he. He tried to explain it to his mind, giving it some second rate logic to chew on. But then, logic being man-made always plays second fiddle to the supreme one—heartfelt and true emotions. No wonder, for him, no amount of logic could win him the war of getting over Avantika. Did he love her? He preferred hiding behind his belief that some relations were beyond the known boundaries and his relation with Avantika was one of them. Though he also knew that articulating his relationship with her and accepting the truth would make his life easier. But how could he love her? He was almost twenty years older than her. While his life was over, life for her had just started looking up. He was just a small time tourist houseboat owner whereas she was a talented and 'on the rise' painter. There wasn't any common ground for their union or even being together.

He took a few long drags. The heaviness was getting worse; therefore, he walked out and inhaled more of the humid yet fresh air. His stomach churned. That reminded him that since morning he had not had anything to eat. He asked himself if he wanted to eat right away or after getting over with the cigarette. His mind chose the latter.

Getting back to his chaotic state of thoughts, did he love her? The heart and mind knew the answer, it was only his physical being that was afraid to accept it. Just admitting the fact that he was afraid of something was such an alien thought. All his life, he had been the brave one. But then he knew that all his life he had also never been in love. But if it was love, then why wasn't he happy for her?

Why was he trying to hold on to her? He pressed his left upper arm as a surge of pain hit him.

Was he jealous of her success? No!

Was he feeling left out? No!

Was he feeling cheated? No!

Was he jealous to think that she was with someone else? Maybe yes!

Would he do anything to be with her? Yes, he would!

Was he in love with her? Well… yes.

Captain's mind could not figure out what true love was all about. Giving each other space and the freedom to make a choice, to explore and express oneself, to fly high and see and discover the world? Then why was he intending to strangulate her with his way of life, thought and choice? If love was a selfless expression, then why was he asking for something in return? If his love was above everything, then why was he lowering it to a physical level? If he really loved her, then did it really matter if she was with him or someone else?

The pain in the left arm was spreading to his shoulder. He massaged his upper arm and inhaled few deep breaths. He could not breathe and began to gasp for air. Like a ripple in pool, the circumference of the pain radiated and increased. With every passing second, it was becoming acute and unbearable. His vision blurred and he staggered towards his phone. With his right hand, he clenched his chest, and with the left, he dialled Sudhakar's number.

The moon started getting dimmer and suddenly like an electricity bulb, it was turned off.

Face Off

"But how can you pull out of my exhibitions, at this moment, like this?" Her voice soft, yet rasp, reeked of betrayal and was laced with fear of anticipated hardships.

"Ms Sen, your reaction was much politer when I agreed to sponsor them. Remember?" Mr Khurana made it amply clear that he was in no mood to tolerate any sort of theatrics or creative mood swings.

They were in a private gallery in Gurgaon, Images, which was currently exhibiting her collection, 'Meera'. Mr Khurana was expecting a business delegation from a leading Singapore construction company, Sembawag & Tamchi, today at the gallery. This was supposed to be a walk-through and casual business warm-up niceties, which was to be followed by lunch at 'The Diya' in Leela Kempinski.

His mood nose-dived when the marketing director for the Indian subsidiary of Sembawag & Tamchi called about an hour ago and apologized for calling off the meeting at such a short notice. Mr Khurana could smell foul in the light of the termination of some civil works contract in Singapore. Such news usually adopted mammoth proportions within a short duration.

"I'm sorry Sir. I did not mean to offend you. But, I mean, we are just eight weeks from my six-city exhibition in Asia. Pulling out at this juncture will affect my career and even Orchid's brand image."

"I understand Avantika. But this global meltdown and recession has hit every single business. Real estate and construction are no exception." He paused and momentarily grimaced at the thought of the failed meeting of that day. "I hope you understand that when there is no money in the market, the purchasing power is squeezed. Moreover, this affects the big-time buyers who buy real estate solely for investment purpose. As you know, most of our projects are high-end luxury projects and, therefore, we are facing the heat more than the companies who are into run of the mill townships and condominiums. You must be aware that Orchid's stocks have taken a big time hit on the NSE and BSE."

He glanced at Francois, who pretended to be immersed in the gold nose pin of 'Meera', yet was half turned to face their conversation. Dressed immaculately in a charcoal grey suit, his face had creases of troubled thoughts.

"But Sir, these exhibitions did so well for Orchid's brand image. And I think during troubled times, a company like yours should be spending more on the consolidation of their brand image. If you ask me, pulling out of these exhibitions will send out a wrong signal which could make the sensitive stock exchange jitterier." She looked at Francois for support.

Francois was amused at her articulation. Till a few months back, not even in the wildest of his dreams, he ever expected the simpleton

Avantika Sengupta to have a point of view on esoteric topics like 'brand image' and 'jittery sensex'. Deep in his heart, he respected her for her stupendous growth; both as a painter and as a woman. However, the task right now was far more complex. As per the brief of Mr Khurana, he was supposed to help him in phasing out Avantika, without creating any bad publicity for his company. He cleared his throat and took a few careful steps towards them, trying to weigh his thoughts, before they shaped as words.

"Ms Sen, we fully realize and understand that this news would be quite a blow, rather a setback for you. But trust me, there is no way out. During such a situation, the endeavour of any company is to consolidate its money outflow and to concentrate only on necessary expenses and creditors. Everything else takes a back seat. I run a company myself and I am not doing any different."

"Mr Lancolne, you could be right, but where does all this leave me?" Her voice still had the startle of a bird, which had just seen the storm on the horizon, bound to destroy her nest. He had no answer.

"You know that it has taken me so long to be where I am. Right now, I am just standing and knocking on doors which if open, can catapult me into the big league, real big league. If these exhibitions are cancelled, my credibility will take a severe beating. You have handled so many artists, and without even an iota of doubt, I am sure that you know that if for once an artist loses trust and confidence of buyers and the gallery owners, for him or her, it's lost forever." She tried giving them the real picture, from her perspective.

"Avantika, you need to understand that art for any business house is just an indulgence…" Mr Khurana's phone buzzed and he picked it up after having a good look at the mobile screen. "Yeah would like to meet with our auditors today evening. Yes, it's urgent." He turned his attention towards Avantika again. "Sorry, where were we?"

"Sir, art for a business can be indulgence but for me it's my life." She delivered the statement with a little more conviction than required. No wonder, it provoked a reaction, far greater than expected.

"And do I need to bring it up that it is this very business of mine that gave you this life?" He thundered.

Accepting truth without sugar coating is surely hard to swallow and harder for someone like Avantika who had got too much of everything in too short a time.

"Hold on there for a second, Sir. Are you trying to tell me that you did some kind of a favour by sponsoring my exhibitions?" She felt her stomach churn the morning coffee and boiled eggs.

Francois was quick to intervene. "Gentlemen, please. This is no time to cast aspersions. It's just that when the time is real tough, it requires drastic steps. But I am sure normalcy would be restored in the market soon." He smiled, hoping that it would lighten up the dark cloud of animosity.

Buzz Buzz Buzz. The vibrating phone of Mr Khurana came as a breather.

"Could you please tell him that I am in a meeting and will call him back shortly?"

During the course of the entire discussion, Avantika's instincts helped her in identifying Francois as the softer target; therefore, she knew that to save her career, she had to win him over by any means.

"But Mr Lancolne, the venue has been booked, invites have been sent. I mean... I do understand that there is something called a global recession going on. But do you think it should affect something as small as my exhibitions?" She pleaded.

"With your kind permission Mr Lancolne, may I take this one?" Mr Khurana interrupted quickly. Francois was generous enough to let him do the explaining part, though he knew the precise content of the answer on the block.

"Avantika, I think it is time we spoke of rupees and euros in the true light. Do you know the cost of your exhibitions?" He looked in her eyes. "Maybe this would get your perspective right." He flipped open his laptop and punched some keys to get it activated. While it whirred and buzzed, with the left hand, he picked the phone and called someone, "Raj, yes, can you walk in, yes, I am inside the gallery. Yeah the Red Room."

Avantika waited, trying to fathom a lot of things at the same time. They were sitting in the corner of the large hall, which was called the Red Room; strangely, the walls were white, but the central pillar was stark red. The mock branches held up the ceiling. It was probably the colour of the central pillar that contributed to its name.

The silence in the hall was getting unbearable. Thankfully, the gloved waiter entered the room, breaking the dour silence with his "With milk?" and "How much sugar?" one liners. As they sipped their respective drinks, each mind was toying with their own plan of action, apprehensions and future roadblocks. Avantika was looking at 'Meera' in grey and white, just her dab of vermilion on the forehead stood out.

Each personal reverie in the hall was disturbed by the turning of a doorknob. "Raj come in, he is the accounts manager." Mr Khurana announced generally. "Here Raj, I have the account details. Could you please explain to Madam the broad heads and the expenses against them for the art exhibitions which we sponsored in Europe and India?" Avantika did not fail to notice the extra stress on the word 'Madam', which was slightly bordering on a sneer.

With each passing moment, her disbelief multiplied as she had no clue that some thing as innocuous as an exhibition could ask for such a huge investment. Raj held the laptop in the cradle of his arms and his expert eyes flirted between the lines, rattling away the numbers.

"Could you tell us the total amount spent so far?" Mr Khurana asked Raj, staring into the large uncut diamond on his middle finger.

"Sir, on a rough estimate, it is about three crore sixty lakh. If you want the exact figure, I can further drill down to get the numbers." He tried to make the best use of the freak opportunity that he had got with the CEO of the company. He was asked to be available near the boss, just in case help was needed during the Singapore delegation visit. However, such a personal interface was not something he had imagined.

Avantika could not believe the figure which was just quoted. "Are you sure that the figures are correct. I mean, are you sure that there is no error?"

"When a guy from accounts shares figures from a published statement of account, be assured that they are precise" Francois clarified coldly. The artist in him was swinging between embarrassment and nonchalance. After all, she was his recommendation and he did love her work. This entire episode was getting slightly distasteful. If he had a choice, he would be miles away from this discussion, but Mr Khurana had specifically requested for his presence.

"So Ms Sen, there you go. I am four crores down fuelling this life of yours! So, as you can see success comes with a price tag. And in your case, it was my company who was picking up the tab while you partied with wine and cheese in Vienna, Paris and Stockholm."

"Mr Khurana, I agree that you pumped in all the money, contact, media and your PR machinery to prop me up. But my paintings are selling at a decent price." Her tone was rock solid and that of a believer. "I am quite sure that you would have recovered this amount or at least a large part of it. So please don't make it sound like a one way thing, making me feel as if I am painter with no talent, just riding high on your money, promotion and PR." Her gaze was cold and with a touch of indifference. "And if money could make a painter look good, for your indulgence, you could have picked any painter and invested in him." She completed her string of defence.

The king size ego of a super successful businessman was bruised. He pushed back the upholstered chair and looked at her line of 'Meera'—the tears, the music, the romance, the love, which inundated every canvas—but all that his eyes could see were not the colours, but the flushed investment. It was a slow and deliberate talk.

"Ms Sen, I am sure you would appreciate the fact that there are a million painters, much more talented than you, trying hard to make both ends meet. If I recall correctly, not very long ago, more or less, you too were in the same state." Francois stepped forward and opened his mouth to interrupt. But with the raise of his hand, Mr Khurana cut him short. He continued, "And even with all that talent of yours, of which you are so proud today, your career was going nowhere. From selling a canvas for a meagre sum of twenty thousand rupees now you are commanding twenty to thirty lakh for the same. Don't you think if it were only for your talent, you would have managed this success long back, on your own?"

His eyes pierced her while he adjusted his tie knot. Avantika was flabbergasted. She was trying hard to control her instincts. She knew that she was in no position to afford her ill-temper, as now she had a world to lose. Mr Khurana looked at Francois and gave a finalistic smile, as the meeting was concluded, and like most of them, he was the winner.

Suddenly, something made Mr Khurana turn towards Avantika. He smiled, a sarcastic one and moved closer. While she was sitting, his figure loomed over her. "I think it's time you know why I chose you over any other painter. I know this will hurt you."

Something in his tone scared her. "You know Avantika, famous management guru, Phillip Andrew in one of his recent writings said that recession is positive as it makes us face the truth, even if it is our worst fear or nightmare. I think Ms Sen, your moment of truth has arrived."

Long after he walked out of the Red Room, followed by Francois, she sat there, completely numb with his last line shredding her soul and her entire being. She felt so small and so much used. Instead of the mild Elizabeth Arden, her body reeked of a strange stench. Was she hallucinating? She smelt her hands and she could feel the stench rising. Her neck felt stiff and her forehead was covered with beads of perspiration. She wanted to throw up. Her feet had grown roots as she sat transfixed. Tears rolled down her cheeks like a mad monsoon fed river.

She tried getting away from the last line of Mr Khurana, which was still echoing in her head and multiplying with every second, but failed. She wanted to speak with someone, someone close. Her mind raced. Whom should she call? Damn, she cursed herself. After paying a hefty telephone bill of seven to eight thousand every month, she did not have even one person with whom she could share her pain? Through her foggy teary vision, her thumb scrolled at entries, searching frantically for a friend. But her tear-soaked eyes could only see names—names of big people, important people, rich people, powerful people, politicians, top cops, industrialists, socialites, builders, social activists, all but a friend.

She blundered out in the sun and winced; was it the sun or the pain within, she was not sure. As she got in the cab, she suddenly saw Captain sitting in the rear seat, smiling. She reached out to him, but he wasn't there. Reality dawned upon her that he was gone long ago. Not only physically, but also on a spiritual level, taking away all his guidance and support. She couldn't help but feel guilty as she knew it was her absolute disregard for his existence which made him fade into the oblivion. Where would he be? She started missing him badly, and for some reason, couldn't help but sob. As the cab moved, she could see the blur of the cars whizzing past, just like her friends, who were gone forever.

An absolute feeling of helplessness overtook her. Her silent sob broke into an uncontrollable wail. The cabbie stopped the car and turned around.

"Madam, everything ok?"

She nodded her head.

"Some water?" asked the cabbie.

"No thank you." She gestured him to keep driving.

She dialled Shweta's number, fully knowing that there would be no response and listened to the auto message 'number not in use'. Shweta was gone for good and to a place from where no one comes back. She looked out of the window. Traffic on the other side of the road was zipping past her. As the car snaked around the metro line being installed overhead, as the traffic around her honked, as the vehicles tried to overspeed and beat each other without any specific purpose, she stared on with her vacant look at the magazine, fruit and flower hawkers, who were peering inside the car.

So many people around and not even one whom she could talk to right now?

Her heart weighed almost a ton. All her life, Shweta was there for her; as a friend, mother, guide and a companion. But when she had the opportunity to reciprocate, to share Shweta's inner turmoil, something which could have saved her life, she was too occupied playing the big painter, busy with her interviews and social gatherings.

She felt absolutely miserable and useless. Mr Khurana's closing line was playing havoc, like a bass drum knocking inside her head. She needed to speak with someone; someone to confide in. Her fingers itched to dial Captain's number. But what would she say to him? After all this, would he still bother to take her obtrusive call? Would he still be the same person—nice, warm and compassionate? What if he insulted her? What if he hung up on her? In whichever way he would react, she knew it was time to call him. She would not mind taking his reprimand, insults even abuses, but this pain was killing her. Should she send a quick text message first and then call? But the fingers had a life of their own and kept scrolling the phone book and finally called.

"The number you have dialled is temporarily out of service."

She dialled again.

"The number you have dialled is temporarily out of service."

Again…

"The number you have dialled is temporarily out of service."

Again… Again… Again…

Same response. A fresh rivulet had already started accumulating in her eyes. The wounded beast in her slumped back on the seat and the phone slithered near her foot. All the anguish pent up within was choking her. She was slowly rambling to herself, "Do you know why Mr Khurana chose me over other painters? Because he wanted the girl, me, Avantika Sengupta, whom his son loved to fuck, back in his life."

The scandalized cab driver looked concerned as he glanced in the rearview mirror.

She was still cooing to herself, "Captain, I wanted to be a painter and look what I turned out to be? A whore to a rich *panjoo* brat. I am a whore, Captain. No wonder you left me. Good that Shweta left me too. No one wants a whore as a friend." Her voice was breaking up, and the madness was palpable, "I am a whore. Can you hear me,

Captain? Your sunshine is nothing but a slut, a filthy little whore, who got paid three crores and sixty lakh rupees."

Then it started coming, silently first. Her head was flung back, the cry did not leave her throat, just the hoarse whisper and then a scream of "Avantika whore" followed by another scream of words which could not be deciphered—just cries of a woman in madness.

The Devil Wears Makeup

"Oh dear, I am so sorry about this, but someday I had to break the news to you." Chow flashed his greasy and shameless smile. "Avantika, I hope you will understand my position. But in any case, I am on your payroll for one more month, so don't you worry about anything."

"But Chow, how can you walk out on me now? This is highly unprofessional. I had… I mean, we had a bond and it was you who pleaded to be my manager. Didn't you?" Avantika was confused and angry.

"Well dear, you are partially right and partially wrong." The sudden sponginess in his tone did not fool her. "The wrong part is that I never had any contract or bond with you. If you remember, you had a contract with Orchid, not me." He let out a shrill laughter. "In turn, I had a contract with them, whereby the company appointed me as your manager, which I am still for a month. Now, as Orchid is not sponsoring your shows anymore, therefore, after a month, the company will relieve me from this boring job." He looked directly in her eyes, searching for the hurt look. "Now coming to your being right, yes, I pleaded to be your manager, simply because there was a lot of money riding on you and being the opportunist that I am, I spotted this one and decided to make some money out of it. Nothing personal dear." He grinned.

This was the first time when Avantika witnessed someone change sides so blatantly and shamelessly. Her temples throbbed and she could feel the bile surge and hit up in her throat. Her instinctive reaction was to walk out; however, she decided to rough it out.

"And Chow I am sure you would have assumed, like your Mr Khurana did, that without you, I would be dead. Right?" She tried her best to keep the sneer in her voice, which now was slurring uncontrollably due to anger.

"Oh dear, please don't insult my intelligence by saying that. How can I assume such a stupid thing?" The actor in him took over the stage. "I am willing to sign on a stamp paper certifying that without me and Mr Khurana, you will not only be dead, but dead and gone like this..." He snapped his fingers, the thumb and the middle one, while his eyes were now just slits, due to his broad grin. For the first time, the unflinching confidence in his voice terrified Avantika.

Chow sat down on the couch, stretched his legs, toyed around with his cuff links and looked at her. There she stood, dainty and slender, wrapped in a grey spun sarong and a light linen jacket. He gave his leering smile again. The leer gradually turning into threat. Avantika shivered as she knew that he was making a mental note of her confidence and courage before he made his move.

"Remember, when you came to me for the first time, I told you that art is like marketing with a complex matrix? I also told you that artists are created, not born. I am sure by now you have seen it for yourself. But there was something of grave importance which I forgot to tell you." He laughed. His hysterical laughter filled the lounge of Avantika's designer apartment.

"You know Avantika, the unsaid rule of the art world is that if the first mover fails to make a return on his investment, then he ensures that no one else is allowed to reap the rewards." He looked at her. Avantika found the context of his last line hard to understand.

"Let me explain it to you." He sat up on the couch. "If Mr Khurana invested in you, he was the rightful owner of the returns which your paintings generated. Now, as there will be no more exhibitions, he will never let any other company put in their money and ride on the high wave which he created using his money and might." He rolled his eyes and pulled his face long, morphing in a comic expression. "So poor you, no sponsors, no exhibition, no sale, no money. I really pity you darling."

Avantika could see the picture now and it made her go livid with rage. "You wretched creature, you scum of the earth…" But Chow was not even bothered.

"Dear, save all this and more for me as I am not finished as yet." He laughed again as he was loving the cat and mouse game with her. "To promote an artist, we use PR, publicity, TV, Press. But to top it all, we use the grapevine to feed bytes, which generates unexpected curiosity and helps the artist to sell better. Like for your shows, we fed the grapevine that you were in advance stages of negotiation with the Royalty of Jordan to paint an exclusive series for his new palace. As this news was unofficial, there was no legal angle to it. But nevertheless, it pushed up the prices of your paintings by a few more lakhs. Now, when Mr Khurana decided that he was pulling out of your exhibitions, he knew that some other business house would approach you to make their fast buck. Therefore, in his own business interest, it got imperative to render you useless. So to do the same, he hired me for an additional month. Like a smart manager, that I am, only this time for Mr Khurana, I fed the grapevine that Mr Khurana promoted you on a temporary basis just to be a good father to his son, who was having a torrid affair with you. And now with his son's passion tide over, the deal between you and Mr Khurana has also fallen off."

Avantika stood in stunned silence, too shocked to react. "And yes dear, I also fed the ever hungry news channels that most of your paintings were bought by Sunny Khurana himself, just to please you."

Surely, art was not as aesthetic as it seemed, at least not with people like Chow and Khurana.

You Lose Some And Then You Lose More

As the bodies were lowered in the electric furnace of the crematorium, the three odd cops and the mortuary guy started walking towards the exit gate. After all, as experienced mortals, they had been a witness to this eternal truth many a time.

In spite of knowing this, walking away was not possible for Avantika as the bodies were of her late father and his wife Simi. The turn of events had completely drained her; emotionally and physically. Standing there alone, at the Yamuna Crematorium, the chill-laden breeze from the river Yamuna was slicing her thoughts. Her father, Col Sengupta was not a good father. Post her brother's episode, she had disowned him. And she was right in doing so. Right from her childhood, he was never there to support her, hold her hand, guide her, protect her or even just be there for her when she needed him the most. He was the tyrant, who took great pride in his background and sought refuge in the fact that he was one of the most decorated and gallant officers of the Armoured Core. Maybe it was this gallantry that overshadowed his tender and emotional side.

Avantika put her hands in the fur-lined pocket of her jacket. Delhi winter was notorious for its thick fog and today was the first day of the long drawn foggy season. It was close to eight am but the fog was so thick that the visibility was not more than a few feet.

The day before, since morning, when one of her clients informed her that news channels were breaking news that the couple who had shot themselves was related to the famous painter Avantika Sengupta, life changed for her yet again.

As she rushed to switch on her television set, to get a first-hand report, her mobile started ringing incessantly. Clients, journalists, acquaintances—all of them lining to express their condolences and to get some more gossip out of her. Even the intercom of her apartment wouldn't stop ringing. From her window, she could see the OB vans of various news channels parked outside her condominium gate. She thanked the three-tier security, which kept the media guys away from her.

She desperately wanted to get in touch with someone whom she could count on. There was no one. The last straw, Sunny, was also lost. After all, she could never have someone as her man who rushed to his father for everything, even for getting love back into his life. Post her discussion with Mr Khurana and Francois, she was sure that Sunny would have got the message that the game was over. What shocked her the most was that he did not even call her up to clarify things. Knowing the mama's boy that he was, she was not surprised at all. Out of sheer desperation, she called up Mr Lancolne.

"Avantika, I am really sorry to hear about this unfortunate event. I was just about to call you myself." His reassuring voice made her feel a little better. Though on a business tour to Europe, he was kind enough to listen to her and offered whatever little he could do. He told her that he would send his lawyer over to her house. Mr Lancolne's lawyer instructed her to go to Gurgaon Police Station and to complete the paper work and other formalities which were required to claim the bodies. He also assured her that he would be there shortly. She thanked him and just fell on the couch, out of exhaustion and weakness. A huge wave of depression hit her. Now, there was no one whom she could think of as her own. Though she never had anything to do with Col Sengupta, but nevertheless, he was her father. With him dead and gone, she was all alone.

Every news channel was reporting the same incident under the garb of breaking news. She wanted to cry but her anger wouldn't let her do so. Interacting with media during press conferences and social get-togethers was something which she loved. It was the first time when they had encroached upon her private space. What was news to them was a loss for her, although she was not too sure of the loss bit. One overenthusiastic channel had branded the incident as '*Katil pati, suhagan sati*'. She felt disgusted. After surfing through a couple of channels, she could weave the pieces together. It seemed that her father and Simi were going through a rough patch in their marriage. The night before the incident, after an altercation, which the neighbours claimed to be a daily affair, in a fit of rage her father shot Simi first and then himself. It was also reported that at the time of this ghastly incident, both of them were drunk. What a sad and cowardly way to die for a gallant Armoured Core stalwart.

The entire day was spent at the Gurgaon Police Station, answering their questions, filling numerous forms. All this while, more than a dozen news channels' OB vans and around three dozen journalists waited like hawks for their pound of flesh. All they wanted was to get her reply to their famous, moronic question: 'So how does it feel?' She knew that whatever she said would become the 'breaking news' of every single news channel.

Mr Lancolne's lawyer was present with her for every single minute which she spent at the police station. He also accompanied her to the government hospital, where they had to wait for hours to get the postmortem report and then the possession of the bodies. As it was well past midnight, he suggested that it would be wise to keep the bodies in the mortuary and then take them the next day, early morning for cremation. Avantika nodded as she had no better option. After completing all the formalities, he left her, leaving his car behind and with a promise that he will be back the next morning.

In the wee hours of Delhi winter, a hot shower felt so refreshing. It opened every pore in her body which was clogged with memories, distraught, fear, trauma and heart-breaks. As the water ran towards the corner of the shower cubicle, from where it went down hundreds of feet, God only knew where, it took away all her sorrows, leaving her fresh to face the challenges of a new day.

As it was decided between her and Mr Lancolne's lawyer to meet at the Yamuna Ghat Crematorium at eight am, there was hardly any time for her to sleep. Lying on the couch, she just watched her entire life play itself in front of her. From being a scared little girl to an independent girl who was mentally ready to perform the last rites of her father and step-mother. Her late father would never have imagined that someday, he will have to depend on her for his last journey and rites. She made a mental note of the fact that in her next painting series, she should try to explore the strange relationship between man and woman. Also, she decided to get all her father's medals framed and to put them up in her sitting area. For some odd reason, she was missing him, though she never felt the same while he was around.

She shifted her focus to Simi. Though she hated her for replacing her mother, but as a woman, now she felt bad for her. She knew that in her hey days, she was a good looking girl who hailed from a respectable family. Her only fault was that she fell for her father's irresistible charm, for which she had to pay with her life. At times, Avantika wondered what made a woman like Simi dump her career, her home, her future—practically everything for a man like Col Sengupta. She had no answer. Or maybe the reason was the same as her flipping for someone as old as Captain. After all these years, today, she really felt sorry for Simi.

Beep beep, beep beep.

Who could be texting her so early? Surely one more condolence message. She picked up her mobile. It was 4.30 am.

"On the tragic demise of your father, Col Sengupta and his wife Simi, I offer my heartfelt condolence. Regarding the same, I have something important to discuss and share with you. Would request you to get in touch with me ASAP.

Advocate Bhushan, Tees Hazari Court, Delhi."

She thought of dialling him right away but then it was too early for a call.

'Thank you Dad for being my father. May your soul rest in

peace. Thank you Simi for being there with my father. May your soul rest in peace.'

Before she closed her eyes for a short nap, she tried Captain's number again.

"The number you have dialled is temporarily out of service."

She made a mental note to sort out the 'out of service' mystery tomorrow.

Windfall

To understand why getting justice on time, or at all, was still a tall claim in India, one had to visit the bustling hub of justice, the *Tees Hazari Court*. Located near the ISBT, it presented a sight which could wreck the nerves of anyone who came there seeking anything, leave alone justice. The road itself that led to the court premises was a glaring showcase of blatant encroachment and unauthorized construction galore. Small shacks and semi-permanent structures dotted both sides of the street. Rickshaws, handcarts, buses, trucks, cars, pedestrians, cattle, dogs—just about everyone jostled for their share of space on the pot-holed road. The mixed noise created by this assorted crowd was loud enough to rupture the ear-drums of any sensitive person.

Even inside the court premises, it was no better. Under every tree, wooden cots were strewn across and on them with aluminium boxes their names painted on them, sat advocates, soliciting clients. Wearing their customary black coat and white band, their activities ranged from sipping tea, discussing some case, haggling over their fee, or just idling there.

Dodging a maddening crowd of a rare mix, plaintiff, accused, defendant, cops, lawyers, hawkers and dogs, Avantika was finally able to locate chamber number 114 as the board on the door announced,

Advocate L Bhushan

MA, LLB, LLM

Chamber no. 114, Tees Hazari Court, Delhi

Mobile: 9810467245

She decided to knock the rusted iron door but then decided against it as she knew that amidst the prevailing cacophony, her gentle rap would be quite abortive.

Advocate Bhushan was expecting her. He greeted her and offered her a seat. She noticed that it was a very small room, maybe 8 × 8. It was occupied by a small table and a high back chair for Mr Bhushan. On one side, there was another small table where two other advocates wearing black coat were busy writing something. Adjacent to their table, there was an iron cabinet which was overflowing with dusty files. Nearby, on a plastic stool, a water dispenser was placed which leaked continuously.

Advocate Bhushan was a middle aged man in his early 50s. His salt and pepper hair suited his age and imparted his aura more credibility.

"Ms Sen, I am sorry for whatever happened. It was indeed very tragic. Please accept my heartfelt condolences."

Avantika tried to look more serious and glum.

Advocate Bhushan continued, "You see Ms Sen, I don't know if you are aware, but I have been your father's legal counsel for quite some time now. A few months back, exactly a week before he was getting married, he had come over here," he pointed the room, "and asked me to draft his will. It took me three-four days for the same and if my memory serves me right, just a day before he got married, he signed his will and instructed me to hand it over to you, in case of any eventuality." He stopped and pulled out an envelope.

Avantika was too puzzled by whatever he had said and waited anxiously for the content of the envelope. He pulled out few sheets and held them in his hand as he looked at Avantika. "This is his will. You want me to read it?"

The answer was obvious.

"I will skip the legal terminology and language and will come to the point. His will states that all his property: a flat in Gurgaon, one in Shimla, a small farmland in 24 Parghanas in Bengal, the money from all his shares, mutual bonds, fixed deposit, saving accounts, his car, will go to his daughter, Ms Avantika Sengupta, you."

She was too stunned to speak anything or even to react.

"On a conservative estimate, after deducting all the expense for paper work and my fees, all this would amount close to four crore."

Still in a state of shock, she signed wherever she was asked to and walked out of the madhouse, oblivious to whatever happened around her.

Her journey from the Tees Hazari Court to her Gurgaon apartment was a long one. Sitting on the back seat of the cab, as it negotiated the heavy traffic, she wondered at the surprises that life has in store for everyone. A father, whom she loathed, detested and abhorred, still left all his worldly possessions for her. Was it due to the fact that runs deeper than anything or could this action be attributed to his guilt of not being able to play the role of a loving father? The picture of her father, dressed in his ceremonial army uniform, flashed in her mind. For some reason, it made her feel good and for a moment she missed him.

Four crore for anyone was a lot of money. Her lips and cheeks tightened as revenge flickered in her eyes. She knew that with four crore she could turn the table on the Khuranas. With all this money, she did not need them. She could paint on her own, hold her own exhibitions and sell on her own terms. As her hatred towards them grew, her face contorted more and more. Though she knew that hatred fuelled by money was the sure shot way to self destruction, but then she also knew that there were times when cost became inconsequential.

Her mind was busy calculating the allocation of the money and how to pull off the exhibition again. Contrary to the age old adage, she was convinced that revenge was best, when served piping hot.

During the course of the long day ahead, it was sure that permutations and combinations would assume varied proportions and would play separate tunes—one to appease her conscience and a different one for her mind.

Reality Dawns

Dial...

Redial...

Redial...

Redial...

Redial...

Every time she dialled Captain's number, the recorded voice gave the same reply: 'the number you have dialled is temporarily out of service.'

Where is he? Why is he not answering the phone? Has he changed his phone number? And then she shuddered. Is he all right?

She flipped on her back and stared at the ceiling, tracing imaginary lines on the chandelier above and redesigning it in her mind. Her mind wandered over a zillion things—a new line she had been thinking for her paintings, a motif she wanted to paint on one of her skirts, trying to remember if she had any other contact in Kochi who could check Captain's whereabouts for her. His thoughts made her very restless. While her toes, like her mind, endlessly wandered on the satin sheet, she was startled; strangely, the cool satin sheets were not looking and feeling as good as they used to earlier. She smiled as her eyes drifted along with her mind to the time when Captain did up her small studio apartment in Defence Colony. They had picked up the lovely cotton and linen bedspreads from Fabindia and Anokhi. She must remember to pull them out from the storeroom; the earthy textures gave her more comfort and homelike feel. She particularly loved the one with red and blue flowers, which Captain had selected himself.

For some reason, before this moment, it had never occurred to her that something could ever happen to Captain. To her, he was the epitome of knowledge, inner strength and discipline. She thought that nothing happened to such people. Restlessness enveloped her.

She desperately wanted to speak to Captain for guidance. She knew that if he were around, with his clear and sorted out logic, he could give her the most pragmatic way forward. Why did she let him go? Why didn't he tell her that she was going wrong? Why couldn't he be around again to tell her right from wrong?

Suddenly, she sat up as she felt fuzzy in her head. She managed to hunt the cigarette packet which she had hidden from her view at the rear of the cupboard. With a long puff, she walked to the terrace. With no image of any God in her mind, she just looked at the stars above and stared at them very hard. "Please God, send him back to me." It was only after her heart and eyes made this desperate cry did she realize that this was the third time that she was asking something from God. In the last thirty plus years, as far as her memory scanned, never had she asked for any favour. Not even when she cringed behind the side board, watching her mother being beaten like an animal.

As the smoke rings disappeared into the already hazy Gurgaon skies, the lonely moon looked down at her as if identifying with her loneliness.

"Please God, take care of Captain. Ensure his safety and make him call me."

Only time would tell if God responded to the prayers of opportunists.

Life Before Life

"As I count from one to ten, with each number, you will go deeper in your sleep and will feel lighter.

One, you are feeling light.

Two, your brain is calm.

Three, your eyes are feeling heavy.

Four, your mind is relaxed.

Five, you are totally calm.

Six, every part of your body is relaxed.

Seven, you are light and almost floating.

Eight, you can see yourself lying here.

Nine, you are ready to take this journey with your angels and guides.

And deep sleep." Chauhan Sir tapped Avantika's forehead with his index finger.

To a large extent, his authoritative yet gentle voice had already pacified her traumatized senses. Deep in hypnotic sleep, she felt relaxed and at peace.

"I pray to your angels and guides to come down and to help you in this journey by showing only what is good for you and what the future has to offer you."

With a few more invocations, he empowered Avantika to start her journey into a world which was way beyond the realms of present time.

A week back, when she had come to see Chauhan sir, he was very much in tune with her mental state. He comforted her by telling that the recent incidences in her life were more out of wrong decisions, than being a manifestation of some past life *karma*. Somewhere she knew that he was right. They spent quite some time together discussing the same. He assured her that whatever will come out of the turbulence will be for her good, provided she accepted it without any apprehensions. Though she was a non-believer, an atheist as she termed herself, but she did remember that whatever she had seen or was told during her first session by Chauhan sir—name, fame and fortune part did come true. This time, with the present deluge of problems, she again wanted a past life therapy session, seeking eternal peace and wisdom. Somehow she had also figured out that whatever little joy she expected out of life was only possible if she surrendered herself to Captain, for good and forever. But unfortunately, she took too long to realize this cardinal truth.

"What do you see?"

"It's hazy, can't see clearly," she murmured.

"I will give you a torch. Here is your torch. I have lighted it for you. Hold it and see what lies ahead of you." He handed her an imaginary torch.

"Greenery, water, palm trees."

"Good. Can you identify the place? Have you been there in the past? Maybe in this lifetime or one of your previous lives?"

Her eyelids flickered rapidly as he strained to decipher the scene more vividly.

"I think I have been to this place."

"Good. Where is this place? Can you name it?"

"Yes."

"Tell me its name."

"Vembanad Lake, Kerala."

"What else do you see there?"

"Bright colours. Red, blue, orange, purple, gold, green and more. They are floating on water."

"Why are colours floating on water?"

"I don't know."

"Ask your guides and angels to help you understand the significance of this scene in your life."

Her eyelids flickered again.

"Avantika, what are they telling you?"

Silence. From the corner of her eyes, tears started to roll. He took a tissue and wiped her eyes.

"Avantika, you have to ask them as to why are they showing you this."

"I can see the houseboat."

"Which houseboat?"

"The Voyager. Captain's houseboat. My houseboat. Our houseboat."

"What do you see?"

"It's deserted, just anchored there. The polish and paint has come off. It looks like a haunted boat."

"Go inside the boat. See, if you can find anyone."

"The sofa is tattered, the rug is faded and torn, the paintings on the walls are crooked, and the dining table is covered with moss." She sobbed.

He used the paper tissue again.

"What more do you see?"

"The brass name plate, just adjacent to Captain's chair, is rusted. His driving chair is gone, the staircase is not there. His room is ransacked; everything is covered with moss and fungus. There are plates, saucers, spoons, gas stove lying all over the place, dirty and unused from a very long time."

"Do you see Captain in there?"

Her tears multiplied.

"No, he is no where."

"Do you see anyone else?"

"No."

"Do you see yourself?"

"Yes."

"What are you doing?"

"Watching the sun set over the horizon, waiting for Captain."

"Where is he?"

"I don't know but something in me tells that he is gone forever."

"Go back to the scene where you saw colours floating on water. Try to see anything else."

"The floating colours are my paintings."

"Which paintings?"

"The series I am currently working on."

"But what are they doing there?"

"I have given back the lake what I took from it—the essence of my life, my paintings, my name, fame and fortune—my truth."

Nature has its own way of balancing life. Whenever it gives something from its kitty, it definitely takes something away. She had to find Captain fast. But only after she was all clean, guilt free and only for him.

Q & A

Post her session with Chauhan sir, Avantika was feeling very restless. It was a mixture of fear, apprehension, guilt and uncertainty, which was making her feel empty and miserable. She looked out of the window. The skyline of Gurgaon was as alluring as ever. Lights were shimmering all over like stars. Only from her 22nd floor apartment, the stars were down, not in the sky, and moving.

Would all the stars be still as soothing and mystical if they were inspected from close quarters? She knew the obvious answer and suddenly had this urge of having something to eat as she thought it would take her mind off the growing restlessness. She walked into the small kitchenette and opened the door of the small, red coloured refrigerator. All she could see was some eggs, a can of tuna and a few bottles of aerated drinks. She felt dejected till her eyes met a red coloured blessing, tucked between the soft drink bottles. Holding the Sula bottle in her hands, she weighed the pros and cons of having it.

A few minutes later, she walked back to the balcony, sipping wine straight from the bottle. She wanted to get drunk due to a plethora of reasons - to unwind, to run away from the truth, which was fast catching up to clear her mind, to straighten her life and a lot more. Fermented grape juice was doing its best to soothe her worked nerves. She placed the wine bottle on the railing and went inside the hall to get her phone. As she dialled the same number again, she got the same answer. 'The number you have dialled is temporarily out of service.' Frustrated, she took a large swig straight from the bottle. Some of the wine trickled down her lips which she wiped with her sleeves. She knew for sure that tonight her sleeves would surely wipe more than the dripping wine.

Looking around, for the first time she noticed the concrete jungle around her. Her view was dotted with high-rise apartments which looked like small matchboxes, stacked together. She wondered how distance made things look close and snug, just like the high-rise buildings. Some more wine was needed in her system to clear the cobwebs from her mind and life.

Half a bottle down, she realized that she had four crores in her bank account now. An amount she never even dreamt of. Though she was not a finance whiz kid, she knew that even half of that amount would last anyone a lifetime. If that was the truth, then why wasn't she celebrating the same? Just due to the fact that it came from her late father whom she did not hold in very high esteem? But then she never asked for it. Her father gave it to her on his own, voluntarily. She was confused and sought the assistance of another sip to clear her thought process. Would she accept anything from a person whom she did not love? Instinctively, she knew that she had asked herself the wrong question.

A couple of quick sips and she could feel the warm lethargy of Sula crawling up her body. She came inside the hall and looked around her studio. Her own studio! Just like the one she had always wanted. Her mother would have been so proud of her. But would her mother, who never ever took anything from her legally wedded husband, just because she did not love him, feel happy to see her daughter leading a life full of compromises? Would she be happy to meet her friends, her agent, her promoter or for that matter even her boyfriend?

Avantika looked at the canvas, which was mounted on the aisle, standing in a corner. White and clean, it attracted her. She walked towards it. As her eyes caressed the coarse texture of the canvas, she thought if it was mandatory for every single canvas to get painted? Just because it happens to be a canvas, does it mean that it has to stand there, coated with layers and layers of paint? Why can't it remain blank yet fulfill its life purpose? Similarly, can a mortal live without hankering after name and fame, yet lead a life of contentment by fulfilling his life's purpose?

She emptied the wine bottle and slumped on the couch thinking if colours were beautiful, so could be the lack of them. The blank canvas looked more appealing to her than any of the ones she had painted. Did the canvas look barren yet beautiful because it was destined to echo silence? She knew that there would be canvases which would be more content just staying blank, untouched, because staying bereft of colours could be the truth of their life and it was an acceptance of this truth which would give them contentment. During all these months of name and money, she was clear that if anything was bigger than happiness, it was peace and contentment. She knew that an average person could not be an inspiration for others but without any name and fame, he could be the most content man if he were in sync with the truth of his life. Were happiness and contentment the same expressions or did they connote something entirely different? Was happiness a physical state of being while the other a more spiritual state? Could a person be happy yet not content or the other way around? Her mind was producing million of questions and then answers for them, too.

If she were to choose between four crores and Captain, what would she do? Would she like to be a successful painter and still be unhappy or just be a painter and live life the way God intended?

She looked at the blank canvas and smiled. Her mind was made up, finally.

Forgive And Live

Mr Khurana looked around the place, De Café, the rendezvous point with Avantika. Wearing his formal, pin stripe business suit, amidst tattered jeans, funky sneakers and tattoos, he was sticking out like a sore thumb. For some odd reason, Avantika insisted upon meeting him there only. And for some odd reason, he agreed to the same. Maybe the guilt in him made him do so.

Contrary to his earlier apprehension, which he had while entering the crowded and 'not his kind of place', he quite liked the ambience. To him, it was so open and inviting, letting everyone be his or her own self. No one seemed to be bothered about anyone or anything. Even the décor followed the same philosophy. Bright colours—red, orange, green and blue—casually splashed on the walls, with no prior colour scheme or pattern. Each chair, every single table was different from the other. Walls had an assortment of pictures, paintings, posters; none of them even remotely related to each other. Even the menu was as diverse as it could be. *Keema-pao* to the finest scotch.

His eyes caught Avantika who was hurriedly walking in, looking around for him. He smiled and waved. She reciprocated. He was pleasantly surprised to see her dressed in her earlier *avtaar*—Fabindia *kurti*, Levis denims and embroidered *jootis*. Her iPod was back, dangling around her neck. The only addition to her age-old attire was a notebook which was stashed away neatly in a smart carry bag, slung around her shoulder. As she took a seat, there was an uncomfortable silence.

"Would you like to have some *keema-pao* with cutting *chai*?" It was one of the best ice breakers that he had come across in a very long time. They laughed. Avantika placed the order and booted her Apple notebook. She looked at Mr Khurana. A man in his late 50s, but still handsome. His face had an air of honesty about it. A just face that could never do anything wrong.

"Sir, while we wait for your *keema-pao* and cutting *chai*, I would like to take this opportunity to let you know that in spite of whatever transpired between us the other day, I am really thankful to you for trusting my skill and putting your money on me." Avantika's voice was straight and honest, just like the face of Mr Khurana.

"Avantika, now stop embarrassing me."

"No Sir, I really mean it. You were right when you said that if it were only for my talent, I would have become successful long ago, and on my own. I am fully with you on this. But you know Sir, this success did change my entire life. The way I looked at art, people, society, relationship, even my own self. On one hand, it helped me in discovering a new me, but at the same time, it killed the other me, the real me. It wrecked havoc with my ethos and belief system. But nevertheless, I know without being successful, I would have never realized all this."

Mr Khurana was listening to her intently.

"You know something Avantika, everything in life comes with a price tag, specially success. At times, the price is huge. I have known people who are not ready to pay this price and, therefore, make a conscious decision to lead a non-descript life. But, even leading this life has its own share of good things. Quality family life, peaceful sleep, stopping by the baker to pick a cake for your loved one, playing cricket with your kid and many such things. When I wanted to be successful, I was aware of the price tag. Constant pressure, travel, staying away from family and friends, dining with people whom I hated, smiling for the Press when my heart bled, and I can go on adding more to this list." he continued.

"I don't know if you are aware of my earlier days, but I come from a lower middle class, Pakistani Punjabi family. After Partition, all we had was fifty rupees. My father was ailing. With that fifty rupees, I set out to become the man I am today. I am fully aware that along this long journey, I have also hurt people, cheated them; either emotionally or financially, not always been truthful, and have pulled people down to go up. All this sits heavy on my soul. Every morning, I beg God to forgive me for all my wrong doings, which were done either intentionally or un-intentionally. Don't know if I deserve to be forgiven."

The waiter served the *keema-pao* and cutting *chai*. Avantika was shocked to see Mr Khurana use his bare hands to polish off the spicy *keema-pao* with the extra sweetened cutting *chai*. During his entire feast, he did not utter even a single word. As he licked his fingers to savour the last bit of thick *keema* gravy, he looked at Avantika and smiled.

"Thanks a ton. You have made my day. You know, some 35 years ago, in Mumbai, I used to catch the local train from Juhu to Churchgate to visit this Irani café which served the most amazing *keema-pao*. This one, if not better, was as good. Thank you again." She accepted the compliment and smiled graciously.

"You have pleased the child in me. And as a return gift, I want to make a confession."

"Sir, now it's you who is on an embarrassing spree. And if you did like this *keema-pao* so much, I am just wondering what your reaction would be if you get to eat the one that I make."

"You must be kidding? You mean you can make better *keema-pao* than this? Damn you, Sunny!"

Avantika was surprised at the mention of Sunny without any context.

"I know you would be wondering why did I curse Sunny." He smiled. "He is such a big idiot that he could not even handle you. Forget his love and liking part, at least he should have handled you for the sumptuous *keema-pao* bit."

They both laughed.

"Getting back to my confession part, and please don't stop me from doing it as it will make me feel better. Please." He requested. She had no option but to listen to what he had to say.

"When Sunny walked up to me, sharing his most recurring and frightful nightmare, I was surprised to learn that it was the fear of losing you." Avantika was taken aback. "I have made my fortune due to various talents of mine. But trust me when I say this to you, identifying people with courage, conviction and vision and making them join my business has been foremost strength. The day I met you, along with Sunny and his mother, within the first thirty seconds, I was sure that you are too good, too strong and too straight a girl to be with him. When you walked out on him, my judgment about you was validated. But for some reason, Sunny was not being able to get over you. I am sorry to accept this, but the father in me couldn't see him depressed. And I knew that like every single thing in his life, I was supposed to buy even this fantasy of his—you. Please pardon the use of my last expression." He stopped and looked at her. Her eyes were all confused.

"From day one, I knew that you were a woman of character. I also knew that if you had walked out on Sunny, there was nothing that could bring you back. Nothing but your own dreams! I hate to say this, but I have seen how far people go to fulfill their dreams. Dream is the biggest drug we thrive on. It changes everything, people included. I am sure that now even you have seen and experienced how far your dream got you." Avantika nodded and he continued. "I made a simple plan. Over a drink, I mentioned to Francois that I was keen to sponsor some painter as a part of PR and brand building exercise. I was sure that he would recommend you, as he was highly impressed with your integrity, thought and work. No wonder, he did the same. Post that, it was all a cakewalk. You got used to money, name and fame and silently Sunny slipped back into your life. But having said and done that, now I don't feel like a father. I feel like a pimp. How I wish if Sunny was lucky to have you by his side, as his partner. But knowing the man he is, he never deserved someone as precious as you."

Avantika was flabbergasted. She could not decide if she should thank Mr Khurana for all the rich compliments he paid her, at the expense of his son, or slap him for screwing her life.

"Avantika, should I tell you something? I know it's kind of personal and I am no one to tell you this, but during the Europe tour, I did notice a man by your side. A middle-aged man."

"He was... is my friend, Captain." She blundered.

"Grab him. Don't let him go. He is the man for you. Trust me, I can read people well."

Her heart cried silently and she got uncomfortable. She wanted to hug Mr Khurana and weep, requesting him to help her in finding him and getting him back into her life. But then she knew that it was her journey.

"Sir, can I tell you something?"

"Surely, by all means."

"I wish you were my father. I would have been so lucky." A lonely tear managed to escape the confines of her eyes. Mr Khurana smiled, a soft smile, which was laden with emotion. "And you know Avantika, I wish I had a daughter like you. It would have made me so proud." He took her hands and squeezed them tight.

"Can this daughter make a request?"

"Ask for it. Just anything that you want."

"Promise?"

"You have my word."

She pulled out an envelope from her laptop bag and kept it on the table.

"Out of whatever reason, but like a father, you helped me in realizing the biggest dream of my life. You gave me whatever I always longed for; name, fame and money. You gave me immense joy by letting me see people appreciate my work. You empowered me to take my work across the globe. You also made me understand that life is not about name and money alone. I truly value your every gesture. A few minutes back, you rightly pointed out that I will be happy only with the man whom you saw with me in Europe. Your daughter is going to find him and start a whole new life. A life where her happiness will not depend on money or fame, but on some thing more substantial. A life in which she will be so content that she will never need to look out. And for this life, I just need your blessings, not this." She opened the envelope and pulled out a draft and respectfully handed it over.

"Avantika, are you out of your mind? Why have you got this draft in my name?" And that too for three crores. I can't take it. I mean how did you ever think that I will stoop so low?"

She looked at him with soft eyes. Her face glowed with inner beauty, honesty and strength of character.

"I can never think of insulting you after what you have done for me. I truly value and appreciate every single gesture of yours and I know that I can never pay you back. This money has been left to me by my late father. But on the journey which I am all set to embark on, I don't need this. In fact, I do not need any of the material things. Therefore, I think this money will be safe and put to some good use by you."

"But what will I do with this money Avantika?" He was falling short of words.

"Please use this to promote genuine talent, some bright artists. I am sure Mr Lancolne will again help you find one. Please don't say no. Remember, you have given me your word?"

Tears, at times, act as the best adhesive to bind two people. It did the same for Mr Khurana and Avantika.

A New Sun

What does it take to enjoy a sound sleep?

Just a bed, a happy heart and a guilt-free soul. However, it took Avantika thirty long years to decipher this simple formula. Her only saving grace was that she finally did, unlike millions of others. Last night, after very long, she slept like a log. Her meeting with Mr Khurana left her feeling so warm and complete. For the first time in her life, she realized that the act of giving was far more joyous than that of receiving. Also, she realized that the more you gave, the more joy came your way. Going by the same logic, after giving away three crore, no wonder she felt like one of the happiest person on this earth. To ensure the state of happiness for the rest of her life, she knew that now she had to bring back the man who would guarantee it for her—the one and only, Captain.

The moment she opened her eyes, feeling fresh and energetic, she dialled Captain's number. The same pre-recorded response. Instead of getting worked up, she took a deep breath and moved to her pre-chalked out next step.

With a cup of green tea, she sat down to search, plan and execute. She googled the name of the resort where she stayed during her earlier visit and blessed Google for being so effective.

"Hi, my name is Avantika. A few months back I stayed at your resort."

"What can I do to help you Ma'am?"

"During my stay, I stayed at a houseboat named 'The Voyager'. I want to get in touch with its owner…" She was cut short.

"Who? Drego Verghesse? After suffering a heart attack, he has stopped running his houseboat service Ma'am."

Her heart missed a beat.

"A heart attack? When?"

"It has been a while Ma'am. If you want, I can arrange another houseboat, a better one at a better price."

"Thanks but can you tell me how can I reach Drego Verghesse?"

"No clue Ma'am. For quite some time, no one in the village has seen him."

"He had his helper named Sudhakar. Is there anyway of getting in touch with him?" she probed.

"He has joined another company 'Kovalam Waters'. If you want, I can book the boat from them. What dates are you looking at?"

His hard sell was irritating Avantika. But she maintained her composure.

"I will let you know of the dates. By any chance, do you have Sudhakar's number?"

"Sorry Ma'am. I do have the number of 'Kovalam Waters'."

"Do you mind sharing the same?"

"Ma'am, if you book the houseboat through us, you will get a better rate. Also, as a special case, I will give you one night free."

"Can I have the number please?"

"09042044504, 08012639131."

Before even asking him the number, Avantika knew that he would rattle it off and would never repeat it. Therefore, she was ready with a pen and paper and got it right the very first time.

"Thanks a ton."

The news of Captain having suffered a heart attack was almost killing her. She knew it well that she was the reason. How could she get so insensitive towards the man who was responsible for giving her a new vision, direction and a new life? She remembered how without even thinking twice, he had left everything, just to be by her side when she was going through a bad health phase. Her eyes got misty. She could vividly see how for months, he would wake her up every morning, take her for morning walks, cook breakfast, shop for fresh fruits and green veggies, cook them in no oil and maintain a strict diet chart, just to keep her healthy. How for days he would sit there quietly, watching her paint and keep her pepped up with a regular supply of fresh, hot vegetable soup and stew. How he would overlook her tantrums and how gracefully, without any complaints, he would be her errand boy, manager and assistant.

Where would he be at this moment? Who would be taking care of him? With no business, how would he be supporting himself? She knew that he was too dignified a man to ask anyone for any kind of help, under any circumstance. God, please be with him. Please

God, give him courage and strength till I reach him. Please God help him.

Google hand held her to a travel agent, and the next thing she knew, she was inching towards Captain.

***

The flight from Delhi to Kochi was a long one. Her flying business class was the only saving grace. Throughout the flight, different thoughts kept pulling her in different directions. Some of them were laden with hope while others confronted her. Though in a minority, some of them made her happy, but at the very next moment, the majority took over.

The montage of her thoughts was largely interspersed with memories of her last Kerala trip, how she met him, the good times they had, the memorable moments in Delhi and Europe, his culinary skills, affection, love and their never ending conversations.

However, there were two thoughts which took away everything from her; every time they hit her like a hurricane. The first one was Mr Khurana's observation about Captain. To him, Captain was a man of self-faith and conviction, and therefore, he would never take a U-turn on life's highway. Whatever went past for him would be a lesson and post that he would just move on. She knew how precise Mr Khurana was in understanding people and their immediate behaviour. If he were even fifty per cent correct in profiling Captain, then there would be absolutely no looking back for him. Deep in her heart, she knew how for weeks, though unknowingly, she had humiliated him by doing exactly the opposite of whatever he stood for. Success made her treat him like a piece of scrap, out of her redundant past. His silent departure, though then it was a big relief for her as she never wanted to confront him and create any unpleasantness, said a lot about his trauma.

"God please, give me one more chance," she pleaded again.

Her second menacing thought traced its genesis to her last session with Chauhan sir. Why was she shown dilapidated images of the Voyager? Why could she not see Captain even after trying so hard? Why during those two long hours was she unable to see even one image that was comforting? If the experiences of these sessions were true, and going by her past experience, they were very close to it, was her last session an indicator of a bleak and blank future with Captain? Was Captain already dead? She scrolled the play list on her iPod and shut herself with Mark Knofler and his husky yet melodic voice belting '*Money for Nothing*'.

***

In the cab, on her way to Kumarakom, Avantika was a busy woman. She knew that by the time she would reach the Golden Water Resort, it would be close to 4 pm. Under no circumstance did she want to waste the evening, sitting at the resort, just crossing her fingers and praying for the well being of Captain. From Delhi, she had managed to get Captain's old time assistant Sudhakar's number. But for some reason, it was continuously out of coverage area. Why can't the pug follow Sudhakar now? She cursed the advertisement for telling nothing but blatant lies. It was only when she called up Kovalam Waters again did she figure out the reason for the pug's failure. Sudhakar was on a week-long boat trip with a group from Sweden. No wonder, the poor pug couldn't have swum that far.

She dialled the front office of Golden Waters.

"Hi, this is Avantika. I will be staying with you for a couple of days and for the same I have my reservations. It's in the name of Avantika. Thanks. I'm on my way to the resort. I just wanted to check if you guys have arranged a boat for me? That's right. I will leave right after checking in. Yes, I do understand that during the middle of the night, it's not safe to sail, but during my conversation yesterday, I had told your manager categorically that I am a sound recordist and I need to record the sound of waves, insects and night birds for an upcoming project of mine. If everything was as per your convenience, why am I paying you guys thrice your going rates?"

If she had her way, she would have slapped the girl who was there to welcome her the traditional way. But then, Avantika knew that she was just doing her job. Five minutes were wasted in the *tilak*, garland and *aarti* ceremony. She looked at her watch. It was almost five. She signed the check-in form at the reception and dumped her luggage in the room and rushed to the spot where the boat waited for her.

Sitting in the cabin of the small house boat, with its driver, she looked out. The engine made a lot of noise and spitted substantial amount of fume.

"I hope the resort guys have explained you the vicinity where I want to go?

"Yes Madam. But if you want to record some really scary night sound, I can take you to a better spot."

"Thanks. If I think it is needed, I will let you know. What's your name?"

"Murali, Madam." He smiled. He was a man in his early 40s, lean and was wearing a faded T-shirt and shorts.

Avantika scrambled her play list but then decided against it. She was feeling restless. Every now and then, negative thoughts sent her scurrying for cover. With nothing better to do, she dialled Sudhakar again. The pug had still not reached him.

She dialled Captain's number. Same reply.

She looked around. Both sides of the backwaters were flanked by small brightly coloured houses, houseboats, big boats, small boats, palm trees. But unlike the earlier time, her eyes had no admiration for God's creation or his own country.

She put on her earplugs and tried immersing herself in the soulful and haunting melody of '*Wish you were here*'.

It took her many more melodies—spanning from Pink Floyd to Nirvana and Bob Dylan to Led Zepplin—before her pilot for the day, Murali, cut the engine. She looked outside the boat cabin. It was dark and the bright moonlight made the entire lake look like a fantasy, silver lake. She removed her earplugs. Her eardrums were hit by the roaring sound of waves, vehemently complaining against the breach of privacy, at that ungodly hour.

"How far are we from that spot?"

"Almost there." Murali switched on the powerful searchlight mounted on the roof of the boat.

Avantika looked out. She could see nothing but water, ahead of her for miles. The boat was swaying with the waves and moving towards left.

"Murali, by any chance are you aware of a Kovalam Waters boat docked nearby?"

"Yes Madam. They are anchored here for the last three days. Some foreigners are on it. You want to go there?"

It was indeed a small world, especially in the backwaters.

Murali steered the boat further left. As it slowly moved towards the bank, the strange sound of insects grew louder.

"Madam, what are you here for? I know for sure you are not here to record insects. If that was the case, you would have come with big mikes, recorders and computers. Last year, I had taken a foreigner who wanted to record the sound of birds. He had lots of gadgets."

Avantika felt ashamed for lying.

"I am sorry Murali. You are right. I am not here to record any sound. I will pay you extra money. Don't you worry." She tried to cover up her guilt.

"I don't want money Madam. You are already paying me. If I wanted more money, I would have refused you when you got on my boat. I knew it from that very moment that you are here searching for something very important as there are few women who would dare to take this journey, at this time of the hour."

"You are right Murali. I am indeed searching for something very precious. Maybe more precious than my own life." The moon passed a cloud and, for a moment, it got pitch dark.

***

Locating the 'Kovalam Waters' boat was tougher and scarier than she had imagined. Though it was a moon-lit night, but with sounds of the waves crashing against each other, a million insects in various stages of life cycle and nocturnal birds blended into one to form a scary background score. The powerful searchlight was trying its best to cut through the darkness. It took Avantika and Murali nearly two hours to locate the boat.

As her boat scrapped side with Kovalam Waters boat, it was nearly midnight.

Seeing another boat pull by its side, the crew of the Kovalam boat turned on their powerful torches. As the beam of light hit Avantika's face, she was almost blinded. To shield her eyes, she put her hands over them. A short conversation happened between Murali and the Kovalam boat crew. As the beam of light moved away from her face, she removed her hands and tried to adjust her eyes back.

"Avantika Madam?" She was greeted by a voice which had more question and surprise than welcome to it.

Instinctively, she knew that it was Sudhakar's. "Hi Sudhakar."

"Sir told me that now you have become a very famous painter. See, I know all about you." He giggled sheepishly.

She smiled back. Her vocal chords ached to ask the straight question, for which she had come so far.

"Sudhakar, could you tell me where can I find Drego, I mean Captain?" His smiling face ceased to exist as a huge wave of melancholy drowned it.

"He is no more. He is gone."

Her heart almost stopped and her expressions froze.

"No no, not that." Sudhakar realized his erroneous statement, as he could see devastating effect on her face, and rectified it immediately.

"I mean, he is no more here. God knows where he is."

Murali looked at Avantika, who was almost shattered, in tears. "Madam, you should have told me earlier that you are looking for Drego Verghesse," he joined the conversation.

"Do you know where he is?" Hope held her arms again.

Murali got embarrassed as he knew that his statement would break her heart. "No, I don't know about his whereabouts, but what I know is that he has left this place. His boat is with one of my cousins who is reworking on it for a new buyer. Before Drego moved away from here, he sold off everything."

"But where did he go? Please tell me, please." Avantika was getting almost hysterical.

Murali and Sudhakar were not accustomed to handling such situations and, therefore, had no clue what to do.

"We really don't know Madam. There are many stories in the village. Some say that he drowned himself in the middle of this lake, some claim that they had seen him during one of their boat expeditions, some say that he has joined some *ashram* and has become a saint."

"Madam," suddenly Sudhakar exclaimed, his eyes shining, "before he left, he had come to see me. He gave me an envelope, a sealed one, and instructed me to only give it to you. When I asked him what if you don't show up, he smiled and said..." he tried remembering the precise expression of Captain, "yes, I remember now," his eyes had the spark of a winner, "he said that soon, for sure, the truth of the hilsa will bring her to these waters, as it was from here that her flight began."

***

'*Dear Avantika,*

I am glad my heart was not wrong and you are back."

As she read the first line, she could almost hear the familiar voice of Captain; deep yet kind, jolting her from the chain of thoughts which were crowding her mind. Murali steered the boat and she sat there, in the boat cabin, with a solitary lamp as her companion.

"As I write this, I am wearing the black 'Superman' T-shirt which you had bought for me. Back then, I felt a little odd wearing it (after all, who would like to see an elderly superman with a beard), but now it has become my favourite. Wish if I had more of them. Wearing and washing it every alternate day has made the Superman logo become a little dull.

When I thought of writing to you, suddenly I realized that for years, I have not written anything. So please, forgive me for my atrocious handwriting. As this is a special occasion, I have taken out the Mont Blanc which my father had gifted me. If you look at this page, maybe you will realize that it is from the same writing pad which you had bought for me at Khan Market, to write South Indian recipes for you. Only if I knew that time would fly so swiftly, I would have definitely done the needful. I am sure that back then, even in our wildest of dreams, we never anticipated that someday I will have to write to you to share my inner most thoughts. Somehow, then it seemed that the moments would exist for ever. No wonder, time is referred as nimble footed.

You know Avantika, the small lantern kept on the table is fighting hard to compete with the moonlight and the moon. I feel like telling the poor thing to take it a little slow, as I know for sure that it's only your face which can win this competition. You remember the times when we held each other's gaze for what seemed like eternity? During those encounters,

I always felt that your face had more radiance, more attraction and more captive power than the moon. Did I ever tell you the same? Anyway, it's never too late and trust me, this statement comes from someone who knows that few people would have watched the moon or you, so closely and for so long.

As you read this, irrespective of the physical miles between us, I am overwhelmed to have my old Avi—the one in Fabindia kurti, jooti and with her iPod back. I am so glad that, she did choose the right path.

You know Avantika, a few days ago, due to no reason, I was just inspecting myself in the mirror. To my horror and dismay, both my wrinkles and gray hair have multiplied. Do you think I am getting old? But let me assure you that you need not worry. My biggest asset, the one you loved so much, the sparkle in my eyes is still intact. Till the time it is there, a few more wrinkles here and there are fine. Remember, you had once said that it was this spark which had fuelled your persona and journey? I was really touched at that statement of yours and promised myself to make it my life's purpose to preserve this sparkle.

While reading all this and in the anticipation of more to come, your heart would be overflowing with a plethora of emotions. But I am also sure that your mind would be numb. Am I right? Maybe, there is so much to say and words only have limited power of expression. To keep myself from meandering off the course, let me give you a systematic update. I am sure you must be aware of my cardiac attack. It was nothing major, just a minor one. I blame it on the lobster-cheese-cream laden food during our Europe tour followed by the tikka-curry-naan fare during my Delhi stay. So, now like a good South Indian man, I am back to my staple fish-rice fare. Courtesy yoga and swimming, I have almost recovered.

Here I would like to stop and warn you that not even for a single moment you need to feel guilty about this and with tear-filled, beautiful doe eyes whisper, "Captain, is sorry too weak a word to say now?" You know what, you are a darling. Let me assure you that whatever happened is not because of you. After all, who are you? For that matter, who are we? Just two dots on the face of this vast earth! We all come with our own personal agendas and merely manage to influence each other in some way; either positively or negatively. Post that, we carry on with our pre-defined paths. I know, if you were here, you would have appreciated a straight answer. But then I really wish the answer to life was so simple. If you look at it; life itself is so simple, without any questions. But then, being the confused, greedy mortals that we are, we choose to go against it, complicating it in the process.

Do you remember the lines I recited for you in Paris?

'And stand together, yet not too near together,
for the pillars of the temple stand apart,
And the oak tree and the cypress grow not in each other's shadow.'

The answer lies somewhere in these lines. To explain it to you, in our context, I attempted giving you strength, yet when you were getting swayed by the flow, I could not afford to remote control your life anymore. The two wheels of any vehicle need to be at a reasonable distance, to maintain the balance, yet they need to move in perfect unison to maintain harmony. Though I could have nudged your shoulders and warned you, which I did to a great extent, I knew the futility of it. Even the higher source can just show you the right path but can never force you to walk on it. It is like when you are about to start a fresh task, if someone commands or pushes you to do the same task, in spite of having all the right intentions, you will have a sudden wall which will prevent you from attempting the task, which you were going to do anyway a minute ago.

Things when done on a self initiative are done. Teachers can attempt to teach you how a thorn can harm you, but you will truly learn if you play with the rose. You could argue with me that here the context is of the path to be chosen where as you were not unlearning something but changing tracks. Correct, but you were changing tracks by unlearning and rejecting the call of your heart. You were getting into a comfort zone with the behaviour which you previously detested. If a person cannot hear the voice from within, it is impossible for him to hear what is being said externally. If I did tell you then that Sunny met me earlier this year and tried to convince me to leave Delhi, would you have believed me? Believe, probably yes, but you may have ignored to see the intention behind it. His father had built the pedestal for you, which was leading you to all your dreams. It surely may have been a very tough proposition for any mortal to battle.

Are you surprised and shocked to learn about the Sunny twist? I need not tell you that I left Delhi not because I was scared, but because I wanted you to learn your own lessons. We learn best when we want to, not when we are forced to. If you ask me if I love you or else why did I selflessly give away those few months of my life to breathe into you the fire to exist, to create, to be your best, here's the thing.

Avantika, love is such a vague word. It encompasses the universe, yet it can be just a touch, a look, a concern. To different people, love has different connotation. To some it may mean being married for years; to some it is to keep someone in their thoughts, or to have someone to appreciate a mutually admired thing. To some, love is a synonym for having sex. Love can be spiritual, selfless like what Meera had for Krishna. She did not want anything in return for her love. Love for a mother is endless hours of tending, to watch patiently every sleeping moment, every flicker of the baby's eyelids. This is a relation which sustains over years. Love is also what you do to your pet. For someone who owns and loves his dog, the bond, the relationship they both share is completely inexplicable. However, it does not mean that their love for their partner or children diminishes. Tell me something, why do you think a married Radha fell in love with Krishna? Not only she, but most of the Gopis whom Lord Krishna romanced were married. However, Radha's passionate love does bring to fore one thing: that unconditional love can be immortal. Meera's unending love found its goal in her music and spirituality as she never had a physical person by her side to express her love. So when you ask if I love you or not, we both may have different connotations. What it means for you could not ring a bell with me and vice-versa.

Let us say we both admit to loving each other. The next predictable question from you would be about our marriage. Avantika, what is marriage? Union of two souls? Their names inscribed together on the nameplate which gets nailed on the door? Or is it a certificate from the court of law, which merely defines that you can stay together legally? For two willing souls to unite, do you need a certificate? If the souls are pure to each other, they will get together anyway, irrespective of any legal sanction or external intervention. So let's say we marry, uprooting ourselves from our own environment to share the space of the other. We try to start liking what the other likes to simulate peaceful co-existence, gradually ignoring our personal choice. Eventually, there will be a day we will miss our own little world, and this will get in the way of how we exist. You will yearn for the pandemonium of the Delhi roads, or I for the cry of the seagulls. Getting lost in the labyrinth of like and dislike and adjustments, we will start doubting our love for each other. And mind you, I am not showing you the pessimistic side of being together, I am merely telling you that love is very powerful. It can exist on its own. It can define its own rules for every unique relationship. It does not have to follow the predefined and established boundaries of acceptance and union.

Let me ask you a question Avantika.

If you thought me to be your love, now what would you do without me? Think hard. Won't you go back to painting with a vengeance and a new found passion? I know you would. Why? Because painting is your real love. You are among the very lucky few on this earth who have actually discovered what they truly love. You and your tryst with colours! That is your love, your passion, your life's calling. That is what you were born to do, that is what will keep breathing life into you. Every time you strike your brush on a blank canvas, you breathe. Every time a colour coats another, you add a hue to your life, every painting you make is a self discovery for you as long as you do it for yourself. When you do an honest painting, you live a million lives with it. The moment you start doing it for reasons you don't identify with, you will land up doing something like what kept your last year busy.

Now with this answer, you would ask me if painting is your love, then what is my love of life? Love for me is life. I love living. I like giving back to the world, what I take in everyday. My affection for you is incomparable, cannot be described. I saw life in you. If your life is a rope, every relation you establish is like a knot, but the knot does not become a roadblock in the journey of life, it merely serves as a foothold to climb on. I have within me the vivacity from our intense closeness and that will stay on with me forever. Every moment I spent with you brought fresh vigour in me, the energy to achieve the unattainable, to experiment with life, to move on. Our passionate bond is something time cannot wear away so I will be there for you, always.

Tonight is my last night on this boat.

Don't panic. It's just that I sold this baby last week. Tomorrow the new owners will be here to take her possession. As far as I am concerned, till I fathom a way ahead, I am temporarily moving in with a friend in Kochi. With the liveliness you have rekindled inside me, I may plan to test new waters. If you remember, my father's friend in Canada had helped me out of crisis so I could buy this boat. A few years ago, on his insistence and sponsorship, I had filed for Canadian immigration. I personally never gave it a serious thought, but he, Uncle Willy, wants me to be a part of his shipping business in Canada. The papers are nearly processed and getting to a stage when I soon need to take a decision.

Coming to your last question, will we ever meet again?

Let me ask you, will we ever separate? Is there a day you don't think of your mother? Is there a day you don't think of the Almighty. Some relations go beyond words; they cannot be confined to the realms of friendship and marriage. These relations just exist. There is no palpable reason for them to remain. There is no shelf life. They are kind of eternal as these bonds are created with existence itself. Mutual thoughts will exist in the heart which will fuel our lives.

And finally thanks for coming all the way to meet me. I would have lost the confidence and hope in life if you had succumbed to the circumstances and had not bounced back. That is what I meant when I said I love life and want to give back to this universe the strength and the positive energy."

P.S. I will also put this Mont Blanc in the envelope for you. I know, post this letter, I won't be writing again for a very long time. God bless.

Captain.'

She looked out of the cabin. Amber colour was getting darker and was spreading on the horizon. She pulled out the iPod from her satchel and scrolled down its play list till she found the anthem of her life. As Bob Dylan's gruff vocals told her again; for the millionth time, that every answer was blowing in the wind, she looked at the rising sun. A new sun, a new day.

The End Is Just The Beginning

Avantika joined Sacred Heart Convent as an arts teacher. With her College of Arts degree and her passion and flair for painting, it was the most obvious profession. During her leisure, she started painting various dimensions of love. Now, with her first hand understanding of it, in its true hue, her depiction of the same touched hearts of the art critics, art enthusiasts and buyers alike.

Captain faded into oblivion, never to be seen again.

Sunny married a rich *panjoo* girl. On their nuptial night, he nicknamed her 'Avi'.

Post-recession, as promised, Mr Khurana started promoting young and upcoming painters. He also appointed Avantika as an art consultant to his company. Once in a while, they met at De Café to enjoy *keema-pao* with cutting *chai.*

Every morning, when Avantika signed the school attendance register, the black Mont Blanc made her reaffirm her faith that Captain was still close to her, still holding her hands and guiding her at every step.

***